WATERLOO

A novel based on the
Dino De Laurentiis film:
WATERLOO

Riding Marengo, his white Arab steed, Napoleon paraded across the French forward slope. Regimental bands crashed out their martial airs, gold braid and polished metal glittered in the sun, cavalrymen brandished their lances and sabres, standard bearers inclined their eagles. Their god-like Emperor was in command, what army on earth could check them?

Spurring his horse to the edge of the ridge, Wellington raised two fingers to his cocked hat. The cheering from the British lines grew louder . . .

Frederick E. Smith, author of *633 Squadron* and *A Killing for the Hawks* whose nine other novels are continually in demand, and a writer noted for his interest in matters military, has created a superb novel based on Dino De Laurentiis' most spectacular motion picture WATERLOO – one of history's most significant battles – starring Rod Steiger as Napoleon and Christopher Plummer as Wellington.

THE FILM

Waterloo is a co-production by Dino De Laurentiis Cinematografica S.p.A. and Mosfilm, produced by Dino De Laurentiis on locations in Caserta (Italy) and Uzghorod (USSR) and at Dino De Laurentiis Studios, Rome. The film is in Technicolor ® and Panavision ®.

Producer	DINO DE LAURENTIIS
Director	SERGEI BONDARCHUK
Screenplay	H. A. L. CRAIG, in collaboration with SERGEI BONDARCHUK
Associate Producer	THOMAS CARLILE
Production Supervisors	ALFREDO DE LAURENTIIS and MARK RISS (Russia), GUY LUONGO (Italy)
Production Managers	GUGLIELMO AMBROSI and MARIO ABUSSI
Director of Photography	ARMANDO NANNUZZI
Editorial Supervision	RICHARD C. MEYER, A.C.E.
Assistant Directors	VLADIMIR DOSTAL and ALLAN ELLEDGE
Production Co-ordinator	ANNA POPOVA
Production Designer	MARIO GARBUGLIA
Art Director	FERDINANDO GIOVANNONI
Film Score	Composed and conducted by NINA ROTA
Set Decorators	EMILIO D'ANDRIA and KENNETH MUGGLESTON
Costume Designers	MARIA DE MATTEIS and UGO PERICOLI
Makeup Artist	ALBERTO DE ROSSI
Hair Stylist	PAOLO BORZELLI
Special Effects	V. A. LIKHACHOV
Sound Mixer	GORDON EVERETT and MURATORI PRIMIANO
Film Editor	E. V. MICHAJLOVA
Unit Photographers	PAUL RONALD and ALFONSO AVINCOLA
Dialogue Director	WILLIAM SLATER
Military Consultant	WILLOUGHBY GRAY
Continuity	ELVIRA D'AMICO

THE CAST

Napoleon	ROD STEIGER
Wellington	CHRISTOPHER PLUMMER
Louis XVIII	ORSON WELLES
Duchess of Richmond	VIRGINIA MCKENNA
Ney	DAN O'HERLIHY
Picton	JACK HAWKINS
Ponsonby	MICHAEL WILDING
Uxbridge	TERENCE ALEXANDER
O'Connor	DONAL DONNELLY
Gordon	RUPERT DAVIES
Soult	IVO GARRANI
Drouot	GIANNI GARKO
Cambronne	EUGHENJ SAMOILOV
De Lancey	IAN OGILVY
Blücher	SERGEI ZAKHARIADZE
La Bédoyère	PHILIPPE FORQUET
Sauret	ANDREA CHECCHI
Maria	IRINA SKOBZEVA
Müffling	JOHN SAVIDENT
Sarah	SUSAN WOOD
Lord Hay	PETER DAVIES
Tomlinson	OLEG VIDOV
Grouchy	CHARLES MILLOT
Gérard	VLADIMIR DRUZHNIKOV
Constant	ORAZIO ORLANDO
Colborne	JEFFRY WICKHAM
Ramsey	WILLOUGHBY GRAY
Normyle	ADRIAN DRINE
Duncan	ROGER GREEN
Gneisenau	KARL LIEPINSC
Mercer	RICHARD HEFFER
McKevitt	COLIN WATSON
Mulholland	CHARLES BORROMEL
Delessart	FRANCO FANTASIA
Berthier	GIORGIO SCIOLETTE
Oudinot	JEAN LOUIS
Percy	VASILI LIVANOV
Somerset	VICTOR MURGANOV
Magdalene de Lancey	VERONICA DE LAURENTIIS

By the same author in Pan Books

A KILLING FOR THE HAWKS

FREDERICK E. SMITH

WATERLOO

*A novel based on the screenplay by
H. A. L. Craig for the
Dino De Laurentiis film:
WATERLOO*

A PAN ORIGINAL

PAN BOOKS LTD · LONDON

First published 1970 by Pan Books Ltd,
33 Tothill Street, London, S.W.1

ISBN 0 330 02544 9

To John and Elaine

Printed in Great Britain by
Richard Clay (The Chaucer Press), Ltd, Bungay, Suffolk

ACKNOWLEDGEMENTS

The author wishes to acknowledge his debt to the
following biographies and works of reference:

The Hundred Days
by Edith Saunders

Napoleon
by Felix Markham

Wellington
by S. G. P. Ward

The Age of Wellington
by Leonard Cooper

Men of Waterloo
by John Sutherland

Waterloo
by John Naylor

A Near-Run Thing
by David Howarth

Eighteen Fifteen
by John Fisher

Napoleon
by André Maurois

Les Derniers Jours de l'Empire
by Henry Lachouque

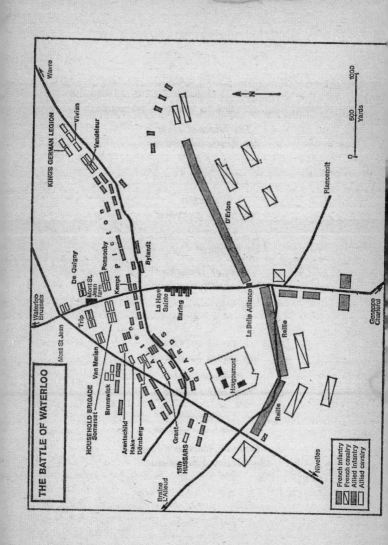

THE BATTLE OF WATERLOO

Wavre

KING'S GERMAN LEGION

Vivian

Vandeleur

De Quigny

Waterloo
Brussels

Mont St Jean

Mont St.
Jean
farm

Trip

Ponsonby

Kempt

Bylandt

P i c t o n

La Haye
Sainte

Baring

D'Erlon

Plancenoit

La Belle Alliance

Reille

HOUSEHOLD BRIGADE
Somerset

Van Merlen

Brunswick

Arentschild
Hake
Dörnberg

G U A R D S

Hougoumont

Reille

Genappe
Charleroi

Mont St Jean

Braine
L'Alleud

15th HUSSARS

Grant

Reille

Nivelles

N

0   500   1000
Yards

French infantry
French cavalry
Allied infantry
Allied cavalry

PROLOGUE

The destiny that brought Napoleon and Wellington to their bloody and fateful confrontation at Waterloo will fascinate men as long as mankind retains its sense of drama. Like Germany 150 years later, France had conquered Europe. Only Britain, protected by the narrow seas, remained undefeated. From her isolation she sought to revive, by money and by the use of her sea power, the nations that lay at the brilliant Napoleon's feet. While Napoleon crushed each revolt he knew only the defeat of Britain, his implacable enemy, could ensure the permanence of his European Empire. It was more than fitting, therefore, that when he, France's greatest general, came face to face at last with a British Army, it should be led by Britain's greatest soldier of the day, Wellington. Each man knew he must win or be destroyed: each man knew the fate of Europe rested on his victory. And in one incredibly bloody afternoon the issue was decided. History has nothing to offer that is more dramatic.

A playwright would have difficulty in conceiving two protagonists more dissimilar. Napoleon, short of stature, impulsive, demonstrative, a student of law, a brilliant opportunist, a visionary with a weakness for pomp and ceremony. Wellington, tall, aristocratic, aloof and curt, contemptuous of praise or ceremony, and almost an ascetic in his personal habits. Napoleon possessing earthy Corsican ingredients that won and held the love of his common soldiers. Wellington, never hiding his aristocratic disdain for the rank and file, yet winning their confidence if not their affection by his sheer military skill. Were it not for the two men's insatiable desire for knowledge, their incisive minds, their courage and powers of leadership, one would be wrongly tempted to think the strange coincidence that brought both of them into the world in 1769 was the only thing they had in common.

9

Yet for all their qualities it is quite possible that neither man would have earned more than a mention in history had the traditional old dynasties that had kept Europe in a state of apathy for centuries remained in power during their lifetimes. It was the earth-shaking events of 1789, when the French peasants stormed the Bastille and a hated monarchy and church were overthrown, that provided the opportunities both men were to seize. Overnight a young republic, bursting with revolutionary zeal, appeared in the heart of Europe's senile monarchies and empires. Its colossal energy, its glee in overthrowing traditional institutions, terrified the old hierarchies who drew together for protection. War soon followed but, although outnumbered by the coalition ranged against it, the tattered French Army was fired by a zeal and faith the monarchies' professional armies could not match, and a breathing space was won for the turbulent young republic to consolidate itself.

It was a consolidation that proved difficult. Leaders rose and fell and dragged down with them the Army officers they had promoted. The opportunities such a climate provided for a brilliant and ambitious young officer without political scruples were obvious, and Napoleon began to make his name heard. After a few reverses, he won favour with the Convention for his ruthless 'whiff of grapeshot' suppression of the royalist uprising. Soon afterwards he met and married the influential (and unfaithful) Josephine de Beauharnais and from then on his progress was phenomenal. He received the command of the French Army in Italy at the age of twenty-six and his success there, particularly against the Austrians at Lodi, was to establish his military genius.

That his political skills matched his military talents was soon in evidence. After throwing the mighty Austrian Empire out of Italy he gained command of an army to invade Egypt with the object of marching on towards British India. Defying Nelson's blockade of the Mediterranean – and missing detection and destruction by a hair's breadth – he landed 40,000 men in Egypt and soon captured Cairo. He brought with him lawyers, administrators, and specialists in all fields, and with his immense energy created a new society in Egypt, part of which remains to this day.

Checked by the Englishman Sydney Smith before Acre – and exhibiting the ruthlessness that was in him by killing prisoners before retreating – Napoleon abandoned his grandiose plan to conquer the Orient, left his army, and returned alone to France. Sensing that she was looking for a strong leader he entered into complicated political intrigues that ended with his emerging as First Consul of France, a post as powerful as that of a monarch. During this period, one of France's 'golden ages', he demonstrated his extraordinary talent for administration by reorganizing the central government, stabilizing the currency, establishing a system of education, and drawing up the famous Code Napoleon which gave the country a greatly improved legal system. Conscious that after nearly ten years of war France wanted peace, he allowed the once-hated aristocrats to return and even toyed with the idea of bringing back the priests.

During these years England, isolated on the periphery of a cowed Europe, had been busy forming coalitions of states to overthrow the French 'ursurper'. But, in war, Napoleon seemed invincible and the Austrians, Prussians, even the Russians, were all forced to accept his terms. England, however, refused to legalize his occupation of Belgium and Napoleon threatened to close Europe's ports to British trade.

The Treaty of Amiens provided an uneasy truce between the two countries, only for war to break out again in 1803. Alarmed by the attempts to assassinate him and conscious Josephine had borne him no heir, Napoleon accepted the Imperial Crown from the Senate and to the amazement of Europe as well as France, insisted on being consecrated by the Pope in Notre Dame cathedral. The wheel had turned its full ironic circle: the young republic's most militant son had assumed the throne that it had cost so many French lives to overthrow.

Napoleon naïvely believed his coronation in Notre Dame would gain him admittance at last into the hostile camp of legitimate monarchs. The reverse was true: the European aristocrats were determined to break this 'parvenu soldier' and England was able to create a third coalition of nations whose purpose was to drive France back to her original frontiers. Napoleon had now only one purpose in life: to destroy the English before they could destroy him.

He built 2,000 flat-bottomed boats to invade England. Success depended on enticing the English fleet out of the Channel for three days, and he ordered Villeneuve to draw Nelson off to the Antilles and then set full sail for home. But with the plan failing to disperse the English fleet, Napoleon was forced to abandon his invasion plans and instead marched his Grand Armée to the Danube. Two months later Nelson's victory at Trafalgar made a French invasion of England impossible.

But it was not impossible for Napoleon to smash England's allies and smash them he did. He defeated the Austrians at Ulm with hardly a shot fired and became master of the German Empire and Italy. He enticed the Russian armies on to the frozen lakes at Austerlitz and shattered the ice with his cannon fire. This brilliant victory blew the coalition to pieces and killed its English architect, Pitt. On land it seemed no power on earth could defeat the 'little Emperor'. With all this success came the inevitable corruption in character. At the height of his power he is said to have boasted he had 100,000 men and 10,000,000 francs to spend every year. In 1813 he told Metternich, a minister of Austria, that a man such as he was not much concerned over the lives of a million men. His love of ostentation grew, and his famous Champs de Mai, held after his return from Elba to celebrate the new constitution, was in effect nothing but a huge military display whose purpose, like Hitler's Nuremberg rallies in later years, was to incite militarism in the civil population.

His invincible reputation brought terror to the most valiant of soldiers. Yet there is no doubt part of his success lay in his contempt for the established codes of war. For centuries Europe had observed these codes until military tactics were as predictable as the steps of a minuet. Now, as was again to happen 150 years later, a New Order had appeared that cared nothing for tradition. Napoleon fought to win – to win in any way he could – and it was his luck and destiny that he appeared at a moment in history when a young republic was uninhibited enough to follow him. It would be no exaggeration to say that during his years of power Europe had her first taste of Total War.

During these momentous years Wellington was learning his profession as a soldier in India. Fortunate in having his elder brother, Lord Mornington, sent out to Calcutta as Governor-General, he soon found himself responsible for the equipping of a field force sent to attack Tipu Sultan, a powerful native prince who was known to be negotiating with the French. The success of this expedition was early evidence of Wellington's mastery over supply problems.

In 1800 he suffered a disappointment when his brother took from him the command of a major naval operation against the French in Egypt: an experience so bitter to him that some historians say it explained his curt and crusty behaviour afterwards. Certainly it broke his health and estranged him from his brother for years. But he was soon to earn an immortal place in Indian history during the British war against the powerful Mahratta nation. The pitched battles he fought in this campaign in difficult country, the sieges, the forced marches, the setbacks, the negotiations with reluctant allies, even the conclusion of peace treaties, were all valuable experiences for the great European adventure soon to come. That he profited from them is shown in his victory at Assaye where, against 40,000 men and an apparently impregnable position, he led 7,000 men to victory. One of his outstanding qualities as a field commander was his habit of staying in the centre of the battle, so keeping in direct control of his army's flanks. As a consequence his personal staff was always small.

In 1805, suffering from rheumatism caused by hardships during the Mahratta campaign, he returned to England and married the faithful Kitty Pakenham who had waited ten long years for him. For the next three years he was engaged in politics and then sent into northern Europe as part of

Britain's contribution to Pitt's third and last coalition. Napoleon's shattering victories at Ulm and Austerlitz destroyed the project and Wellington had barely embarked before the expedition was recalled. A more successful campaign in Denmark earned him a command in Portugal which, because it was still trading with Britain, was invaded by the French. This was little more than a token expedition by the English, who expected defeat and evacuation, and as a result Wellington was only given second-rate soldiers. In this climate he made his first direct contact with the French armies.

During this time Napoleon was undisputed master of Europe. In a blitzkrieg attack he had defeated the Prussians at Jena and triumphantly entered Berlin. For the moment only two nations threatened him: Russia to the east and Britain to the west. Unable to crush Britain because of her storm-tossed 'wooden walls', he passed his famous decree in 1806 that forbade all European ports to trade with her. To make the Russians comply he invaded Poland and later defeated the Russians at Friedland, forcing the Czar, Alexander, to make terms at Tilsit.

But although he was now at the peak of his glory, with the whole of Europe at his feet, the trade blockade that was hurting England was also hurting his empire, and when Portugal defied him he sent an expedition to crush her. Soon afterwards he dethroned the Spanish king and put his brother Joseph in his place.

It was a grave error of judgement which led to war with Spain. Wellington, brilliant at keeping his lines of supply and communications open, held on in Portugal, forcing Napoleon to send more and more men into the Peninsula. His best generals – the red-headed Ney ('the bravest of the brave' who was to have five horses killed beneath him at Waterloo), the clever but cautious Soult – none of them made progress against Wellington who was now proving that British infantry were more than a match for any soldiers in Europe.

Napoleon had made an alliance with Austria by divorcing

Josephine and marrying the Austrian princess, Marie Louise. She bore him a son and the French Empire an heir in 1811, and for a while Napoleon was happy. But with the continental blockade causing great discontent and unemployment in his empire he knew that any relaxation on his part might cause the whole edifice to crumble. Consequently when he learned Russia had defected by allowing in 150 British ships flying the American flag, he decided to invade her. Like Hitler after him, he had long feared the enigmatic Russia at his back, and felt that once he had finally crushed her he could contain his last enemy, England.

His Grand Army as he now called it, of 600,000 men, was the greatest he had commanded. His plan was to crush the Russians in one massive battle, but by burning their crops and withdrawing they drew him deeper into the vast steppes. At Borodino he caught up with them but although the charges of his magnificent generals, Ney, Murat, and Davout, broke up the enemy positions, Napoleon was too afraid of the vast spaces behind him to throw in his Guard and the Russians were able to continue their retreat.

Moscow was in flames when he reached it but still the Russians did not sue for peace. He waited a fateful month and then, realizing at last his peace terms were rejected, began the long march back to France. But it was October: he had left the retreat too late. The terrible Russian winter reduced his army to a rabble, and Napoleon abandoned it and made for Paris. For this disaster he blamed England, whose implacable refusal to make peace had forced his hand.

He performed miracles on his return, raising and re-equipping another army in less than a year, but the writing was now on the wall. Wellington was in Madrid and moving up to the Pyrenees. Finding fresh courage, the Austrians, the Prussians, the Russians, all were threatening France's frontiers. Leading his reduced army brilliantly, Napoleon still won battles but the end was near. After the battle of Leipzig, 600,000 Russians, Austrians, Germans, and English invaded France from every side. In March 1814, with the Prussians and Austrians at the gates of Paris, Napoleon's own generals, led by his loved and loyal Ney, demanded his abdication. This defection of his generals, particularly Ney, was the bitterest blow of all and one he did not forget in the days to come. He made a last appeal to them to fight: when they kept an icy silence he knew all was lost.

His ambition had brought ruin to France and death to countless thousands all over Europe, and only his Old Guard, veterans who had grown to middle age in his service, wept when an English frigate carried him away. From the throne of the mightiest empire modern Europe had seen, the 'Little Emperor' was given the sovereignty of the tiny island of Elba. And the fat, gouty Bourbon, Louis XVIII, was put on the throne of France.

But the incredible flame of ambition had not yet burned out. While sovereigns and diplomats, with Wellington in high prominence among them, struggled at the Congress of Vienna to put Europe together again, Napoleon, in between giving Elba a new road system, a hospital, and a theatre, was brooding over past glories. He had many grievances. Marie Louise had not come and brought his son, and the pension he had been promised had not been paid. In addition he feared for his life, for he knew that while he lived the Bourbons would never feel safe. Hearing from France of their unpopularity and that there was already a move to dethrone them, learning with new heart that his old soldiers had remained faithful to his memory, Napoleon decided on a last great gamble. Assembling his tiny army of less than 1,000 men at Porto Ferrajo, he sailed for France to take back his crown and his glory. The Hundred Days, the last tremendous act of the epic drama that was to end at Waterloo, had begun.

CHAPTER ONE

The young Austrian envoy, standing before Louis XVIII, turned at the urgent knock on the door. A second later an old nobleman burst into the audience chamber, followed by two middle-aged marshals. All three men looked upset and alarmed. Ignoring the King's raised eyebrows the old man, Baron de Vitrolles, hurried forward and held out an envelope in a trembling hand.

His voice was shrill. 'Sire, the monster has escaped from Elba. A courier brought the news and this dispatch a few minutes ago.'

For a moment the King froze. Then he reached out and took the dispatch. 'Where has he landed?'

'In France, Sire. In the Golfe Juan. The news was sent by aerial telegraph from Lyons.'

Louis's eyes moved to the pale faces of the two men standing behind the nobleman. One was Ney, the other Soult, both ex-generals of Napoleon. With his powerful build, red hair, and weather-beaten face, Ney could not be mistaken for anyone but a soldier. A passionate, quick-tempered man who could occasionally be both brash and boorish, he had displayed brilliant qualities of leadership under Napoleon and his reckless courage was legend in the French Army. His companion Soult, also a soldier with a high reputation, tended to favour more caution in his military campaigns. With his high forehead, receding hair, and furrowed face he resembled a worried academic as he met the King's gaze. He was the first to speak.

'At least we can thank God he is mad enough to land in France, Sire.'

Louis's blue eyes gave him a significant look before concentrating on the dispatch. The young envoy, unable to contain his excitement, turned on Baron de Vitrolles. 'Are you saying that Napoleon Bonaparte has returned to France, Votre Excellence?'

The old man motioned him to be quiet. Louis, a sufferer from gout, was having difficulty in breaking the seal of the dispatch and his brother, the future Charles X, who was standing behind his chair, moved forward to help him. Louis waved him back. He was a man of gross dimensions, with a huge stomach and arms that hung with fat. Reputed to consume at least two gallons of wine a day, he had the florid complexion of a heavy drinker and a forehead that seemed to rise in a smooth arc to the dome of his powdered head. As a protection against his gout, he was wearing bundles of velvet around his legs.

He had now succeeded in opening the envelope, and as he read the contents a tense silence fell in the magnificently ornate room. Ney, pale and still, looked like a man awaiting sentence. As Louis finished reading the dispatch and his gouty hand fell on his stomach, Ney could be seen swallowing to lubricate his throat.

Louis's voice was composed. 'We must be careful not to dramatize this event, gentlemen. General Bonaparte and his followers – a mere thousand men – are not very dangerous yet. Marshal Soult, you will keep command of the troops here in Paris. Marshal Ney, you will be the first to confront the werewolf. Leave as soon as possible and travel with all haste.'

As the red-headed marshal stared at the King, his eyes betrayed a turmoil of conscience. Louis, intelligent enough to recognize it, nodded. 'I know how you have loved this man. But now you see how little he cares for peace, you will do your duty to France.'

Ney drew himself erect. 'Sire, I hate him for the evil he is doing. I will bring him back in an iron cage.'

Stepping forward, he kissed the King's jewelled hand. Then, with face dark and angry, he left the chamber, followed by Soult. Moving a leg painfully, Louis grimaced at Baron de Vitrolles.

'How these soldiers exaggerate. In an iron cage! Who asked for that?'

The old man moved anxiously forward. 'Sire, he is dangerous. Already his proclamations are nailed up in the streets of Seranon.'

The excited young envoy tried again. 'Sire, what message can I take to my Emperor?'

Louis turned to him with a shrug. 'You can say a mutual acquaintance is paying an unexpected visit to France – a visit that will be of short duration. Tell your Emperor you found me entirely unperturbed, for I am convinced the event will have as little effect on the tranquillity of Europe as it has on me.'

The short, stout man in the grey redingote reined back his horse and waited for the officer of the Polish lancers to approach him. The man cantered alongside, wheeled his horse, and pointed at the defile ahead.

'It is only a line regiment, Sire. But they have cannon and Marshal Ney commands them.'

Napoleon nodded and rode ahead of his troop of stationary cavalry. The officer followed him. The road into the defile began to unwind and reveal its perils. On the right was a steep mountainside, on the left a long, narrow lake. Deep into the defile a battery of cannon and a regiment of soldiers effectively blocked the pass. Even at that distance the unnatural stillness of the men was noticeable.

The Polish officer, a grizzled Napoleonic veteran, gave a grunt of contempt. 'They are nervous, Sire. Let me make a charge and they will run like rabbits.'

Napoleon lifted his telescope. He sounded amused. 'Where have you been these fifteen years, Captain? Did you miss Lutzen, Elchingen, were you not at the Moskowa? I tell you I have known men more loyal than Ney but none more brave.'

Beneath his shako the veteran's bearded cheeks were flushed. 'I have been in your service long enough, Sire, to know that no enemy officer can withstand you when his men desert him.'

Napoleon sounded quizzical as he lowered his telescope. 'You are right about that, Captain. Go and tell my

Infantry of the Guard to form up behind me. We are going to present our simple, heroic Ney with a problem he has never faced before.'

Deep in the defile, erect on his horse alongside the regiment of young soldiers, Ney was experiencing spasms of trembling that racked his whole body. It was caused, he told himself angrily, by the chilly morning air. There was still snow on the surrounding mountains and an icy wind was blowing off the lake.

He was staring at the empty road ahead, down which Napoleon's van of lancers had withdrawn. What would be his next move, he wondered. The Old Guard with their bayonets at the ready? Glancing at the young soldiers who barred the road and the mountainside above, Ney tried to find confidence in their superior numbers and their cannon. Yet would they stand fast against Napoleon's terrifying Old Guard, small though the Corsican's Elba contingent was? As trainees they had been reared on the legend of the Guard's invincibility, and to Ney resistance suddenly seemed too much to expect of them.

Their excited murmur drew Ney's attention back to the road. Three hundred yards ahead two horsemen had appeared round the bend. One was wearing a bicorne and a grey redingote and at the sight of him Ney felt his heart contract. God, the nostalgia and the irony of it! Fifteen years of following that little figure all over Europe and the steppes of Russia . . . The plod of weary horses, the jingle of harness, the smell of sweat and leather . . . The camp fires and the picket lines, under moons like melons and moons of pitiless ice. The fear, the grapeshot, the pain, the victories that made a man feel like God; the elements that had welded them together in a way only soldiers could understand.

Fifteen years, and every day of it he had been willing to give his life that the little Corsican could extend his empire from Normandy to the Urals. Until that black morning when it had become clear France could suffer no more and he of all men had been forced to place the papers of abdication in his hands.

It should not have ended like that. Nor should this happen – that he, the soldier Napoleon loved most of all, should be chosen as the obstacle between him and the throne he wished to recover. Watching the distant Corsican through eyes that were blurred in the wind, Ney felt sick with bitterness.

The two horsemen vanished around the bend. Ney glanced at Delessart, his second-in-command. The colonel's face was pale but determined. Ney edged his horse towards him, keeping his voice low. 'It'll be his Guard first. Then his cavalry. You understand that?'

Delessart nodded. Ney's eyes flickered to the motionless soldiers. 'Will they fight?'

The Colonel gave a grim nod. 'They will fight. I have trained many of them myself.'

Ney sat back, sighed, and waited. Beside him buds were green on the branches of a bay willow. The chain curb of his bridle jingled as his horse stirred nervously. Ney calmed him with a pat. For a moment the only sounds were the soughing of the wind and an occasional nervous cough. Then Ney heard a thudding sound, like the sudden beating of a heart. As it grew louder Ney felt tension snap tight among the young soldiers. He hissed at Delessart from the corner of his mouth.

'Talk to them, man. Hearten them or when they see the Guard come round that corner they'll freeze.'

Delessart wheeled his horse. 'All France's eyes are on you today, mes gars. Hold steady and before the hour's over we'll have the tyrant trussed up and ready for the Marshal's cage.'

Ney had already regretted his impetuous remark to Louis and the thin cheers that broke out, confirming it had become common knowledge, made him wince.

The leading ranks of the Old Guard, their shakos making them look unnaturally tall, were now appearing round the bend. Marching in perfect formation, their muskets at the ready, they looked living proof of their legendary invincibility. Ney's eyes, however, were fastened on the dismounted man who was marching a few paces ahead of them. His voice had a strangled sound as he turned to Delessart.

'You see that? He is leading them on foot.'

Delessart nodded eagerly. 'It's better this way, sir. We can dispose of him more quickly.' He turned to his men. 'Ready! Present!'

There was a loud slap of hands as the leading ranks of the young soldiers brought their muskets up across their chests. The van of the Guard, with its diminutive leader, was now little more than a hundred paces away and the tramp-tramp of marching feet reverberated from the mountainside. A few seconds passed and then Delessart's voice rang out again.

'Aim!'

As his soldiers brought their muskets to their shoulders, a command followed like an echo down the defile and the Old Guard halted as one man. At a second command their muskets rose to cover the barrier of men before them. The impasse was now complete, another aggressive order or a nervous trigger finger would turn the pass into a slaughterhouse. Heedless of his own danger, Ney watched in fascination.

It was then a new voice, but to Ney one as familiar as his own, rang down the defile. 'Infantry of the Guard! Reverse arms!'

With discipline concealing their surprise, the Old Guard swung their muskets harmlessly beneath their left arms. As Ney gave a start and a great sigh of relief sounded from Delessart's young soldiers, Napoleon began walking alone down the road towards them.

As he drew nearer, Delessart heard Ney's hoarse whisper: 'The unexpected – always the unexpected' and his glance showed the Marshal's face full of torment.

Napoleon was well within pistol range before he halted. Removing his hat, he set his hands on his hips. 'Soldiers of the Fifth! Do you not recognize me?'

Muskets were wavering, some falling away. Cursing, Delessart raised an arm. 'Aim at that man! Fire!'

A terrible silence followed. Delessart stared at his troops in disbelief. 'I said fire!'

Men closed their eyes. A young soldier swayed and fainted,

his musket clattering to the ground. Napoleon, his voice casual, pointed at his crumpled figure. 'Pick that boy up!'

Three men stooped to obey. Moving a few steps nearer, the Corsican opened the breast of his redingote. 'You all know me now. If there is any man wishes to kill his Emperor, he may shoot. History will not forget his name.'

In spite of the frantic shouts of regimental officers, musket after musket wavered and fell. From the mountainside someone shouted 'Vive l'Empereur' and the cry was taken up by those below. Discipline faltered then collapsed like a broken dam as soldiers surged forward. Some dropped at Napoleon's feet, others kissed his hands. Men lifted their shakos on the barrels of their muskets, and deliriously shouted their allegiance. Erect on his horse, Ney sat with glazed eyes. Napoleon gave him a glance of triumph, then called for silence.

'Soldiers, it is not ambition that brings me back to you. Leading members of the Paris government have called for me and my return is supported by England and Austria. To join me is not to desert France but to help her find justice again. The fat Bourbon has seen the inevitable and is already in flight.'

There was a tremendous cheer. Men pushed and fought to touch the Corsican's clothes and only parted when Ney rode among them. He dropped his sword at Napoleon's feet, then dismounted and faced him. His words were heard only by the men nearby. 'You lie, Sire. It was Louis who sent me here.'

He received a mocking stare. 'My messengers move faster than yours. I tell you Louis is already fleeing towards Belgium.'

Unable to verify the falsehood, Ney hesitated. 'At least you lie about your reason for returning. Nothing called you back but your own ambition.'

Napoleon motioned a soldier to pick up Ney's sword. He took it and felt the edge of the blade. 'Yours was the last face I saw before I left and now it is the first I see on my return.'

There was the clatter of hoofbeats as Delessart and three

other officers wheeled their horses and galloped down the defile. Knocking aside eager muskets, Napoleon raised his voice. 'Let those men go! I want no blood spilled on my way to Paris.'

Ney was holding out his pistol. 'You should not have come back, Sire. God knows what new suffering it will bring to France.'

Napoleon showed his contempt. 'France and I are the same being. Do you think I could stay away from myself?'

He handed Ney's pistol to a soldier alongside him. The sword was still in his hand: he gazed at it for a moment then suddenly threw it at Ney. As Ney caught it, the Corsican gave another contemptuous laugh. 'For your treachery I give you your life. Now join me and follow me to Grenoble.'

CHAPTER TWO

The crowd outside the town hall of Grenoble was in a state of rare excitement. Townsfolk, peasants, and soldiers were jammed together in the huge cobbled square and more were pouring in by the minute through the narrow streets. Pigeons, used to having domain there, were perched indignantly on the roof tops and on surrounding windowsills, where more spectators were gathered. At the side opposite the town hall an enterprising citizen had been playing revolutionary airs on a barrel organ and filled his beret with coins before a tall moustached sergeant had pushed him aside and called for silence. Other sergeants, also carrying proclamations, were placing themselves at strategic points around the square.

The crowd jostling round the barrel organ had quietened and were now facing the sergeant. Drawing himself to his full, imposing height, he unrolled his sheet of parchment. His voice, fruity with the accent of the Dordogne, boomed across the square to the annoyance of the other sergeants who were made redundant before they spoke.

The first proclamation was Napoleon's address to the people of France, and the crowd listened raptly as the sonorous voice rolled out the dramatic phrases. 'Men of France, your complaints and your desires reached me in exile. I have braved every risk to cross the sea and return to you. I shall disregard all that misguided men have done, written, or said since the fall of Paris – events transcend human beings, and I shall remember only the important services men have rendered ... No man shall have cause to regret my return except those who were put on the throne of France with the help of foreign bayonets. At this moment they are trying to sweep away your rights and replace them by the old feudal system you hated. To you, the patriots, are going the burdens. To the emigrés are going wealth and distinction. All these wrongs I have returned to sweep away ...'

A great cheer broke out as the sergeant finished the proclamation and laid it aside. As he unrolled the message to the Army, soldiers pushed back civilians and kept them silent as the sergeant began reading again.

'Soldiers, we have not been defeated. Our tribulations were due to traitors. Your General, called to the throne by the people's choice and lifted there on your shields, has come back to you. Tear down the hated Bourbon colours the nation has rejected – flaunt the tricolor that we wore together in our days of glory and form up with me beneath it. My life is yours. My interest, my honour, my glory are your interest, honour, and glory ... Victory will go with me – my eagle will fly from steeple to steeple to the towers of Notre Dame itself. Then you can show your scars with honour, for you will be the liberators of your country.'

Another great cheer broke out. Hats were flung into the air and soldiers raised their muskets and shook them joyously. A women let out an ecstatic scream and the whole crowd turned as one to face the balcony of the town hall. As a small, bareheaded figure was seen walking towards the rail, women fainted in their joy and the very ground itself trembled with the cheering.

* * *

Inside the town hall Napoleon was exhibiting his restless energy as he paced up and down a large room crowded with local personages. He was holding the arm of a young colonel as he walked. La Bédoyère, in command of the 7th Line Regiment in Grenoble, had once been his aide-de-camp and had gone over to him when he approached the town. As the two men paced backward and forward, with the ingratiating assemblage making passage for them, Napoleon was talking in low tones to the young colonel.

'I want you to go to Austria, La Bédoyère. Tell the Emperor Europe has nothing to fear from me. France wants peace and I want peace. Tell it well, La Bédoyère. Much might depend on it.'

The door behind Napoleon opened. Local celebrities whispered excitedly among themselves as they saw who was standing there. Napoleon noticed their interest, but did not turn. Instead his voice rose above the buzz of excitement.

'Is that you, Ney?'

The Marshal stepped forward. 'Yes, Sire.'

Napoleon turned mockingly. 'Then you haven't emigrated yet?'

Ney flushed. 'No, Sire.'

'I hope you have kept all your men here?'

'Everyone. To the last drummer boy.'

Napoleon nodded and then glanced at La Bédoyère. 'Start your journey. Remember, I want peace. Tell it to him well, La Bédoyère.'

As the colonel saluted and withdrew, Napoleon turned to the mayor alongside him. 'It is time to show my face. Open all the windows.'

Men hurried to obey. Napoleon took Ney's arm. 'Uncover your head and follow me out on the balcony. I want them to see the Army has come over to me.'

He walked out alone to the balcony rail. The explosion of cheering from below made the windows rattle. Ney, his red hair shining in the sunlight, followed him. The square below was a tossing sea of wine bottles, hats, tricolors, and waving muskets. Napoleon made a gesture for silence, but

26

the shouts of welcome redoubled. Frightened pigeons, circling the square, added to the din.

It was the army sergeants who finally quietened the delirious crowd. Hushed at last, they listened to the small man with the Corsican accent. 'Citizens, I heard your complaints and your desires in my exile. So what choice had I but to come back?'

An enormous roar interrupted him and sent the pigeons circling the square again. As it died down, Napoleon went on: 'I am here among you to resume my rights which are your rights. I have come back only to make France happy.'

Another demonstration broke out. As Napoleon waved both arms in response, he whispered coldly to Ney at his side.

'I shall never forget how you looked that day at Fontaine-bleau, Ney. You, of all men – forcing me to abdicate.'

Ney looked drawn and pale. 'I did only what I had to do, Sire. France would not have followed us into another battle.'

'Not have followed?' The Corsican's voice was icy with contempt. 'When I had given France another victory, she would have followed me to the stars.'

The crowd was quietening and Napoleon turned back to them. 'Men of France! No nation in history has hesitated to rid itself of a ruler put there by foreign bayonets. I know what France wants. I know the very beating of her heart. That is why I stand here today.'

As another wild cheer broke out, the Corsican's low voice taunted Ney. 'I have heard of your boast – to put me down before the King's throne in an iron cage.'

Ney winced. 'I said it, yes. But it was to hide my true feelings.'

The crowd were waiting again. Napoleon's hiss was like a thin whip across the Marshal's face. 'Your feelings are those of a whore, Ney. You sell them to those who pay you best.' He turned back to the crowd. 'Citizens, the fat King in Paris has corrupted the honour of Frenchmen. If he cannot run, he will be carried from his throne.'

It was an insult the crowd loved. There was a scuffle among them and a moment later a fat man, kicking his legs frantically, was lifted high by a dozen arms. As the crowd roared their laughter, Ney's expression betrayed his conflict of conscience. 'You wrong me, Sire. All I have ever done was for France.'

'Are you sure?' the taunting voice asked. 'Is that the reason you are standing at my side now?'

Ney's troubled expression grew. 'I believe it is, Sire. I believe France does not want the Bourbons. But this assumes you will reign with justice. If you continue to govern tyrannically, then I am your prisoner rather than your supporter.'

The Corsican gave him an amused stare. 'At least you believe that France wants me.'

Ney's eyes moved to the fat man still struggling in the arms of his tormentors. 'If I am wrong I shall pay for my mistake. They will be quick to shoot me.'

Napoleon's reply was cynical. 'If it's any comfort to you, you won't die alone. They might even shoot me first.'

He gave a last wave to the crowd and then made a brusque gesture to the obsequious dignitaries lined up behind him. 'That's enough for one day. Have the windows closed to keep out the noise.'

He and Ney vanished from the balcony. But the crowd had not had enough. Cheers of 'Vive l'Empereur' mingled with shouts of: 'Down with the priests', 'Death to the Royalists', 'The Bourbons to the scaffold'. As dogs barked hysterically and tricolors waved, a chant began that was taken up by townsfolk and soldiers alike. 'Ah, ça ira . . . ça ira . . . ça ira . . .' Teenage boys and girls skipped to the tune; middle-aged men and women sang it with wet eyes. 'Vive le son, vive le son; Dansons la Carmagnole, vive le son du canon . . .' The crowd sang the Carmagnole song in chorus as it had been sung in 1793.

It was a sound that reached Napoleon inside the town hall in spite of the closed windows. His eyes glowed as he stared at Ney. 'Listen to them! Soon all France will be singing the old songs. How many regiments have I gained in Grenoble?'

'Five, Sire. All well-trained and armed.'

Napoleon's expression as he turned towards the balcony

window suggested he was talking to himself but Ney caught his exultant murmur. 'Until Grenoble I was a mere adventurer. Now I am a reigning prince again.'

From Grenoble, Napoleon's triumphant march took him to Lyons. Here, on March 10th, Marshal MacDonald was trying to rally the King's forces to stand and fight the Corsican. While reviewing and talking to the troops he was reinforced by Comte d'Artois, the King's brother. The sympathies of the soldiers and their officers were undoubtedly for Napoleon, but the officers had sworn an oath of allegiance to the King and the rank and file were conditioned into obedience. It was the civilian population who swung the balance. In Lyons there were many silk workers who owed their former prosperity to Napoleon and they put massive pressure on the uncertain troops. The crisis came that evening when the van of Napoleon's party reached the city and white Bourbon cockades were thrown down and trampled into the mud. Egged on by the exultant populace the troops laid down their arms and refused to fight. By nightfall, with MacDonald and d'Artois fleeing for their lives, Napoleon took possession of the city.

It was in Lyons, after taking up residence in the archbishop's palace, that Napoleon resumed the title of Emperor. He dismissed all emigrés from the Army, banned the white cockade of the Bourbons, and abolished all the orders, decorations, and promotions made in the Army during the last year. He sequestered the Bourbon estates and abolished the title of nobility. He also sent an order that disbanded the King's Household troops and demanded that the Swiss Guard should leave Paris.

The jubilant citizens of Lyons broke into the Café Bourbon, a popular meeting place for the city's nobler citizens, and smashed the windows of their private houses. Villages for many miles around the city became deserted as the peasants flocked into Lyons to see their legendary Emperor. Even the chicken bones from his plate were kept and treasured as relics. The old magic seemed as potent as ever.

It had already reached Paris, which was in a fever. Gleeful Bonapartists tied white cockades to the tails of dogs and sent them racing through the streets. In retaliation royalists began a campaign of terror against them and any of their like who might support Napoleon. Fouché, the former left-wing leader, only escaped by fleeing down a secret staircase in his house to a neighbour's garden.

With the help of his Minister of War, Marshal Soult, Louis sent out three expeditions to stop Napoleon and all failed. Soult, whose conduct was particularly inept during the crisis, resigned soon afterwards. As Napoleon neared Paris, advice came to Louis from all sides, but in his ineffectual way he accepted little of it. In some cases he could hardly be blamed. One suggestion was that he should shut himself and his supporters in the Tuileries and resist all attempts to remove him, thus forcing Napoleon to enact either a farce or a tragedy! An even more absurd suggestion was that he should ride out in state to meet the usurper at the gates of Paris, where the upstart would be so overawed by the sight of his majesty that he would beat an ignominious retreat! Confusion began to reign everywhere. Men asked their officers for orders, officers turned to their equally unbriefed superiors. Part of the trouble was that the Duc de Blacas, who was the King's chief adviser, still refused to believe the danger from Napoleon was real and kept many of the alarming facts from him.

But the truth reached him nevertheless and he had his diamonds packed into ammunition boxes. Together with four million francs, they were sent north under an escort of gendarmes. That same morning a notice was found tied to the railings round the column in the Place Vendôme. It read: 'From Napoleon to Louis XVIII. My good brother, there is no need to send me any more troops. I have enough already.'

That night, a few minutes before midnight, the Guarde Nationale in the Reserve Guard House saw the King's gilt carriage draw up outside the Pavilion de Flore. Although it was raining hard and a gusty wind was blowing, the courtyard as well as the hall of the Pavilion was crowded with the

King's supporters. The wind of change, which made most men now see Louis as a tedious old man with gout, had not reached them: ardent catholics and royalists, they still believed him God's representative in France. As his gross body, supported by the Duc de Blacas and another nobleman, appeared at the Pavilion entrance, men and women sank to their knees on the wet cobblestones.

A page, carrying a torch whose flame blew horizontally in the wind, led him down the steps to his carriage. There he paused and turned to the sobbing assemblage. 'I am deeply touched by your devotion, my children. But spare me, for I lack strength.'

It took three men to get him into the carriage. As he lay back, gasping on the thick cushions, the Duc de Duras gazed in anxiously. 'Are you all right, Sire?'

Louis's row of chins wobbled as he nodded. He moved anxiously towards Duras. 'How do you think it will be outside? The people are letting him come without bloodshed – will they allow me to leave the same way?'

'I think so, Sire. But it would have been dangerous to wait any longer. The monster is already at Auxerre.'

A sign was made to the coachman and the horses' wet flanks tightened as they took the strain. As the carriage rumbled over the cobblestones a white-haired old man, kneeling in a pool of water, crossed himself. A minute later the Tuileries gate closed. Once more the Bourbon king had fled to exile: once more the throne of France sat empty for the little Emperor.

CHAPTER THREE

At nine o'clock the following evening, Monday, March 20th, a travelling coach, led by an escort of lancers, was seen approaching the Tuileries at speed. Men at the gateway saw its lanterns and a great wave of excitement swept over the crowd of people gathered inside the great courtyard. Most of them were former members and servants of the Imperial Court who had been converging all day on the Tuileries to take up their old quarters and welcome back their master. Many half-pay officers were among them, some on horseback, others waiting on the Tuileries' steps.

The frenzied cheer that greeted the coach as it swept through the gates caused the startled horses to rear and almost throw one of the postillion riders. As in the days of Imperial Rome, it was the soldiers who claimed the right to welcome back their Emperor. Drawing their swords, forcing the crowd back, they swept forward in a frenzy of idolatry, one officer even throwing himself beneath the wheels of the coach. Shouting, cheering, they helped the Corsican reverently to the ground and passed him from hand to hand to the Pavilion de Flore where other officers lifted him shoulder high and carried him up the steps.

Inside the Pavilion emotion turned even more delirious. As the tide of officers swept the small Corsican up the staircase, an hysterical mob of men and women began flooding down it. Seeing the danger, one of the officers turned and screamed to a comrade.

'For God's sake, get in front of him. Quickly, before he is crushed!'

An officer, by name Lavellette, flung himself in front of the advancing party and took the full pressure of the descending crowd. As he forced himself back up the staircase, step by painful step, his laboured voice could be heard gasping. 'It's you, my Emperor. It's you . . . you at last!'

And the object of all this idolatry, carried high on the shoulders of his officers, had his eyes closed and a fixed smile on his face. He looked like a sleepwalker – or a man drunk on the excess of his triumph.

Yet Napoleon was soon to learn this feverish welcome was not typical of the citizens of Paris as a whole. It had been given him by those who stood to gain everything by his return, his old soldiers whom Louis had stood down on half-pay, his servants, and place-seekers. Unlike the provinces, Paris itself had not taken part, and in the coming weeks Napoleon discovered his main followers there were either thoughtless sightseers or dangerous street mobs thirsting for excitement or violence.

Nevertheless he was able to form a government immediately, since most of the ministers who had previously served him were ready to take office again. Cambaceres became Minister of Justice, Calaincourt Minister of Foreign Affairs, Bassano Secretary of State. Fouché became Minister of Police. In two new appointments Carnot accepted the Minister of the Interior and Marshal Davout the important post of Minister of War. In addition, Napoleon gained the support of General Drouot, a stooping short-sighted soldier who was nevertheless the greatest artillery-man of his day. And although Soult had been one of the marshals who had forced Napoleon's abdication, a shortage of experienced officers forced the Corsican to make Soult his Chief of Staff.

On his journey to Paris from Elba Napoleon had stressed to the crowds that he was a soldier of the Revolution and had come back from exile to deliver the country from the nobles and priests who wished to enslave it again. Once back in the Tuileries, however, his reinstatement of palace prefects, pages, heralds, and all the rest of palace pageantry gave evidence of his monarchical tendencies. The steady, hard-working people of Paris showed themselves either opposed to him or indifferent. The legal profession was openly hostile.

To France and the rest of the world during those early momentous days Napoleon adopted the role of a dove. In the same way that he had won support en route to Paris by assuring the war-weary populace they would have peace under his sovereignty, he tried to pacify the Allied Heads of State with letters assuring them his only wish was to keep the peace of Europe. He forgave his old enemies and drew up an Additional Act of the Constitution to provide for free elections and the freedom of the Press: a concession unpopular among his army officers who, like army officers anywhere, wanted a return of autocracy. It was these very

33

men, who had previously betrayed him, that he had been forced to restore to their old positions, and it did not add up to a very strong team with which to oppose the combined might of England, Prussia, Austria, and Russia.

For in spite of his pacific letters and assurances, a shrewd politician like Napoleon must have guessed all along that his return to the French throne would bring massive retaliation against France, and the interview he had with Davout on March 21st, weeks before his appeasing letters to Austria and England were returned unacknowledged, showed how his mind was working.

Davout was one of the most brilliant of Napoleon's generals and had retired on the first restoration of Louis. He was a stern disciplinarian and the severity of his conduct in occupied countries, although carried out under Napoleon's orders, had made him feared in Europe. In his role of Minister of War he listened to his Emperor's summing up of the situation.

'If war comes, Davout, we strike at Belgium. France needs it to protect her northern flank. How long do you think we have to prepare?'

'Until June, Sire. Not longer.'

Napoleon shook his head. 'I say July. The second or third week. A large part of England's best troops are in America, the Russians camp in Poland, and Murat in Italy can hamper Austria if she decides to fight.'

'Do you think she will, Sire?'

Napoleon rose from his chair and moved over to the window. 'It will depend on the fate of my letter that offers peace and asks for the return of my son.'

'What if they do not agree, Sire?'

Unseen by Davout, the Corsican winced. 'Let us not meet obstacles before they appear.' Recovering, he swung round. 'We must divide our enemies, Davout. Keep them from war until the early autumn and we will have 800,000 men under arms.'

Davout looked anxious. 'That will mean conscription again, Sire.'

'And so?'

'Sire, the King's most popular measure was its abolition. The people will not accept its revival.'

'Are you saying I have no authority over France?'

In his anxiety Davout moved towards the Emperor. 'Things have changed in France, Your Majesty. The people are weary of war: they want their sons back on the land. We have 200,000 men under arms at the moment. Let the gap be filled by volunteers.'

'600,000 volunteers? Are you in your cups this morning, Davout?'

The Marshal flushed. 'The Garde Nationale can give us 230,000 men. And your old veterans will provide another 25,000.'

'And with less than 500,000 men I might have to fight four nations? I want the 1815 conscripts, Davout. They are already mustered and not yet demobilized. See they are trained and ready.'

Biting his lip, Davout nodded. Napoleon, who had moved back to the desk, was studying a report. 'Arms, cartridges, uniforms – all as scarce as soldiers. I shall need 400,000 new muskets by the end of the year. Make what we can – buy the rest from foreign manufacturers and ship them on barges down the Rhine. And the men must have at least a hundred cartridges each. Work the factories, particularly Vincennes, twenty-four hours a day.'

Building up armies swiftly was a speciality of Napoleon's. During his reign as Emperor he had standardized military equipment throughout the country. The types of artillery wheels had been reduced from twenty-two to eight and the same principles applied to saddlery, harnesses, and tools, with enormous improvement in efficiency.

His training methods were equally standardized, reducing the problems if regiments were forced to combine with one another or were scattered into smaller units. Even the battle tactics he used during the latter half of his career were designed to obtain the utmost benefit from unseasoned troops.

'What about your generals, Sire?' Davout asked.

Restless with energy, hands clasped behind his back in characteristic pose, Napoleon was pacing backwards and forwards behind his desk. 'D'Erlon, Reille, Gérard, Lobau, Vandamme, Rapp . . .'

Davout gave a start. 'Rapp!' Rapp was a general who had told Napoleon on his arrival in Paris that he would have shot him if the King had given the order.

Napoleon gave a grim, half-humorous smile. 'The man has courage and that is something we shall need in abundance before the year is out. Tell them to establish their corps in these centres: d'Erlon in Lille, Reille in Valenciennes, Gérard in Metz, Lobau in Paris, Rapp in Strasbourg. Vandamme's centre I'll decide later. If the need arises I shall operate from Maubeuge on the Sambre, where they can march to join me.'

Davout was showing uneasiness again. 'You don't think their presence might provoke our enemies into action, Sire?'

He received another grim smile. 'Don't you think the crown of France on my head is enough provocation, Davout? Call them Corps d'Observation and spread the word they are only to keep the royalists quiet in the provinces.'

The scene that April day in Napoleon's study was one of feverish activity. Five male secretaries, quill pens poised, were bent over five small tables. In the centre of the room, a large table was covered with reports, letters, petitions, lists, and miscellaneous government papers. Napoleon, the freshest man present, was prowling among the secretaries dictating several letters simultaneously.

He paused over secretary No 1. 'I have come to make peace. Nothing more.'

He moved over to secretary No 2 whose pen was raised. 'To the Countess Barry. Madame, I regret to inform you that your son Ferdinand has been killed during training manoeuvres.'

He glanced at No 5, who was half-turned and waiting, and shook his head curtly. 'Not yet.' He walked past No 3 who was sanding a completed letter and paused by No 4. 'You will also remove Colonel Musset. The conscripts from

36

the Macon province are insufficient. You will sweep the area again. Signature.'

He returned to No 2, signing on the way the completed No 3 letter. 'Your son, madame, was brave and persevering in his duties ...' As the man scribbled down the condolences, Napoleon turned to No 3. 'The next one is to the Prince Regent of England.' He glanced back at No 2. 'I am sorry, madame, that Fate has such little discrimination. Signature.'

He moved to secretary No 5 as if ready to complete the letter he had already commenced. The man waited but the Corsican seemed to lose his nerve and turned to No 4, dictating quickly and angrily.

'To the Prince Alexis. You are wrong, Prince. I did not usurp the crown. It was lying in the gutter and I picked it up with my sword. It was the people who placed it on my head. Who saves his country violates no law. Signature.'

Then he appeared ready at last for No 5, although he kept his eyes averted from the paper on which the secretary was writing. 'I beg you again as my wife – even as the daughter of Austria, my enemy – to restore to me my dearest possession, my son.'

No 3 was waiting with an empty paper and Napoleon approached him. 'Your Highness, England has been my generous enemy for twenty years but now I desire only peace with her. Therefore I protest at the presence of the Duke of Wellington on the northern borders of France.'

Moving back to within a few paces of No 5 he paused, his voice betraying his emotion. 'Being my son, he is my future. But I had rather he were thrown from the walls of Schonbrunn than be brought up a captive Austrian prince.'

He turned sharply to No 4. 'To the Quartermaster-General. The boots supplied to the 2nd Corps are a disgrace. I have inspected a pair myself ...' He paused and then went on bleakly as if the awful thought contained in the previous letter were still in his mind. 'And I threw them from the window like as much rubbish!'

*   *   *

37

Napoleon, La Bédoyère, and Drouot were walking slowly past a row of colonnades outside the Tuileries palace. The day was full of spring and blossom was gay in the gardens. A zestful breeze kept brushing a fountain whose cascade glistened in the sunlight.

All three men appeared deep in thought. It was Napoleon who spoke first, addressing La Bédoyère. 'Well, it is done. England, Austria, Russia, Prussia – all Europe has declared war on me. Not on France. A war against one man.'

'They dignify you, Sire, by making you a nation.'

Napoleon paused opposite the fountain. 'They have denied me the civilization of law. Any corporal who can get me beneath the branch of a tree can hang me.' He turned to Drouot. 'What news of Wellington today?'

'Still in Brussels, Sire. Still doing nothing.'

The Emperor's eyes were moving down a bank of red tulips. 'Our meeting will not be long delayed. I feel it.'

From a second-storey window at the opposite side of the gardens three men, Carnot, Soult, and Ney were watching the small party. 'So it has happened,' Carnot muttered. 'Once more we must fight the world alone. And what nation can push back the sea?'

There was a tense silence before Soult answered him. 'You think it is as bad as the last time?'

Carnot shrugged. 'Isn't it?'

Ney was frowning. 'No. Austria and Russia are not ready yet. The danger lies in waiting.'

Soult turned to him. 'The Emperor said the same thing this morning. Wellington is in Brussels, perhaps waiting for Blücher to join him. If we can concentrate an army in secret at Maubeuge and destroy their forces piecemeal, we might then be able to face the Austrians and Russians later. I believe myself it is France's only chance. But the Emperor will have to move like lightning to get the Army to the Belgian frontier in time.'

Carnot looked troubled as he gazed through the window. 'You know that he went to La Malmaison last week?' When both men nodded, Carnot went on: 'He sat alone in the room where Josephine died and spoke not a word to anyone during his journey home. And on Friday evening I found him in tears before a portrait of his son.'

Ney was staring at the Minister of the Interior in dislike. 'What are you trying to say?'

'He has changed since the old days, mon ami. He works now in fits and starts. As energetically, yes, but when he rests it is as if he were dead.'

'What do you expect of a soldier cooped up within these silken walls?' Ney grunted. 'He only needs the smell of gunpowder to turn him into a tiger again.'

Carnot gave another shrug. 'For France's sake I hope you are right.'

Ney turned impatiently to Soult. 'Has he said anything about giving me a command?' When Soult shook his head, Ney's voice rose in frustration. 'Why not? He has forgiven you. Was my crime any worse?'

Down in the gardens Drouot was shaking his head in awe. 'Four nations marching against one man. History can show nothing like it.'

Napoleon's laugh reached the three men at the window. 'You are right, Drouot. I have made quite a mark on this world, haven't I?'

Large wax candles burned in baskets around the walls of the bathroom. Lying in the bath with his hands resting on his swelling stomach, Napoleon looked a small and vulnerable figure. As a cold draught swept across the steam-filled room he opened his eyes to see Constant, his servant, hurrying towards him.

'Marshal Soult is here, Sire. He craves to see you at once.'

The Corsican sat upright. 'Send him in.'

Soult was inside the bathroom before the servant had time to turn around. 'Sire, I have just received reports on the Allied cantonments. Wellington's troops are still grouped round Mons and west and north of Brussels. Blücher's army is based round Namur and Liège, except for the 1st Corps whose headquarters is Charleroi. So they are still apart.'

39

Napoleon's dark eyes glowed with excitement. 'You are sure of this?'

'Certain, Sire. I have it from three separate sources.'

'And their armies? Is their strength confirmed?'

'Wellington has around 67,000 men. Blücher has slightly fewer.'

The Corsican gave a jubilant laugh. 'Then I was right. My 124,000 men is enough if I can catch them apart. And they give me that chance!' Slapping the water in his excitement, he drenched Soult's white trousers. 'What will history say of them?'

His enthusiasm infected even the dour Soult. 'It will be harsh, Sire.'

There was another exultant laugh. 'History will pillory them, Soult. If possible I shall destroy Blücher first. Then Wellington and I will have the day to ourselves, and what a day it will be. Everything will depend on one battle – just as it did at Marengo.' His dark eyes glowed up at the Marshal. 'The stars are still shining for us, Soult.'

'Yes, Sire. It seems they are.'

The Corsican lay contentedly back in the water. 'Wellington and I at last. One battle to settle all accounts.' Then, as his eyes fell on the swelling protuberance of his stomach, his expression changed. 'Only at Marengo I was young. So were we all, Soult. All young.'

As Soult gazed down he remembered Carnot's words, and the rising steam seemed to distort his vision. Instead of his legendary Emperor he saw a small naked man with receding hair and a swelling belly. Pale from lack of fresh air, the Corsican might have been a dead man floating in a ditch. Soult blinked hard and the nightmare image vanished. Napoleon's eyes, staring up at him, were burning coals again.

'For twenty years those shopkeepers have defied me. Their money has bought them assassins and armies and turned even the people of France against me. We must not fail, Soult.'

'We should not, Sire. Our men are in good heart.'

Napoleon motioned the servant, hovering in the background, to bring him a towel. 'Then go and make them ready. We cannot march too soon.'

CHAPTER FOUR

By the night of June 14th, Napoleon's Armée du Nord had bivouacked a few miles from the river Sambre, the frontier into Belgium. The speed of the massive operation seemed a sufficient answer in itself to those who feared the Emperor's powers were declining. So was its secrecy – the first suspicion of the army's existence had come only hours earlier when Prussian sentries south of Charleroi, 28 miles from Brussels, had caught sight of camp fires. The French had been under orders to light them on the reverse side of slopes but a bank of clouds had given the night sky a blood-red tint. But by midnight the fires were doused and an uneasy silence lay over the great French Army.

Young recruits, made restless by the grisly stories told them by old sweats, lay staring up at the waxing, three-quarter moon. Old Guardsmen, veterans of many a bloody campaign, slept like tired children. Occasionally, the bark of a dog could be heard or the sharp call of a sentry. Here and there, in copses of trees or occupied haylofts, the low giggling of a girl broke the silence. The *chattes* that followed the Army always found plenty of customers the night before battle.

At his outpost on the Sambre, old Sauret was leaning against a tree and gazing down at the river with its willows and poplars. Hairy-cheeked, fiercely-moustached, and massively built, fifty-year-old Sauret was a good representative of his Imperial Guard comrades resting two miles away. Well over six feet tall, and with his crested shako making him look even taller, he appeared an almost supernatural figure as the moonlight, filtering through the branches, fell on him.

Sauret had no wife. Nor had he any children, at least not to his knowledge. What life was it for a woman to follow the Army from battle to battle, with the certainty of being raped if a battle was lost? Besides, with the Emperor's policy of making the invaded country provide the food for his armies, a soldier was occupied enough finding food for his own belly. When a woman was available, Sauret slept with her. When one was not, he had learned how to forget about them.

Sauret, who had marched with Napoleon for nearly fifteen years, had seen all there was to see in war. He had stood steadfast against the Black Uhlans of Prussia and the terrible Cossacks from the east. On a score of battlefields and more, in their impregnable squares, he and his comrades had first defended their Emperor and then gone forward to bloody victory with him. In this time he had seen rape, torture, death in every ghastly form, and if he had ever had a religious faith it had long lost any meaning for him.

Nor would he call himself a patriot. What was France to him when, after all the glory his little Emperor had brought her, she had allowed him to be banished into exile? When he, Sauret, had been spat on by townsfolk when he cried his anger at the wrong? When he and his comrades, who had shed so much blood for France, had been kicked out of the Army on a pension too mean to support a dog?

No; the only love in Sauret's life was his little Emperor. The Corsican he had followed without question through the torrid valleys of Italy and into the icy steppes of Russia. Sauret had seen disembowelled men rise at the sight of him and shout 'Vive l'Empereur' before they collapsed in their own coils. Sauret was too simple a man to understand this love. All he knew was that when Napoleon had been betrayed by the cursed generals, the very heart that warmed his blood had seemed to stop. And when the blessed news of his return had reached him, he had gone half mad with joy. The little Emperor was as near a deity as Sauret was likely to see, and he was prepared to die any death for him.

But, soldier-like, he was thinking none of this as he gazed

at the serene, moonlit river. Roach and tench there would certainly be, but was it swift-flowing enough for trout? The thought of a large trout for breakfast made the Guardsman's mouth water.

He pushed the vision away with a soldier's resignation. In a couple of hours, three at the most, reveille would be sounding and with the preparations that had to be made they'd be lucky to get any breakfast at all.

The jingle of bridle bits made him start and listen. Experience told him it was a group of horsemen, four or five at the most. Although the sound came from behind him he melted into the shadow of the tree, raised his loaded musket, and waited. A few seconds later four riders appeared at the far side of the moonlit meadow. As they approached he saw the leading horse was white and ridden by a man in a greatcoat and bicorned hat. Throat dry with excitement, Sauret called out his challenge.

'Halte! Qui va là?'

As the gruff, grim voice carried across the meadow, the four horsemen halted. As one of them called out the password, Sauret took a step forward. 'Avancez!'

The party rode towards the river. As they neared it, the man on the white horse broke away and walked his horse towards the tree.

'All quiet, mon brave?'

Sauret, heart pounding hard, musket at the present, was as stiff as a ramrod. 'All quiet, mon Empereur.'

Under the shadow of his hat, Napoleon's expression was hidden. 'But not tomorrow. The Prussians await us. And the English too. Are you ready to follow me, mon vieux?'

Sauret cleared his throat. 'Where you go, I go, mon Empereur.'

'To death, if need be?'

'I am your soldier, Sire.'

Silence followed the simple words. Then the Corsican gave a laugh of pride. Reaching down he pinched the Guardsman's grizzled cheek. As he rode back to the waiting officers, the granite-like Sauret stared after him with love in his eyes.

The four horsemen rode down to the water's edge. One of them was Soult. 'Have you had news yet of Ney, Sire?'

'Yes. He should arrive tomorrow.'

'And you still intend to give him the left wing of the Army?'

'Who else is there? And who is braver?'

Soult nodded. There was a short silence as the four men gazed at the river. Then Soult stirred. 'We shall need to cross by the bridges. But they should present no problem: the Prussians cannot hold them for long.'

Napoleon, who appeared fascinated by the river, spoke as if he had not heard him. 'So in a few hours we cross the Rubicon. We dry our boots in Belgium.'

The less imaginative Soult nodded. 'Sunrise is about three-thirty. I have set reveille for two-thirty. It will give time for the men to hear your Order of the Day before we march for the bridges.'

Napoleon recovered himself. 'And then to Charleroi. Like an arrow between their armies.'

'It seems now we shall achieve it, Sire.'

Napoleon stared at him, then laughed. 'Achieve it? It is already as good as done, Soult. Neither Wellington nor Blücher has time to move his army now.'

'Might they not retreat?'

The Corsican nodded. 'They might.' In the moonlight his eyes were glittering. 'But it is my hope they do not.'

It was 3 AM. A morning mist lay wet on the grass and the hedges. Shivering, their breath condensing, the soldiers of the Armée du Nord stood listening to their Emperor's Order of the Day.

'Soldiers! Today is the anniversary of Marengo and Friedland, which twice decided the fate of Europe . . . We believed in the oaths of princes we left on the throne – now we know they would destroy the independence and most sacred rights of France. Soldiers, we have forced marches ahead of us, battles to fight, dangers to encounter, but with steadfastness, victory will be ours. The rights, the honour, the happiness of France will be re-conquered. To every

Frenchman of spirit, the moment has come to conquer or perish.'

Column by column, cheering their Emperor, the regiments moved out. Units of cavalry swept ahead of them and, as Soult had predicted, quickly captured the river bridges. By 8 AM the invasion of Belgium was well under way.

The sun had now burned through the mist and it was a glorious June morning. The invading troops saw around them orchards, sunlit fields, and ancient villages, and felt themselves invincible. What could go wrong, with their little Emperor leading them? Men laughed and sang, and thought of the gay time they would soon be having in Brussels.

Small but sharp actions began as units of French cavalry came up against advance Prussian outposts. The Prussians fought stubbornly in the rye and corn fields but by noon Charleroi had fallen and the Prussians were retreating to the north-east.

Napoleon had an early lunch in a small inn on the outskirts of the town. At twelve-thirty he had a chair brought outside and sat watching his assault troops, who had been detailed to clear the villages ahead, marching down the road. Seeing him, the men cheered loudly and some broke ranks to stroke his horse, Desirée, which was tethered near the gate of the inn. Obviously delighted by their reception, Napoleon answered their salutes until his head nodded and he fell asleep. The deafening cheers continued but he slept until two-thirty when Soult and two travel-stained horsemen approached the inn. Waving aside Napoleon's aides, Soult tapped the Emperor on the shoulder.

'Sire, Ney and Grouchy have arrived.' Bending his head, he whispered: 'The Army have received Ney well: there have been shouts of "Vive Rougeot" all along the road.'

As Ney approached, Napoleon's eyes moved mockingly over his crumpled and stained uniform. 'What have you been doing? Sleeping with a *chatte* in a hayloft?'

It was always Ney's habit to answer back. 'There were none left, Sire; they had all followed your Army's advance.

45

I received my order to meet you here but no means of transport arrived with it. So I had to make my own way.'

'Which you have done quickly,' Napoleon conceded.

Beneath his dust-coated red hair, Ney's expression was eager. 'I want to be of service, Sire. Am I to be given a command?'

The Corsican glanced quizzically at Soult. 'What do you think? Can I trust him not to hand my army over to Wellington?' As the hot-tempered Ney stiffened, he went on: 'Yes, you are getting a command. The left wing of my army.'

Stunned, Ney was about to kiss his hand in gratitude when Napoleon waved him back. 'Your army is already advancing on Gosselies. Your orders are to sweep the road past it and occupy strategic villages and crossroads, particularly Quatre Bras. I have already separated Blücher and Wellington – now I must keep them apart while I destroy them.'

At that Grouchy moved forward. 'Sire, there are reports that Blücher and his staff are only a few miles from Sombreffe.'

Napoleon stared at him. 'Sombreffe?'

'Yes, Sire. It seems the old man is looking for a fight.'

The Corsican's hand slapped down on his knee. 'If it is true, it's the way I want it. Blücher and his army first!' Jumping to his feet he motioned sharply to a groom. 'Bring my horse. I must check this myself.'

His eyes were glowing with excitement as he turned back to Soult. 'They are not satisfied that we lie between them – the Prussians march to meet us. If the old fool wants a fight, he shall have one. Either way the road to Brussels is open.'

CHAPTER FIVE

Inside the great hall at No 9, Rue de Centres in Brussels that night of June 15th, all was gaiety, light, and colour. Chandeliers of candles shone down from the vaulted roof: their sparkling light to be caught and imprisoned in polished silverware, in golden buttons and braid, in starry, amorous eyes. Against a background sea of a hundred conversations there rose laughter, the tinkling of glasses, the music from talented violinists.

On the floor, as handsome young officers whirled their pretty partners about, it almost seemed as if the sexes were vying with one another as to who should catch the on-looker's eye. At a quick glance the brilliant scarlet and gold of the men appeared to win the day, but a closer look at the young women proved this impression false. That year (ironically) women of fashion were wearing the classical Empire style that had first appeared at Napoleon's Court and, although its pastel shades could not compete with the masculine colours, the swelling crescents of naked breasts the style demanded were more than compensation.

Other young couples were established in corners where the light from the wax candles did not reach. As the evening progressed, a certain feverishness could be sensed from the extravagant laughter of the officers and the melting eyes of their young girls. Rumour that the Army might soon be in action against the terrifying Bonaparte had been spreading through the assemblage and assisted many a young officer to win a kiss or a promise from his admiring partner.

A group of privates of the Gordon Highlanders had taken over the ballroom floor and were performing a sword dance. All were young, tall, and good-looking. Watching them from a nearby sofa was the Duchess of Richmond, the hostess of the ball, and her younger daughter, Sarah. Standing behind them was the distinguished figure of Sir

William Ponsonby, Colonel of the Scots Greys, in full dress uniform.

The Duchess's eyes were resting reflectively on the powerful legs of the young dancers, surmounted by the billowing kilts and bobbing sporrans. She leaned back to Sir William with a confiding gesture.

'Uncle Gordon paraded his entire regiment for my inspection this morning. So I just rode up and down, in and out, and picked my fancy. Didn't I do well?'

The girl turned to her with a giggle. 'Mama, you chose such big ones.'

The Duchess put her gloved finger on her daughter's lips, quietening her. The effect of the gesture was slightly lewd. On the floor, with a crescendo of music, the dance ended. The Highlanders formed up behind their pipe-major and to a lively skirling tune began to march out through a door guarded by two rough-looking sentries. As a tall strapping Highlander named Duncan passed, a girl in the audience plucked a flower from her bosom and tossed it to him. Immediately other girls began to follow suit and with kilts swinging, the Highlanders made their exit under a hail of flowers.

The floor was quickly occupied by dancing couples. Over the music the two sentries at the door, Mulholland and McKevitt by name, heard eleven striking on a nearby church steeple. As they watched the revelry with the ranker's jaundiced eye, the clatter of hooves and rumble of wheels made both of them turn sharply. A chaise pulled up outside the door and a tall slim officer leapt out and ran up the steps, leaving his equerry still climbing from it. Seeing who he was, Mulholland let out a muffled oath and both men scrambled to attention. As the officer acknowledged the salute and strode through the door, Mulholland gave his companion a silent whistle of relief.

A moment later, the bandleader made a frantic signal to his orchestra, and the music ceased. The dancers paused in some confusion, only for a buzz of excitement to break out from them as the band struck up with: 'See the Conquering Hero Comes.' Men and women turned, then surged forward to form a passageway down the centre of the ballroom.

The officer, who gave the band a curt salute and then strode forward, was Wellington. He was a tall, beaky, handsome man in his middle forties, wearing a dark blue cloak lined with white. There was deprecation in his acknowledgement of his welcome, yet at the same time he pleased the crowd by making it. This was Wellington's way. His casualness was always deceptive: with him polite suggestions would be peremptory orders. He possessed the unique ability of combining good manners with absolute authority.

He had been a busy man that afternoon. At 3 o'clock news had reached him via the Prince of Orange that the French had invaded Belgium. He had immediately called in his Chief of Staff, Colonel de Lancey, and sent orders to all his unit commanders that their troops must hasten to their concentration centres and be ready to march off at a moment's notice. His next move, the concentration of the Army at a given point (which because of the wide dispersion of the cantonments would take at least twenty-four hours), had to wait until Napoleon's objective was known.

Privately, Wellington was certain the Corsican intended to strike westwards through Mons. Success in the west would cut off the English Army's supply lines and also its escape route to the Channel ports, and after his experiences in Spain Wellington was something of an obsessionist about supply lines. It would also ensure that Napoleon had only the English Army to contend with.

This fear that his western flank might be turned, which haunted Wellington even at Waterloo, explains why he took no steps to guard road communications with Blücher: expecting the French attack to come from the opposite direction he did not believe those communications were threatened. Fortunately for him, his forward area commanders near Charleroi did not share his views. Seeing sobbing peasants and wounded Prussians streaming northwards in ever-growing numbers, they became convinced Napoleon was heading straight between the two Allied Armies, and the Belgian general, Baron de Perponcher, disobeyed Wellington's concentration order and sent 4,000 men and eight guns to the Quatre Bras crossroads which he recognized as a key communications centre. Unknown to Wellington that evening, these men caused Ney to postpone his attack on the crossroads for fifteen vital hours, a delay that was to save Wellington's face the following day.

He had been tempted to miss the ball but had decided to attend for two reasons. There was enough fear in the city already over the French invasion and his absence might start a spate of alarmist rumours. In addition, Napoleon's agents were everywhere, and the news that Wellington and his Allied officers were attending frivolous parties might make the Corsican believe his invasion was a complete surprise and so lead to carelessness on his part.

The eyes of all the guests were on Wellington to see what news could be gleaned from his expression, but he was his usual impassive self as he acknowledged their applause. Approaching the Duchess he gave a wry smile as he took the hand she extended to him.

'In none of my campaigns have I had such brilliant company, madame.'

She took his arm affectionately and led him to her sofa. 'This season soldiers are the fashion, Arthur. We ladies just have to follow the drum.'

Wellington's eyes were busy picking out his own officers. 'I think your ladies must be Bonaparte's allies, madame. My entire army must be in the hands of its NCOs tonight.'

For a moment the Duchess's gay mood slipped. 'It was good of you to allow so many of your officers to come, Arthur. God knows what is in store for them soon.' Recovering, she laughed and pointed at the door where McKevitt was inelegantly feeling a rotting tooth. 'Besides, your fellows are the salt of the earth, are they not, and well able to take care of themselves.'

It was a subject on which the Duke's opinion was well known and his answer did not disappoint the amused woman. 'My fellows are scum, Charlotte. Some of them enlist to escape the magistrates, others because they beget bastard children at home. They are poachers, beggars, and thieves. The best of them join up for the free drink. Gin is the spirit of their patriotism.'

'Yet you expect them to die for you.'

'I expect them only to do their duty.'

'But doesn't that entail dying sometimes?'

'Often. But as I say, that is their duty.'

The Duchess wrinkled her nose. 'I doubt if even Napoleon could draw men to him by a sense of duty.'

Wellington's eyes twinkled. 'Napoleon is not a gentleman.'

The Duchess gave a laugh of outrage. 'Arthur! What an Englishman you are.'

He shrugged. 'That is why I give my little Corsican fair play. I admire the enthusiasm he inspires and confess that in a battle the sight of his hat is worth twenty thousand men. But he is not a gentleman.'

The smiling aristocrat waved her fan airily. 'I'd better warn you now – I'm a little bit of a Bonapartist myself.'

Sarah turned to her with a gasp. 'Oh, Mama, how can you say such a thing?'

She received one of the Duke's dry glances. 'Your mother is a duchess, my dear. Napoleon has cheapened life by bringing glory back into war.'

'He's a monster,' Sarah said, with feeling.

Wellington smiled. 'Yes. He eats laurels and drinks blood. Or so they say.' He glanced back at the amused Duchess. 'They have given me an infamous army to fight him with, Charlotte. Only 29,000 British troops and few of them have heard a shot fired, 30,000 Dutch-Belgians whose allegiance is in question, and a hotchpotch of the King's German Legion, Hanoverians, and Brunswickers. All are ill-equipped and my staff is woefully weak.'

'You have pointed this out to Lord Bathurst?'

'Time and again. All I get in reply are more of the Prince Regent's young protégés. And now time has run out.'

The Duchess could not contain her curiosity any longer. She glanced around her, then moved nearer to Wellington. 'What is the latest intelligence, Arthur?'

'Last night the Prussian sentries near Charleroi saw the reflections of a thousand camp fires caught in the clouds. By the late afternoon their wounded were stumbling back to the north-east.'

The Duchess gave a muted gasp. 'Then Brussels is in danger?'

Wellington gave another dry smile. 'So Bonaparte wishes us to think. He wants me to send my army to Blücher's aid while he rides west through Mons and cuts me off from the Channel. I have given orders for concentration to commence and for all roads from Mons to Brussels to be covered.'

The Duchess, whose eyes had strayed to her daughter, gave a sigh of relief. 'Then you think Brussels is safe?'

'I feel certain of it, madame.'

CHAPTER SIX

In a château in Charleroi, Constant was standing alongside Napoleon's bed. 'Sire, Marshal Ney has ridden from Gosselies to see you.'

All his life the Corsican had possessed the enviable ability to awaken lucidly from sleep. That day, however, he had been in the saddle for over sixteen hours and took a moment to regain his faculties.

'Hand me my gown. Tell him to wait in the ante-room.'

Ney, as travel-stained as on his arrival that afternoon, rose from a chair as he entered. 'I thought it as quick to ride here myself as to send a messenger, Sire. Quatre Bras is occupied by the enemy. I reconnoitred it myself this afternoon.'

'How many men?'

'One of my hussars said he believed they were part of Perponcher's Dutch-Belgian division. Perhaps 5,000 men.'

'Why did you not take it?'

'I had only a battalion of infantry and a unit of cavalry within immediate call. It would have been dark before more men could be brought up.'

Napoleon had begun his characteristic striding across the room, hands held behind his back. 'Take it in the morning.

At first light. With the Quatre Bras crossroads in our hands neither Blücher nor Wellington can help the other.'

'What are your plans for Grouchy's army, Sire?'

Napoleon ceased his pacing and turned to him, his voice grimly humorous. 'It depends on Blücher. If he attacks at Ligny, as now looks likely, we'll satisfy that old drunkard's thirst for a long time.'

On the sofa in the great ballroom in Brussels, Wellington was watching seventeen-year-old Lord Hay, one of his Foot Guards, waltzing with Sarah.

'Your daughter is a graceful girl, Charlotte. She's a pretty sight dancing with young Hay.'

The Duchess nodded. 'Don't let young Hay get killed, will you, Arthur?'

Wellington turned towards her. 'What's this? An engagement?'

'Yes. And I don't want the girl to wear black before she's had the chance to wear white.'

Two officers were making their way through the waltzing couples towards the sofa. One was General Picton, commander of the 5th Division, a large, heavy, gruff Welshman of fifty-seven. The other was Lieutenant-Colonel Frederick Ponsonby, an elegant aristocrat. As the two men reached the Duchess and were paying their respects to her, Sarah pulled Lord Hay from the dance, and holding his hand ran in an exhilarated fashion to the sofa.

'Mama, Dicky has promised to get me a cuirassier's helmet as a work basket. Without any blood on it, Mama.'

The Duchess's smile was both grim and playful. 'Get another for me, young man. And I don't mind the blood.'

Wellington leaned forward. 'Where do you intend to stick your Frenchman, Hay?'

Hay coloured. 'I thought under the arm, Your Grace.'

Sarah's voice was triumphant. 'See, Mama, he has it all planned.'

Picton's gruff, scornful voice interrupted them. 'When you meet a cuirassier knee to knee, you'll be lucky if you bring your life away with you, my lad, never mind his helmet.'

53

Wellington and the Duchess looked amused as the blunt Welshman went on: 'Lad, you'll learn the art of fighting from the French.' He turned to Ponsonby, his voice loud with disgust. 'God help us, I never saw such a set of sprats.'

He stalked off ponderously with the smiling Ponsonby. Sarah pulled a face at his broad back in defence of her defeated soldier. 'General Picton doesn't know how to walk properly in a ballroom.'

Wellington's eyes twinkled. 'But he's very good when he's dancing with the French, Sarah.'

The girl tossed her head, winning a schoolgirl victory. 'One dances with *them* in a field.'

As the young couple scampered away, Wellington invited the Duchess to dance. The bandmaster waved his baton as they rose and the music ceased ... The pause lasted until the couples on the floor drew aside. The Duchess laid a hand on Wellington's arm, then the orchestra broke into a spirited waltz.

As Wellington, helped by his long legs, whirled her round and round, the Duchess let out a gasp of amusement. 'Now I know how you win your battles. You dance your enemies to death.'

Wellington gave his dry smile. 'I do, Duchess, I do. The whole secret of combat is in the legs. You stand fast or you run fast. One or the other.'

Wincing in mock horror, the Duchess hid Wellington's face with her fan. 'Run fast! The ladies mustn't hear you say that, Arthur. Imagine all those unwashed Frenchmen here – lusting for partners!'

Unseen by the Duke a young officer in a muddy and stained field uniform had entered the ballroom and was working his tentative way through the splendidly-attired officers and their ladies surrounding the floor. Colonel de Lancey, the Duke's Chief of Staff, who had spent all the afternoon and evening sending out Wellington's concentration orders, noticed the young officer and steered his partner in his direction. The burly General Picton also noticed him but his way across the floor was barred by a whirling line of dancers. The Duchess said casually: 'I'm afraid, Arthur, that that untidy young gentleman who has just arrived is about to spoil my party.'

Wellington gave a start on noticing the embarrassed messenger and drew the Duchess off the floor. The young man came stiffly to attention as he approached. Giving him a curt nod Wellington turned him away.

'Where are you from, sir?'

'Mons, Your Grace. The cavalry has established that the roads before it are clear. The French concentration is at Charleroi and spear-heading north-east and north-west.'

Wellington took the dispatch from him and sank down on an empty sofa. Seeing his expression, anxious officers, among them Picton, de Lancey, and Uxbridge, his Commander of Cavalry, moved within earshot, followed by the Duchess. As Wellington tore open the dispatch, his sharp exclamation reached the nearest of the onlookers. 'He has humbugged me, by God! He has stolen twenty-four hours on us.'

Uxbridge took a step forward. 'What has happened, Wellington?'

Wellington frowned up at him. 'He has split me from Blücher. And is now poised to attack one or the other of us.'

With officer whispering to officer, the alarming news spread like wildfire through the ballroom. Couples ceased dancing and the music faltered. The Duchess moved forward solicitously. 'Do you wish me to stop the ball, Arthur? If you do, I will call for the carriages.'

Wellington jerked his head curtly. 'No. Continue. I want no panic. All officers obliged to ladies will finish their dances.' As the Duchess motioned to the bandleader for the music to continue, Wellington glanced at Lord Edward Somerset who had joined the party.

'Have you a good map with you, Somerset?'

Somerset, Brigade Commander of the 1st and 2nd Life Guards, nodded. 'In my carriage.'

'Then oblige me by fetching it.' Wellington turned to the Duchess. 'With your permission, madame, I would like to make this my temporary headquarters. Is there a room I can use?'

Inside a small ante-room at the rear of the hall Wellington and his party of senior officers gazed down at a map stretched out over a table. Flickering candles, illuminating anxious faces, added to the drama of the scene. One of the most anxious faces belonged to thirty-four-year-old Colonel Sir William Howe de Lancey. Good-looking and talented, with a pleasant personality, de Lancey was an American who had been born in New York of a Huguenot family. He had received a knighthood for his services to Wellington during the Peninsular War. Although extraordinarily young to be Chief of Staff, he was an officer whom Wellington both liked and trusted. He had recently married a girl called Magdelene Hall, but their honeymoon had been interrupted by his mobilization orders. After weeks of effort Magdelene had managed to follow him to Brussels but the joy of their reunion had been destroyed that afternoon by the news of Napoleon's invasion. De Lancey's present anxiety was due to the concentration orders Wellington had given him to send out only a few hours ago. Knowing nothing of Perponcher's decision to disobey them and occupy Quatre Bras, de Lancey was thinking that Napoleon's advance on Brussels would be helped rather than hindered by the orders.

Another anxious face belonged to Major-General Baron von Müffling. Müffling, middle-aged, plump, and loyal, was the Prussian liaison officer attached to British Headquarters and no one was more aware than he of the dangers that would face his fellow-countrymen should Wellington decide to play safe and retreat.

As Wellington examined the map, Uxbridge moved to his shoulder. A Lieutenant-General and an earl, Uxbridge with his curly fair hair, moustache, and debonair behaviour was both a beau with the ladies and a brave and efficient cavalry commander. His voice broke the tense silence.

'Logically, he should have done as you said, Wellington, and attacked through Mons.'

Wellington, who had dropped some of his reserve on leaving the ballroom, threw him a glance. Five years earlier Uxbridge had caused a scandal by having an affair with

56

Wellington's sister-in-law and although time had healed the breach between the two men, friction showed occasionally in moments of stress. 'Logic or not,' the Duke grunted, 'he appears to have won a victory over us at the cost of a few bootlaces.' He studied the map again, then turned to Müffling. 'If Marshal Blücher will stay in Belgium, so shall I. To my last regiment. He has my word on it!'

The plump Müffling showed his relief. 'On that promise, Lord Duke, Marshal Blücher would tie his men to trees – if it were necessary.'

With his preference for understatement, Wellington grimaced at the commitment. Measuring the map with his thumb, he paused and pointed. 'These crossroads here. What are they called?'

De Lancey answered him. 'Quatre Bras, Sir. Bonaparte is certain to cover them.'

'Nevertheless, that is the way I shall try to reach Blücher. Alert all men throughout Brussels and have them on the march before first light. Uxbridge, get your cavalry on the move. Picton, march your division as it has never been marched before.'

'What about our 17,000 men at Hal, Your Grace?' It was de Lancey again. 'As they are no longer needed there, should we not send them to Quatre Bras?'

Wellington hesitated. A man who always found it difficult to change his mind, he was still not entirely convinced that Napoleon would not make some move to cut him off from the Channel ports. His decision to leave 17,000 men idle at Hal was one he was to regret bitterly on the corpse-strewn ridge at Waterloo. 'No. They are my insurance. Alert them but let them remain there.'

As he bent over the map again his low exclamation was heard only by de Lancey and Uxbridge who were standing by his elbow. 'Charleroi! By God, that man does war honour.'

As Napoleon made like a juggernaut towards Brussels, the city became a turmoil of activity. At the ball the orchestra was still playing although the girls were finding it increasingly difficult to find partners as more and more of the young officers left to join their regiments. Some found it hard to drag themselves away. To depart from a brilliant party, with a lovely girl's eyes caressing one, straight to a bloody battlefield awakened a host of conflicting emotions.

Outside, alerted sentries were dashing from house to house and soon the roll of drums, the strident notes of trumpets, and the scream of pipes could be heard all over the city. Townsfolk rushed to windows: some threw on their clothes and hastened out into the streets. NCOs could be seen everywhere, ordering their men to fetch their equipment and make for their assembly points. Some soldiers were so confused that they appeared in the streets without their shirts or trousers. Others, unable to find their NCOs, were running about trying to discover from their equally ignorant comrades what was happening.

Near the ballroom there were comical sights as officers, fresh from the floor, ran around in their dancing pumps trying to find their NCOs. As the cobbled streets became more crowded, artillery caissons and supply carts piled up nose to tail. Dispatch riders tried to fight their way through the confusion. Young girls, tears streaming down their faces, pressed talismen into soldiers' hands. Kindly townsfolk, who had grown fond of the soldiers they had billeted, cried softly as the men waved them goodbye. The Duchess of Richmond, watching the young officers leaving the ballroom one by one, turned to her husband in some distress: 'I wonder how many of these young gallants will be corpses before tomorrow night.'

To add confusion to confusion, the men who were already marching out of the city ran into the train of peasant's carts which were moving in. It was usual for the countryfolk to arrive shortly after midnight so as to find for themselves the best places in the city's market, and soon soldiers, guns, caissons, and carts filled with cabbages, onions, turnips, and strawberries were a struggling mass in the narrow streets. Old Flemish women in their black smocks yelled down imprecations and the occasional soldier, risking a flogging, answered back by stealing a bunch of carrots or a lettuce. Other soldiers, also foreseeing the shortage of food in the days ahead, made hasty purchases while their sergeants bawled at them to get back into line.

O'Connor, an Inniskilling infantryman, was one of those who had already said goodbye to the frantic city and was marching down the long, poplar-lined roads that led to Quatre Bras. He was not with his regiment: they had been quartered north of Brussels and would not reach the crossroads before the next day. O'Connor had been one of a twenty-strong working party sent to Brussels the previous afternoon to collect supplies, and when the mobilization panic had struck the city he and his comrades, much to their disgust, had been pushed into the ranks of the 33rd Regiment and marched away. Soldiers like to fight with their regiments and feel as insecure as bees in a foreign hive when detached from them.

A professional soldier, O'Connor differed from most of his regiment in having already fought the French in Portugal and Spain. Most of the British regiments given to Wellington consisted of inexperienced 2nd battalions stiffened by only a few Peninsular veterans who had not been sent to America in 1814. O'Connor's reason for missing the draft had been an arm injury during training. At the time he had been delighted. Now, as every step took him nearer Bonaparte's Army, he wondered if fate had not played him a dirty trick after all.

In many ways O'Connor was a typical British infantryman of his day. Driven into the Army when he was sixteen by the harsh conditions in Ireland, the Regiment was the only home he had known for nearly twenty years. He was not a dashing soldier – in fact, O'Connor made it almost a point of honour to volunteer for nothing – but he was hardy, dogged, self-reliant, and extremely dependable. He was also very well-trained. While at that time Britain's Army was small in comparison with her incomparable Navy, it was a highly professional unit. Few if any advancing lines of infantry could match its steadiness and rate of fire – at times it seemed the British infantrymen had inherited the same skills with the musket that their ancestors had possessed with the longbow – and these qualities Wellington had learned to exploit to the full in the Peninsular War.

To the superficial observer he did not seem as happy a soldier as the Frenchman, but this was only because he found his amusements in different ways. Grumbling was perhaps his greatest pleasure and because, as to this day, it had a mordant quality, it often gave a false impression of his morale. On the other hand it could be said he had plenty to grumble about, for he could spend ten years from home without leave and unlike the French, who did not believe in capital punishment, he could suffer a hundred lashes and more for seemingly trivial offences. Again, unlike the French, he was not allowed to forage off the land he occupied, and an offence against a civilian, particularly a woman, was often punishable by death.

A further cause for complaint – and this time not without reason – was his dress: designed, it seemed, to hinder him in action as much as possible. His head-dress was a felt shako with a brass plate in front and his regimental colours on the front or sides. His face was wedged between an upstanding collar supported by a leather stock, then came a red coat with short tails but cut away to expose the lower front of his body. A further hindrance to his breathing were the ammunition webbing-belts that criss-crossed his chest. He also carried a heavy glazed knapsack. O'Connor's one relief was that his old breeches and gaiters had been replaced by trousers and short boots. For inclement weather he was issued with a heavy pepper-and-salt greatcoat. In all, when fully kitted, O'Connor carried sixty pounds on his back.

His musket, like the muskets of his French and Prussian counterparts, had changed little in design since the days of the Stuart kings. It was strongly built but weighed a full nine pounds. The round leaden bullet it fired was highly inaccurate over a hundred paces but could kill at over five hundred yards. Because the leaden ball flattened during its trajectory, the wounds it inflicted were appalling.

Provided with it were paper cartridges of gunpowder. These had to be torn open with the teeth, a sprinkling of powder had to be dropped into the firing pan of the musket as a primer. The rest was then emptied down the muzzle of the musket and a ball and paper wad rammed down on top of it with a ramrod. If all had been done properly and the flint on the hammer (which had to be changed every thirty shots) provided the required spark, the musket let out a hollow retort, poured out dense smoke, and recoiled with brutal force on the marksman's shoulder. In tests under ideal conditions, there was one misfire for every four shots. In battle conditions three misfires in four shots were not uncommon.

The reason is not difficult to find. In spite of trembling or exhausted hands, the firing pan had to receive the correct amount of powder. Too much and the infantryman might receive a nasty flash burn: too little and the musket would not fire. Humidity, sweat, or rain would also render the powder useless, and one, if not all, was always present on a battlefield.

These were not the only problems of the infantryman. Room was needed to set the long musket's stock to the ground while he prodded the charge and bullet home. (This was the reason for the seemingly awkward posture of standing and firing from the shoulder.) While performing the operation he was as likely as not to get a comrade's musket stock across his head as each man fought for space. Misfires could also make the musket dangerous. In the heat of battle a desperate man might pile charge after charge on top of the other and it was not an uncommon occurrence for a musket to explode and injure if not kill its owner and the men around him. And even if none of these misfortunes occurred, the musket became virtually useless after fifty to a hundred firings unless a man swabbed out the barrel and carefully cleaned out the priming vent.

In all, it seems a minor miracle that any man's nerve could remain steady enough to perform all these difficult tasks when a yelling horde of cavalrymen, murderous sabres uplifted, might be bearing down on him. With only two shots a minute possible under ideal conditions it is something of a mystery why archers, who could have fired fifteen times as many lethal arrows in the same time, had gone so much out of favour. Certainly it explains the value of highly-trained, battle-seasoned professionals.

The sun was well above the horizon now and its brightness made the day seem more advanced than it was. Seven-thirty or thereabouts was O'Connor's guess – they ought to be getting their five minutes' rest soon. Phlegmatically, he eased a strap that was digging into his shoulder. His nostrils were filled with the familiar smells of marching, the rising dust, and the sweat of his comrades. He was sweating profusely himself; an indication to O'Connor that in spite of the bright morning there was rain on the way.

His countryman's eye was appreciating the gently undulating land around him with its woods, streams, and well-built farm houses. He noted the barley crop was good that year: some of it was as high as a man's shoulders. Now and again they passed peasants working in the fields and he wondered what they were thinking as they stared curiously at the long column of men and carts. They were probably like peasants anywhere, caring little who won as long as the cursed soldiers were soon off their land.

Flies were now buzzing around the sweating men. As he swept one from his cheek O'Connor heard orders being shouted behind him. Unable to look back because of his upturned collar he saw one of his officers bridle his horse and swing it round. A moment later there was a yell for the column to march at attention.

The reason appeared a few seconds later as a glittering group of horsemen swept past at some pace. Among them was a slim, erect figure in a marshal's hat, white waistcoat, blue surtout coat, and half-length boots. Wellington and his staff were riding for Quatre Bras.

There was little cheering, the English infantryman sharing nothing of his French counterpart's love of his Commander-in-Chief. When Wellington was present no one called out 'Vive Beaky' or 'Vive Conky Atty': they kept their eyes to the front and hoped they were not noticed. Nor could this be put down entirely to the different temperaments of the two races. The men knew Wellington thought of them as scum, just as he knew they thought he was a long-nosed aristocratic bastard. Each respected the other's dislike, for in England there had never been the fierce hatred between the peasant and aristocrat that had existed in France. One could say they co-existed: each wondering what God had been up to in making the other species but putting a brave face on it nevertheless.

In any case professional soldiers like O'Connor were less interested in being loved than being fed, and whereas the French had to forage for their meat, old Beaky did appreciate that a man with a filled belly fought better than a man with an empty one. Moreover, O'Connor had respect for Wellington's military common sense. There was none of that nonsense of parading you about on the wrong side of a hill before battle, so their cannon fire could cut bloody swaths through you before you could get a musket shot at the bastards. Beaky kept you on the reverse side of slopes until the last minute and you couldn't ask for more than that. If it had been suggested to O'Connor that Wellington's careful conservation of his army was due to the fact that if he lost it he could not get another, O'Connor would have shrugged his phlegmatic shoulders. If a woman slept with you, who cared what her reason was?

The men had been apprehensive as they left the confusion of Brussels. Now, as the June morning displayed its splendour, their mood began to change. Streams glistened in the sunlight, birds sang in the tall trees, and a kestrel soared in the blue vault of heaven. How could death exist in a world as gold and green and beautiful as this? Men felt the strength of their legs and backs, the deep vigorous beat of their hearts, and knew that whatever might happen to others, they at least were immortal. No one, not even O'Connor, noticed the sudden drop of the kestrel or saw the torn and bleeding thing it carried away in its claws.

CHAPTER SEVEN

It was 10 AM when Wellington reached Quatre Bras. The 6,000 troops he found there were in direct disobedience to his orders, but as their commanders had been right and he wrong about the line of Napoleon's attack he was hardly able to reprimand them. Some might feel he should have congratulated them on their foresight, but perhaps that was asking too much. Instead, as it was now obvious Quatre Bras must be held at all costs if communication with Blücher was to be maintained, he inspected the defences and wrote a number of dispatches urging his oncoming divisions to make all speed for the crossroads. Because of his earlier orders, which confused his unit commanders, it was obviously going to take hours to build up a sizeable concentration, but in spite of this he decided a meeting with Blücher was imperative, and at 1 PM he rode across country to confer with him.

The old Prussian, fierce of appearance and purpose in spite of his seventy-two years, had turned an old mill into his headquarters and from it Wellington could see the glittering panorama of Napoleon's Army lined up for battle. Behind the massive phalanxes of infantry, cavalry, and artillery, the units of the Imperial Guard were standing ready to deliver the *coup de grâce*. In the far distance Gérard's corps, which had been delayed in its deployment, was advancing to further augment the massive Army. The sight was intimidating, particularly when Wellington's telescope picked up a small group of horsemen on a hillside. Napoleon was among them and his presence convinced Wellington his first objective was the destruction of the Prussian Army.

He did not like Blücher's disposition of his forces. They were deployed on the exposed sides of the shallow hills, and the two villages, Ligny and Brye, that the old man had turned into strongpoints were out of musket range of one another. To Wellington, whose strategy was to use every hillock and ditch for cover and always to interlock fields of fire, this was a mistake and he did not hesitate to say so to Blücher.

'Everyone knows their own army best. But if I were to fight with mine here, I should expect to be beaten.'

The old man grinned wickedly. 'I assemble my men this way because they like to see the enemy.'

Shrugging, Wellington turned to other things. 'If he attacks you first I shall come to your assistance as circumstances permit. But first I must build up my strength at Quatre Bras. Once this is done I shall try to advance south to draw some of his strength from you.'

The fierce old warrior, who was both willing and eager to fight Napoleon alone, read Wellington's thoughts. 'We shall help one another as best we can. But both of us know we must see this day through on our own.'

As if to underline his words, artillery fire was heard thundering from the west. Wellington caught the eye of his staff and made for the exit of the mill. 'I must get back. It appears Ney has started his attack on the crossroads.'

In fact Ney's initial attack on the key position was extraordinarily cautious for a man so brave. For this, many historians blame Napoleon who seemed to have given him little if any briefing before putting him in command of so important an assignment. Completely unaware that Wellington's main concentration was north of Mons, Ney took notice of his field-general, Reille, who warned him that the thick woods and luxuriant crops must by this time hide the bulk of the British Army. As a consequence, instead of ordering an all-out attack which must have overwhelmed the small force of Dutch-Belgians, Ney began a bombardment that, while driving huge flocks of birds from the woods, did little else but provide additional time for Wellington's troops to arrive.

In the meanwhile, Napoleon, certain that Ney could easily take care of Quatre Bras, sent him a message to push Wellington back and then turn and envelop the Prussian rear. With his own massive attack driving into the front of Blücher, Napoleon reasoned, with justification, that the Prussians would be massacred. He gave a signal to a battery of the Imperial Guard who fired a salvo as precise as if celebrating a royal occasion. It was the signal for a general French advance on the Prussians.

With 68,000 men and 260 guns before Ligny, Napoleon was full of confidence. His orders were to attack, attack, attack! This way he knew Blücher would be forced to throw in his reserves until the last of them was exhausted. Then, with Ney closing in on the Prussians' right flank, he would call on his Imperial Guard for the *coup de grâce*.

Afterwards, with the Prussians destroyed, the entire French Army in all its invincible might would turn on Wellington at Quatre Bras. In forty-eight hours the campaign would be over and Napoleon undisputed master of Belgium.

The French and Prussians were soon engaged. Charge followed counter-charge until the whole line was aflame. Legendary enemies, they fought to the death. Black-coated Uhlans sabred down French infantrymen and rode them into the ground. French cuirassiers lifted their great horses over stone hedges and scythed down their defenders. Few prisoners were taken, the hatred between the two nations was too great, the wounded men were slashed open as they lay screaming on the ground. With the indomitable Blücher here, there, and everywhere, the Prussian resistance was heroic but their defence positions had been badly sited and as the burning sun moved across the sky they began to lose ground.

At Quatre Bras the outnumbered Dutch-Belgians were also being driven back and fortified farmhouses were falling into French hands. Arriving there just after three o'clock Wellington took personal command and tried to plug the gaps until the first of his British units should arrive. Around three-thirty a cloud of dust was seen to the north and a few minutes later the flash of red coats. It was Picton's division – a part of Wellington's reserve that had been in Brussels the night before. Some of the regiments were Scottish

Highlanders and soon the skirl of their pipes was heard through the cannon fire. The French artillery caught them in an open field and did heavy damage but the rest were deployed by Wellington into woods and natural strong-points.

Across at Ligny Napoleon sent another message to Ney, saying he must manoeuvre immediately to strike at Blücher's side and rear. To spur Ney on, Napoleon told him 'The fate of France might be in your hands.' By this time, however, more and more solid British regiments and Hanoverians were reaching Quatre Bras and with all the cunning he had learned in Spain, Wellington was deploying them in every fold of the countryside. What had earlier been an easy fruit for the picking was now becoming a very hard nut indeed.

Impatient that no help had come from Ney, Napoleon had sent an individual order to d'Erlon, one of Ney's generals who commanded a corps of 20,000 men. These men, who constituted Ney's reserve, had not yet been thrown into battle and Napoleon, certain Ney could take Quatre Bras without them, ordered them to Ligny to outflank Blücher.

Ney had heard nothing of this order and, frantic at the thought of failing his Emperor, he ordered all his reserves forward for an all-out attack. His feelings when he discovered his major reserve had been taken away can only be imagined. Sweat-stained and exhausted from battle, hardly knowing what he was doing, he sent an urgent order for d'Erlon to return, thus ensuring that 20,000 fresh troops who might have turned the tables in either battle spent the whole afternoon marching and counter-marching from one battlefield to the other.

Unable to know if d'Erlon would obey and, in any case, unable to wait, Ney ordered his all-out attack. The British line bowed under the tremendous onslaught but did not break. The Duke himself escaped death only by leaping his horse, Copenhagen, over the bayonets of his Highland division. Almost insane in his desperation Ney threw Kellermann's cavalry forward in a death or glory attack. The terrifying cuirassiers broke right through the 69th Regiment and cut down two entire companies. It was only when they had driven almost into the heart of the British position that they were thrown back. Fanatical soldiers, many of them refused to surrender even when unhorsed, and fought to the death with sword or pistol.

At Ligny the scene might have come from hell. Some of the villages had been captured and re-captured half a dozen times. Men used the cottages as strongpoints, only for the enemy to fire them and incinerate the soldiers inside. Infantrymen fought hand to hand in the streets, the ditches, the rye fields. The savagery was barbaric. Prisoners were sabred, the wounded burned alive in the flaming cottages. Maimed bodies lay everywhere like carcasses of meat.

As the wind changed and storm clouds closed across the sky, the situation became desperate for the Prussians. They had used up all their reserves and Napoleon judged it was the moment to strike. At seven-thirty he gave his signal and a massive cannonade of over two hundred guns smashed at the Prussian centre.

All that afternoon, in both battles, the French artillery had been devastating in its accuracy and firepower. Now it crushed the remaining Prussian batteries and tore great holes in their thinning defences. Fifteen minutes later, at the very moment thunder rolled above, the great phalanx of the Imperial Guard began to move forward. Thousands of cavalry, cuirassiers, lancers, and hussars swarmed round the 'Old Bearskins', as the Guard was affectionately known, to help in the death blow.

Military bands and shrill trumpets mingled with the artillery fire and the thunder above. Through the cannon smoke the first line of the Guard appeared. In a desperate effort to stop them, Blücher charged with twenty-one squadrons of Landwehr cavalry but the bayonets of the Guard brushed them aside.

The sun was sinking behind the black storm clouds. Rallying his bleeding regiments the gallant old Prussian led yet another charge. As he swung his sabre, men could hear his fiery curses. 'Vorwarts – vorwarts in Gottes

Hahmen. Hell and sulphur to the French bastards. Drive them through the gates of hell!'

The square of Imperial Guard remained steady. Reining his horse, Blücher withdrew to reform his troops and charge again. But this time the cuirassiers thundered after them. A shot rang out and Blücher's horse fell. The old man's foot caught in the stirrups and the dying horse rolled over him.

His aide-de-camp, Nostiz, immediately dismounted and prepared to defend his commander as best he could. But the twilight prevented the French from seeing the extent of their success and a moment later a Prussian counter-attack drove the cuirassiers back. Anxious cavalrymen jumped down to help the old man. He had now recovered consciousness and was trying to cut himself free from a tangle of leather by the sword tied to his wrist. Hurriedly lifted on to a horse, he was carried behind the infantry lines to a peasant's cottage and laid on a pallet bed. He lost consciousness again while General Gneisenau, his Chief of Staff, was called for, only to awaken with some spirit as Gneisenau leaned over him.

'Hellfire and damnation, what happened?'

'Your horse was shot, Sire,' Nostiz said, who was standing alongside Gneisenau. 'And it rolled over you.'

Blücher felt his leg and side, and swore again. Gneisenau's voice was anxious. 'Are you all right, Sire?'

'Of course I am,' the old Prussian said testily. 'What news of the battle?'

'They have broken our centre. I have ordered a retreat.'

The old man stiffened, then sat upright. 'Retreat?'

'I had no choice, Sire. Otherwise your whole army would have been lost. As it is, 8,000 men are fleeing eastwards.'

Blücher stared at him, then shook his head in a dazed fashion. 'Retreat,' he muttered. He lay back for a moment, then turned towards Nostiz. 'I'm getting old. Fetch me some gin.'

The aide-de-camp ran from the room. Gneisenau was spreading a map out on the bed but Blücher, head in hands, was not looking at it. 'Retreat,' he muttered again. 'Have I come all this way to meet that runt of a Frenchman only to run away from him?'

Gneisenau was indicating a line on the map with his finger. 'The right road, Marshal, is back to our base at Namur.'

Nostiz returned with a cup of gin. The old man drank deeply and gave a grunt of satisfaction. Then, tearing open his sweat-stained shirt, he rubbed gin on his bruised ribs. Throughout his army it was well known and a standing joke that he used gin as an embrocation. After a few seconds he glanced back at Gneisenau, his guttural voice distressed.

'Namur, you say? If my allies desert me, Gneisenau, it is their dishonour. But if I desert them, the disgrace is mine.' Sitting up, his sparse body trembling from shock, he took hold of the sword still lashed to his wrist. 'This steel is my word, Gneisenau, and at seventy-two I'm surely too old a man to break it.'

Gneisenau showed his disapproval. 'I don't trust the English. If Wellington runs for the coast, none of us will see Berlin again. I say the logical road is Namur, Sire.'

Blücher took an angry gulp of gin. Before he could reply, Gneisenau's voice changed. 'Nevertheless, because I have served with you before, Sire, I have ordered the retreat to Wavre. So you can still cooperate with Wellington. But God help us all if he does not stand.'

With an old man's triumphant laugh, Blücher rose painfully to his feet and clapped his Chief of Staff across the shoulders. Then, grinning at Nostiz, he repeated a performance for which he was famous. 'Do you know I am the only man alive who can kiss his own head?'

As Nostiz smiled his disbelief, Blücher grabbed Gneisenau by the shoulders and implanted a kiss on his forehead. His gruff voice was muted by affection. 'This is my head. Gneisenau, you are the brains of my army.'

Gneisenau cleared his throat. 'You, Prince Blücher, are its heart. Never was that more apparent than this afternoon.'

Embarrassed by the compliment, Blücher turned with a grunt towards Nostiz. 'In that case the heart had better start beating again. Get me a horse, Nostiz. I want the men to see I am still alive.'

In the heavy dusk outside, the Prussian infantry were a sorry sight. Drenched with sweat from their exertions, they were coated with powder, smoke, and dust. Blood was soaking through filthy bandages and hardly a uniform was not split or torn. Although most men still carried their muskets, many had discarded their knapsacks, shakos, and coats. They walked like defeated men, silent, with their heads hanging.

Then a shout was heard from the rear. A cheer followed it, rapidly turning into a wave that swept forward as the white-headed old Marshal, sitting erect on his horse with a pipe in his mouth, galloped along the column. Men stared in disbelief, then their heads lifted and their shoulders came back. Hope and courage could be felt flooding back like blood along a limb when a tourniquet is eased. The Prussians were in full retreat but with the old Father leading them again, all was not yet lost.

CHAPTER EIGHT

Darkness, that fell around 9 PM that night, brought a merciful halt to hostilities. Napoleon, exhausted by the long day and not feeling well, left the battlefield for Fleurus, three miles to the rear, where he rested in a requisitioned house. Although the Prussians were now in full retreat and his officers asked for orders to pursue them, he said there would be time for that in the morning. One of his strange new moods of lethargy, on which Carnot had remarked in Paris, had suddenly fallen on him and seemingly affected his judgement. His last act, before falling into bed, was to send a messenger to Ney, ordering him to report in person at 6 AM the following morning.

Ney, who by this time had also returned to his base, a cottage a few miles behind the lines, had left his troops in roughly the same positions they had occupied before hostilities began. After a light meal with a few of his staff officers, he also dropped into an exhausted sleep.

At Genappe, barely four miles away, Wellington took his customary single glass of port before retiring. As yet no news had reached him of Blücher's fate at Ligny. In order to reach Quatre Bras early, he left instructions to be awakened at 3 AM.

Meanwhile British reinforcements were now pouring into Quatre Bras. All day Wellington had been forced to use non-British artillery and cavalry. Now they were all converging on Quatre Bras, and the night was filled with shouts, orders, and the rumble of caissons. Artillerymen, trying to find a site for their batteries, cursed as their horses stepped on corpses and reared in terror. Men pushing through the fields of rye froze as the hands of wounded men clawed at their boots. One new arrival was O'Connor, congratulating himself that he had missed at least one day's fighting.

In the midst of this chaos, the men who had done battle that day were huddled into groups. For those left with the energy to find fuel, camp fires glowed redly. Some of the Highlanders had discovered the breastplates of dead cuirassiers could be used as receptacles in which to boil their stew. Thinking the Scots were devouring the cuirassiers, the Dutch and Belgian soldiers crossed themselves.

Other men, weary to the bone, huddled in their coats and tried to sleep. Some succeeded, only to live the day again in nightmares. Others lay thinking of their dead friends and wondering what the morrow would bring. A few thought of the wounded, crammed into every empty church, cottage, and cellar in the district. Here and there a lucky casualty had his wife to attend to him. The rest were virtually abandoned for the night and suffered the torments of the damned with pain and thirst. The medical services were totally inadequate and it was a disturbing feature of the time that few soldiers on either side bothered to give succour to wounded comrades. Self-preservation was the order of the day: a man who survived battle fed his gnawing belly, drank his gin ration, got his head down into his greatcoat, and hoped the moans of the wounded would not reach him. Often they did not: by nightfall one side or the other had usually given ground, and so men tended to bivouack well away from the spot where their comrades were lying. To-night, however, they were close by and if a man listened carefully he could hear cries through the hoof beats and rumble of wheels. Mercifully, the storm clouds gave the waxing moon little chance to illuminate the carnage.

Less than a mile away, among the hundreds of camp fires of the French, there was dejection among Ney's soldiers that they had failed to capture Quatre Bras. Although no one blamed the popular Ney, there was talk that other generals had betrayed him, and NCOs and field officers were kept busy quietening the rumours and cheering up the men.

At Ligny morale was high, for had not Blücher been beaten? In the camp of the Imperial Guard, the 'Old Bear-skins' were their usual organized selves. Cunningly-placed muskets and greatcoats made tents that protected them from the occasional light showers that fell during the night. Camp fires burned outside most tents on which stews and soups simmered enticingly. Although the French line regiments carried only bread and had to forage for meat and vege-tables, it was noticeable that the Guard always appeared to have enough food.

Sauret had already eaten. His next task had been to clean his equipment and weapons. His bayonet in particular had needed cleaning: he had run it through the bodies of three Prussians that day. Two had been infantrymen, the third a wounded, unhorsed Uhlan who had taken a slash at him with a sabre as he ran past.

Lying at ease in his makeshift tent, pipe in mouth, he was remembering with professional satisfaction how he had dispatched the second of the infantrymen. A neat side-step, a swing of the stock to shatter the Prussian's jaw, then a bayonet thrust through the stomach to the heart. As quick and painless a kill as he had ever made.

Yawning, he lifted his grizzled head from his knapsack. The two men who shared his tent were still discussing the day's happenings around the fire. They were young enough to waste the precious hours. Tomorrow would be another full day, particularly if they marched against Wellington. Settling his head on his knapsack again Sauret closed his eyes, and in less than two minutes his rumbling snores reached his comrades by the fire.

Meanwhile Brussels was in turmoil. During the afternoon the artillery fire from both battles had been heard but although it had caused apprehension there had been no panic. But just after midnight broken remnants of a Dutch-Belgian cavalry unit began clattering down the cobbled streets. Battle-stained, many with serious wounds, the cavalrymen shouted to all who asked that Wellington's forces had been defeated and Brussels lay open to the French. To make matters worse, deserters from Quatre Bras, followed by cartloads of wounded, began pouring in. Mostly from Dutch-Belgian regiments whose hearts had not been in the battle from the outset, these deserters had created such a traffic jam on the roads that it had taken the British regiments and artillery hours longer than estimated to reach Quatre Bras. With their shouts that Wellington was defeated and everyone should flee for their lives, it spoke highly of the discipline of the British units that with every evidence of disaster ahead they had obeyed orders and marched on.

The same discipline could not be expected in Brussels. Doors were hurled open and half-dressed civilians poured out into the streets as the cartloads of wounded rumbled past. With the deserters shouting their tale of woe, panic spread through the city like a forest fire. The richer of the British tourists helped their servants to pack their bags and find their carriages. Many of the townsfolk whose sympathies had been with the British tried to flee the city. By 2 AM the streets were solid with carts of wounded men, supply wagons, coaches of fleeing tourists, and general flotsam and jetsam. Horses reared, hysterical women screamed, and men fought wildly to free themselves as rumour piled on rumour that Napoleon was only a few miles away.

In fact the cause of all this death and fear did not awake until 6 AM, an hour after Wellington had reached his troops again at Quatre Bras. The first news Napoleon received was from Pajol who had been sent by General Grouchy the previous night to discover Blücher's main line of retreat. Misled by the darkness and by the 8,000 young Prussian deserters who had fled in the direction of Namur, Pajol came back with the incorrect but satisfying report that Blücher's main army was retreating in panic along its supply lines to the east. To Napoleon it seemed his strategy had worked. Blücher had been driven east and every minute was taking him farther from Wellington. The English could now be attacked without fear of Prussian help.

Meanwhile, Wellington arrived at Quatre Bras to discover there was still no news from Ligny. (It came out later that Blücher's dispatch rider had been intercepted and killed by French cavalry.) With his decision to advance or retreat entirely dependent on whether Blücher's army still guarded his flank, Wellington was forced to send a strong force of cavalry to reconnoitre the Ligny battlefield. During the hours he awaited its report, he could do nothing but wait, while his soldiers, cooking their breakfasts, wondered why they were not ordered to attack. Like the French Army opposite them, they were in a sober mood for the morning sun had brought to their eyes the carnage of the previous day.

At Ligny, Napoleon's officers waited confidently and then in growing perplexity for orders to pursue the retreating Prussians. Few of them cared, even in the privacy of their minds, to question their Commander's judgement, and yet those who remembered his strange indecision before the retreat from Moscow were uneasy. He had shown no urgency the previous evening when a general pursuit would have given the *coup de grâce* to the Prussians, and now, even after a night's sleep, he seemed in the same indecisive mood.

Drouot arrived at his billet just before 8 AM with approximate casualty figures. The first piece of paper seemed to awaken the little Corsican whose eyes lifted from it with excitement. 'Sixteen thousand and more Prussian corpses! Let that be slapped up on the walls of Paris.'

75

Drouot passed him a second slip of paper. 'These are our losses, Sire. Twelve thousand dead and wounded.'

Napoleon glanced at it and tossed it aside. 'A field of glory always has its price. Did you say Ney had arrived?' When Drouot nodded, Napoleon sank back into his chair. 'Send him in.'

Across the room La Bédoyère was standing over a map on a table. His eyes flickered uneasily on the Corsican as Drouot left the room. La Bédoyère knew his man well and knew what that slumped posture signified.

Half a minute later Ney appeared. His efforts of the previous afternoon had taken their toll even on one as hardy as he, and his cheeks were shadowed and pale beneath his red hair. The Corsican stared at him with cold, controlled anger.

'You are two hours late.'

'I am sorry, Sire. I had to visit my troops first.'

Napoleon's sarcasm was like acid. 'And what were your troops doing? Sleeping in the sun as they slept yesterday?'

Ney bridled. 'That is unfair. They all fought bravely. But when you took d'Erlon's corps from me, you took away my right arm.'

The slumped figure leaned forward. 'So you blame that for your failure. Why did you not take the crossroads on Thursday evening? Why did you not take it yesterday morning?'

Ney was erect and pale-cheeked with anger. 'I have already given you my reasons.'

'I do not want your reasons. I wanted Quatre Bras. And you have not given it to me.'

Silence would have been wiser but that was never Ney's way. 'Some of my officers felt I did too much when they counted their losses last night. With d'Erlon's corps we would have swept over the English positions like an avalanche.'

Napoleon gave a mocking nod. 'If you had used them, so you would. When you kept them in reserve, I decided to use them myself to outflank and destroy the Prussians. But you were so determined d'Erlon should not be used, you countermanded my orders and took him back again. And so lost me Blücher and 30,000 prisoners.'

The pain the reprimand was causing Ney showed in his expression. 'But you have beaten Blücher. All he needs is pursuing.'

He earned another look of dislike. 'Pajol is already following him. Later Grouchy will take Vandamne and Gérard and a third of my force to Gemblouix and attack him as the situation demands. This will mean he will have no chance to link up with Wellington. In the meantime you will carry out my yesterday's orders and capture Quatre Bras.'

'But British reinforcements have been arriving all night, Sire. I am now heavily outnumbered. My officers are expecting Wellington to attack me.'

He received another disdainful smile. 'Then your officers are going to be disappointed.' Napoleon rose, motioned Ney over to the map, and jabbed a finger at it. 'I shall strike here, at the Englishman's left flank, and between us we shall have him like a nut in a pair of pincers.'

Hope and doubt mingled in Ney's expression. 'Rather than risk being outflanked he will retreat, Sire.'

The Corsican gave a characteristic shrug. 'Let him. He cannot run far – not with Brussels behind him. And once he stops he is ours for the taking.'

CHAPTER NINE

At Quatre Bras the cavalry patrol that Wellington had sent out to reconnoitre Ligny had returned with the report that Blücher had been defeated. Bad news though it was for Wellington, it nevertheless gave him something concrete to work on. A clear-sighted commander and a realist, he knew at once he would be forced to evacuate the hard-won strategic position of Quatre Bras.

With his men having fought so gallantly the previous day and now expecting to take their revenge on the outnumbered French, it was painful news to give them. It was also news that would go down hard in Brussels and London. Perhaps this was the reason Wellington waited until 10 AM before issuing the general order. The French showed no signs of attacking them, and with many wounded still unevacuated and hundreds of corpses still unburied, there was plenty of work to occupy his men.

Of all Wellington's officers, Picton was the most incensed by the order. His division had suffered heavily the previous afternoon in throwing back the French and a withdrawal now, with the time it would give the French to manoeuvre and make up their losses, would mean everything having to be fought for again. Yet some of Picton's acidity might be explained by pain. In the battle the previous day a musket ball had broken three ribs but he had kept all knowledge of it from Wellington and his own men.

Just before 10 AM a Prussian officer rode into Quatre Bras with details of Blücher's retreat. Wellington sent him back to Blücher with the message that he, Wellington, would stand and fight Napoleon at Mont St Jean but to succeed he must be supported by at least one corps of the Prussian Army. If he were denied this support he would be forced to surrender Brussels and retreat northwards. As the Prussian officer galloped off to Blücher with the message, Wellington began his unpopular withdrawal to the ridge south of Waterloo.

During this time morale had somewhat improved in Brussels. That morning the first battalion of the Royal Inniskilling Fusiliers, O'Connor's battalion and part of the 10th British Infantry Brigade, had reached the city. Marching with the 4th and 40th Regiments, disciplined and formidable-looking, they had created an excellent impression as they marched through the streets to the tap of drums.

But by two o'clock, when on the road to Quatre Bras, their smart appearance was drastically altered. The reason was a storm that blew up shortly after noon. It turned the sky almost into night over Brussels and after a preliminary bombardment of lightning and thunder, the rain drenched down. Veterans among the British troops who had known service in India said they had never seen such a downpour.

It was to prove a godsend for Wellington. Although for

the first hour the British withdrawal had been almost un-hindered, Napoleon had then thrown off his strange lethargy and become his dynamic self again. Nothing seemed to move fast enough for him now: after sending Grouchy and 33,000 men chasing after Blücher, he took personal charge of the flank attack on Wellington. Sending a note to Ney telling him to attack, he jumped into his carriage and took the road to Quatre Bras. At Marbais a force he had sent earlier was waiting for him, among them his Imperial Guard. There he mounted his small, wiry horse, Desirée, and with elements of Milhaud's cavalry he went forward like a whirl-wind towards Quatre Bras.

His belief was that Wellington was enmeshed in desperate fighting with Ney. Instead, to his anger and disgust, he discovered only small rearguard units of Wellington's Army were in action while the main bulk of his forces were well north of the crossroads. It was a moment when he must have bitterly regretted the hours he had wasted in Fleurus. Now, however, he was all virile action, galloping his small horse from artillery battery to cavalry unit in an effort to destroy the British rearguards and open the way to Wellington's main force. The British units, particularly the artillery bat-tery commanded by Captain Mercer and the cavalry ele-ments led by Lord Uxbridge, fought doggedly and repulsed attack after attack. The actions fought were too bitter for men to note the darkening skies above but as Mercer's battery fired a salvo at an advancing squadron of French cavalry, it seemed the retort tore open the black clouds. There was a tremendous crash of thunder and a deluge of rain came like a curtain between the opposing forces.

It proved no passing storm: the rain continued to pour down the entire afternoon. Soon the area around Quatre Bras became a quagmire, with men and horses slithering to their knees in the mud and artillery pieces sinking to the axles. With Wellington's main forces already well up the Genappe road that led to Mont St Jean, the conditions were a much greater handicap to the French. Napoleon's inten-tions had been to pursue Wellington through the country-side at top speed and then converge on him on either flank.

With the fields turning into quagmires, he was forced to order the bulk of his attacking force along the *pavé* roads, and while this meant that fighting at the rear of the British column was heavy, it did greatly lesson the danger to the infantry units ahead.

Nevertheless, the ferocity of the French attacks along the Genappe road was causing heavy casualties to the British rearguard, and just north of Genappe village Uxbridge decided to make a stand. His opportunity came when troops of French lancers emerged from the village. With long columns of French units piling up behind them, the lancers could not retreat and Uxbridge ordered a charge of the 7th Hussars.

Initially it proved a disaster. The French lancers stood firm and the light horses of the British hussars could not provide the impact to shatter the French line. Scores of young English cavalrymen were impaled on lances as the two forces clashed. Soon a French artillery battery came into action and blasted great gaps in the British ranks. Realizing his cavalry was too light, Uxbridge ordered a withdrawal. Exultant at their victory, the French lancers charged after them, only in their turn to run into units of the Life Guards that Uxbridge had ordered up. Helped by the 23rd Light Dragoons, the Life Guards succeeded in checking the French charge and then hurling it back with heavy casualties.

In the meantime Napoleon had realized that the massive jam of men and artillery units in Genappe represented a danger should the British bring back artillery, and ordered his commanders to slow down the advance. With the French cavalry also subdued by their reverse the pressure on the British was somewhat eased, although once they were clear of Genappe the French made a new effort to strike at the British flanks. But with regiments like the Inniskillings now linked up with the withdrawing British forces, they had little success.

Wellington ran into the Inniskillings himself in the early evening when, with de Lancey alongside him, he sat on horseback on a small hillock watching his units withdrawing northward along the Genappe–Brussels road. The road ran from a low hill ridge, across half a mile or so of drenched fields, to a second ridge that ran parallel to the first. It was on this northern slope that Wellington had decided to make his stand.

As the two men gazed back along the choked road, they could see a small roadside building on the crest of the southern ridge. It was La Belle Alliance, a small inn that was to gain immortality the following day. It was along this southern slope that Wellington was expecting Napoleon to bivouack his army that night.

A heavy cannonade was in progress. Seeing the British spreading out on the northern slope of the valley, the French were using their artillery to probe their intentions. The fire the British batteries were sending back gave reply they intended to stay.

On the road that ran from hill crest to hill crest, the weary Allied soldiers plodded past. Few could have missed seeing Wellington's familiar figure on the hillock but the drenched, dejected soldiers hardly gave him a second glance. With the rain pouring from his hat to his cape, Wellington turned wryly to de Lancey.

'Blücher gets a hammering and so we have to retreat. Back in England there'll be questions in the House, de Lancey. They'll say we have been beaten too.'

De Lancey knew his commander too well to try to comfort him. 'It's bad luck, Your Grace.'

Wellington shrugged. 'Luck or war. They're much the same coin.'

On the *pavé* road below a battalion of Inniskillings were now marching past. O'Connor was among them and as he caught sight of the two horsemen he turned to the man on his right, shouting to make his voice heard over the cannonade.

'Boney has kicked the Prussians in the arse but it's us who have to do the running. Look at the two of 'em sitting up there. They won't be sleepin' out in the fields tonight. They'll be in a warm bed with a warm wench.' At that moment O'Connor realized the cannonade had betrayed him by falling silent and that his voice would carry towards the two officers. As his muddy face stared upwards in dismay, Wellington gave a sudden laugh.

'A retreating army is never in love with its commander, de Lancey.'

De Lancey laughed with him. 'A few shots from the French and they'll be themselves again.'

Wellington, his voice dry, had raised his telescope and was examining the southern ridge that was half obscured by dusk and falling rain. 'Yes. Napoleon Bonaparte is a wonderful tonic to us all.'

The cannonade had now fallen into an uneasy grumbling. As the Inniskillings, bitter and resentful at having to retreat, faded into the mist, the skirl of bagpipes could be heard. A moment later a battalion of Gordon Highlanders appeared. Led and encouraged by old Colonel Gordon, a stoutly-built Scot with a florid, indomitable face, their virile appearance belied their circumstances. The bagpipes were playing *MacPherson's Lament* and the men were singing lustily. Among them Duncan, one of the handsome young soldiers who had danced at the Duchess of Richmond's ball, was prominent. As Celts so often do, he sang the saddest song with the most enjoyment and his strong tenor rang out above the gruffer voices of his comrades.

> *Sae rantingly, sae vaultingly,*
> *Sae gallantly, gaed he.*
> *He played a tune and danced it roun*
> *Beneath the gallows tree.*

The old Colonel was riding in the middle of his men. As Wellington beckoned to him he edged his horse out and spurred up the hillock.

'Congratulations on the cut of your men, Gordon,' the Duke smiled.

The old Scot beamed his pleasure. 'They're damned forward fellows with the bayonet, Wellington. Meat and eggs from the cradle up – an' a lemon a month. All from me own acres. Bred 'em myself.' Merriment spread across his florid face. 'Some of 'em might call me something more than Colonel, eh?'

Wellington gave his dry nod. 'More congratulations.'

As Gordon rejoined his men and his wheezy voice picked up their song, Wellington glanced up at the darkening sky and then at the misty ridge to the north. 'It's a relief we have reached it at this hour. There'll be some hard fighting tomorrow.'

De Lancey sounded vaguely apprehensive. 'Are you determined to make your stand there?'

The Duke was wheeling his horse towards the ridge. 'If Blücher can promise help in time, I must. Otherwise we shall lose Brussels.'

'But what if he cannot?'

Wellington spurred his horse forward. 'We have until dawn to hear from him. Let us pray we hear in time.'

As the two men rode past the weary Allied troops they passed a quarry and then, six hundred yards farther on, a farmhouse and orchard on the left of the road. It was La Haye Sainte, another name that was to become history before the following night. A sandpit lay on the right of the road which sank into a cutting as it approached the ridge. Riding along the sunken road with difficulty, for it was choked with troops, the two men climbed up to a crossroad. A lane, sunken into another cutting so as to be on the same level as the Brussels road, ran along the full length of the ridge. Eastwards it soon surfaced and was flanked only by holly hedges. Westwards it continued below the level of the ridge almost as far as the Nivelles road which ran in a south-westerly direction across the valley.

The Duke rode a few yards westwards along the lane and then put his horse to the slippery bank of the cutting. After a scramble the animal emerged on the hill crest. De Lancey followed. An elm tree stood nearby and to gain shelter from the rain the two men rode beneath it. Below to their left they could see the farmhouse of La Haye Sainte, and beyond it the Genappe road full of marching men and caissons. To the left of the road the valley curved out of sight behind the farmhouse and the ridge; to its right the terrain folded into small undulations and valleys. Some of the fields were growing clover but the majority bore rye. On the rainswept ridge opposite, dark clumps of trees could be seen and the tiny silhouette of La Belle Alliance.

With night now closing in rapidly, the cannon fire had ceased and allowed spasmodic musket fire to be heard. The troops who were already in position in the fields behind the ridge were clearing the charges in their muskets in the quickest way they knew. Wellington, who had not spoken a word to de Lancey since leaving the crossroads, now turned to him. 'I shall make this my observation post tomorrow. Have a chair and tables brought out at first light.'

Before de Lancey could answer, the thud of hooves along the ridge made both men turn. An officer was galloping towards them, his heavy chestnut throwing clods of mud in all directions. It was Picton, Wellington's tough infantry commander, and his burly face was agitated as he reined back his snorting horse.

'Wellington, I must protest. This place is unsound. It's no position to make a stand.'

No one could sound colder than Wellington when his dispositions were questioned. 'No position, sir? Then know that I noticed this ground a year ago and have been keeping it in my pocket for just such a moment as this.'

Showing his disbelief, Picton pointed at the long wood that ran along the rear of the ridge. It was the Forest of Soignes and in the falling dusk looked thick and impenetrable.

'But, dammit, Sir, have you seen that wood? If they push us back our whole army will be shot against it.'

'There is no undergrowth in that wood. The army can slip through it like rain through a grate.'

Picton wheeled his horse to face the valley. 'Then what about the two roads down there from Nivelles and Genappe? They will help the French to bring up their artillery.'

Wellington nodded coldly and swung his arm in an arc. 'Down there in the valley are three strongpoints: the château Hougoumont to the right of the ridge, the farmhouse below us, and another farm called Papelotte on our far left. Garrisoned, they will protect our centre and our flanks. And in case of a breakthrough this sunken lane will help to check their cavalry.'

Breathing heavily from his ride and the pain of his wound, Picton still looked unconvinced. 'I don't like it, Wellington. Nor do some of my officers.'

'The opinion of your officers, sir, is of little concern to me. Behind us the way lies open right to Brussels. Unless Blücher fails us, this is where we must make our stand.' The Duke's cold voice ran on without a change of expression. 'See your men are in position and then join me at the inn three miles up the road. We have much to discuss before the morning.'

There were others who thought Wellington's choice of position unsound. On the low, rainswept rise to the south, four horsemen had spurred to the head of the advancing French troops and were gazing across the valley. The smallest of the men, Napoleon, had his telescope raised.

'His whole army is there. Or so it seems.'

Ney turned towards him eagerly. 'He appears to be positioning his troops, Sire.'

The Corsican leaned forward on his horse's neck in an attitude of thought. His reflective voice barely reached La Bédoyère who was alongside him. 'He is ignorant of Caesar's basic principle, standing there with the trees in the small of his back.' He straightened as if coming to a logical decision. 'When your enemy is making a mistake it is poor policy to interrupt or provoke him. Order "rest", Soult. And show him no strength. We want him there when we awaken in the morning. What do they call this place?'

Unfolding a map beneath his cape, Soult had some difficulty in reading it because of the poor light. 'That plateau is called Mont St Jean. And beyond it I can see a hamlet called Waterloo.'

Napoleon nodded and turned back to the dark ridge. Allied camp fires were beginning to twinkle along its entire length. Suddenly a jagged bolt of lightning stabbed down at the plateau, giving the four men a flashlight glimpse of its woods and fields. Before the clap of thunder followed that shook the ground, they heard the Corsican's amused laugh.

'It seems the gods and I are in accord, gentlemen.'

CHAPTER TEN

Few soldiers on either side could remember a more miserable night than that night of June 17th. Because of the appalling conditions, the cavalry and artillery were given priority on the roads and on both sides the infantry were left to make their way across the flooded fields. Many had not eaten since the early morning and, with the British in urgent need of a defence position and the French anxious to catch them before they found one, neither commander allowed his men to rest. As they grew more and more tired, mud became their greatest enemy as it did to many a famous army in years to come. The soil in that part of Belgium makes a particularly glutinous compound, and as men slid, stumbled, and fell, it added pounds to the weight of their boots and clothing. Here and there it sucked a soldier's boots clean off his feet, and with ranks of men pressing him forward, he had no option but to stumble on barefoot.

On the roads conditions were not much better. As wagons broke down and gun caissons tried to pass them, they sank to their axles in the roadside mud. Men sweated and swore and some ruptured themselves trying to heave the caissons free. Others were injured by the flying hooves of panic-stricken mules. Cavalrymen were thrown to the ground and sometimes rolled on by their falling horses. Yet in spite of the occasional deserter who traded his chance of a firing squad for a few hours' rest, men struggled on knowing their only reward would be another bloody battle on the morrow.

The British and Allied soldiers were slightly better off than the French, not only because they reached their positions sooner but because the wiser ones still had some rations left. But on neither side, even with camp fires alight, was it possible to keep warm. Men tried to make small tents of their greatcoats but the incessant rain flooded beneath them. A few ingenious ones, bivouacked near trees, made themselves racks of branches to lie on, but they still could not escape the wind and the rain. Most men gave up trying. Huddling themselves under their single, sodden blanket, they sought for the sleep that would help them forget their misery.

Among the Allied lines there were a few realists like O'Connor who, deciding the whole busines of trying to sleep was a waste of time, risked a flogging or worse by slipping off into the darkness to see what he could find to make the night more bearable. A mile to the south, with their only ration a cake of hard bread, the incoming French had little choice but to forage. The operation was usually carried out by groups of friends: as soon as a place was staked out among the thousands of bivouacking troops, one man stayed behind to guard his comrades' kit while the others stirred their weary limbs again and went off into the night. With so many men hunting the same essentials, it was an expedition that might take hours. Any cattle or chickens encountered were given short shrift with the bayonet. Houses and cottages, deserted that day as the Armies drew nearer, were broken into and everything consumable dragged away. Even doors and window shutters were hacked off for fuel. For peasants in the early nineteenth century, a plague of locusts would have been infinitely preferable to a visit by Napoleon's Army.

To his disgust, for the rain and long march had turned his legs into leaden weights, Sauret was one who had to forage for his group that evening. As he dropped his sodden pack alongside Poirot, the lucky one who would lie down and rest, he felt as if his aching back would never straighten. Growling a curse to hide his discomfort, gripping his dead pipe between his teeth, the old Guardsman moved stiffly away.

Many men were without camp fires, either because they could find no fuel or were too weary to search for it. Sauret came across such a couple on his way out of the encampment. They were two young drummer boys, huddled with their drums beneath drenched blankets. Muttering to himself, the old Guardsman paused over them.

'If I were your daddy, I'd give you both a kick in the arse. War's not a game for children.'

Feeling his gaze, one of the boys woke up. He gave a violent shiver. 'It's cold.'

Sauret motioned him to sit up. Showing nervousness at the appearance of the fierce soldier, the boy obeyed. Kneeling down, Sauret pointed across the valley at the Allied camp fires. Then, holding out his hands, he rubbed them together vigorously. 'Our old trick in Russia, boy. The Cossack fires would be all around us, and us, we'd be icicles. So this is what we'd do. Come on, boy – warm yourself.'

Losing his fear, the boy smiled at him and obeyed energetically. Sauret patted him on the shoulder and moved on.

A mile to the east of the Mont St Jean plateau, O'Connor had convinced himself that the Blessed Saints had recognized his qualities at last. Emerging cautiously from a wood he had come across the astonishing sight of an undisturbed cottage. As he crept round the wattle fence searching for a way of entry, he heard the scamper of feet and a grunting sound. A few seconds later the snout of a small pig was pressing through a gap in the wattles and sucking the finger O'Connor offered it. The gratified Irishman's comment was rich with affection.

'You poor little friendly crathur. You're nosing yourself right into the pot.'

Jamming the butt of his musket into the gap, O'Connor swung his weight on the muzzle. There was a splintering sound as the wattles disintegrated. As O'Connor assisted the pig through the gap, a woman's voice suddenly screamed at him from the cottage.

'Eh là! Veux tu laisser mon cochon. Sale voleur!'

With the pig under one arm and his musket under the other, O'Connor bolted back to the wood. There, sitting on a fallen tree to regain his breath, he lowered the pig to the ground and felt the skin of its back and shoulders with affection.

'There, there, me little darlin'. You'll give O'Connor some nice, crisp cracklin', won't you?'

The little pig, as if suddenly realizing things were not all they seemed, let out a squeal and bolted with astonishing speed out into the darkness. O'Connor stared after it in dismay then, grabbing his musket, floundered across the fields in pursuit. In his concern he was unaware he was heading straight towards the French lines.

Sauret was disgusted as well as tired. Being the Emperor's crack regiment, the Guard were not often called on to forage for their own food. But on this campaign it seemed none of the normal conventions applied. First the generals had not followed on the heels of the defeated Prussians, and now even the Old Bearskins had to join in the undignified foraging.

But as the thing had to be done, Sauret did it well. Walking farther east than most of the weary men, he came across a stray hen brooding in a flooded ditch. With that in his empty knapsack and his pockets full of potatoes, Sauret was turning back to camp with a lighter heart. Whatever might happen tomorrow they would eat well tonight, and an old sweat like Sauret had long learned the wise soldier lives only for the moment.

He had just reached a large oak and was preparing to plunge into a shoulder-high growth of rye when he heard a peculiar pleading sound coming from the side of the surrounding ditch. A man was calling softly 'sucksucksucksuck-suck' and repeating the invitation as he advanced towards the Guardsman. Fascinated, Sauret stepped behind the oak and waited.

A moment later the man appeared from the darkness. His arms were extended enticingly towards a small animal that kept stopping, then running a few steps away. As the two of them neared the tree, Sauret stiffened as he saw the animal was a pig and the man a British soldier. As he raised his musket to take aim, the pig turned and bolted past the tree. Letting out an oath, the pursuing soldier dropped his musket and ran full-pelt after it. The squealing pig tried to alter course but the man, diving full length, grabbed one of its legs. Muddy but triumphant he sat up with the struggling animal in his arms.

'There, there, me little darlin'. But shame on ye for leading O'Connor such a dance.'

Sauret chose that moment to step from behind the tree. O'Connor's grin froze as he saw the massive Guardsman loom out of the darkness. Still clutching the pig, he leapt to his feet, only to realize his musket was at the other side of the tree. His horrified murmur broke the silence. 'Mother o' God, little one, will you take a look at that? Tell me it's a ghost or that I'm dreamin'.'

Sauret, who had already attached his bayonet, was now only a few paces away. O'Connor, too frozen by shock to run, could only think of holding out the pig in a silent appeal for his life.

The two men were now thrusting distance apart, the white appealing face of O'Connor staring into the grizzled visage of the Imperial Guardsman. Sauret, who had killed more men in hand-to-hand combat than he had fingers and toes, never understood why he experienced such reluctance to drive his bayonet into the helpless man. Unarmed or not, the Englishman was an enemy of his little Emperor and his duty was clear enough. Perhaps it was the absurdity of the situation that checked him. Or perhaps it was the sentiment that O'Connor, breaking the tense silence, hopefully expressed.

'There'll be enough killing tomorrow, matey. So can't we forget you an' me are on different sides tonight?'

As he once again offered the pig to the Frenchman, Sauret suddenly growled something and jabbed his bayonet fiercely towards the British lines. O'Connor stared at him in awe. 'Holy Mother o' God, he's going to let me go.'

Sauret was staring uneasily around at the darkness. His growl came more fiercely this time. 'Allez! Allez vite!'

Once again O'Connor pushed the pig at him. 'Don't you want it?'

'Non. Dépêche toi!'

O'Connor backed past the tree and picked up his musket. He walked away a few paces, then suddenly turned, causing the watchful Frenchman to lift his musket. Shaking his head, O'Connor fished in his pocket and brought out a hunk of tobacco. Breaking off a generous piece, he presented it to the Frenchman with a good deal of exaggerated courtesy. Sauret hesitated, then took it from him.

O'Connor was now his old self again. He peered at Sauret's face, then jabbed a finger at his own. 'Take a good look, matey. Just in case we meet tomorrow.'

He turned his face in both directions and then with a wink hurried away. For a full fifteen seconds Sauret did not move. Puzzled by his behaviour, he was now feeling guilty at letting one of his Emperor's enemies escape. With a last uneasy look around, he pushed the plug of tobacco into his empty pouch and started back for camp.

Hurrying back towards the Allied lines, O'Connor was wondering what to do with the squealing piglet tucked under his arm. A bayonet across the throat was the obvious solution but although O'Connor was no sentimentalist, the narrowness of his escape had given him an affection for the small creature and he found himself squeamish about killing it. For the briefest of moments he considered the supreme sacrifice, but thoughts of delicious gravy and crackling defeated him. His solution was full of human frailty. He would hand the piglet over to Patsy Macmahon, who had no sentimental attachments to the animal. Pushing it carefully into his knapsack, O'Connor continued on his way.

In spite of the rain, which was now a steady drizzle, camp fires and flares were glowing in their hundreds on the plateau. With his regiment on the western end of the ridge, O'Connor pondered on his best way of reaching them. Wending his way through the camp fires of the forward areas he might be spotted as a forager, in which case he faced death or a hundred lashes of the cat. On the other hand, although the valley lay in darkness, it probably teemed with French foragers and he could not hope for a second amnesty that night. Deciding the devil he knew was his better choice, O'Connor made his way up the hill.

The top of the ridge was alive with activity as unit commanders prepared their positions for the likely battle on the morrow. With camp fires and flares making concealment impossible, O'Connor decided boldness was the best policy and joined the detachment of men moving guns and ammunition along the narrow lane. On the forward side of the lane, working in the light of flares, fatigue parties were clearing gaps in the holly hedges and preparing gun emplacements. As he neared the third working party O'Connor saw his troubles were not over that night. The digging men were Inniskillings from his own company.

Recognizing his friend Patsy in the party, O'Connor edged furtively towards him. 'What's been happenin'?' he hissed.

Patsy, shovel in hand, took a quick look around. 'You're in trouble. The sergeant came for a workin' party ten minutes after you left. Your name was on it.' His eyes moved to O'Connor's bulging pack. 'Whatcha got in there?'

As O'Connor told him, Patsy's eyes glinted. 'You're a darlin' of a boy, Michael. Whatever happens to you, I'll see you get a piece of cracklin'.'

O'Connor seized a shovel and began hacking desperately at the holly-hedge. 'You'll tell the sergeant I was back in the woods relievin' myself. Otherwise I'll set the poor crathur loose.'

A group of horsemen were forcing their way along the crowded lane: Wellington, de Lancey, and a group of unit commanders were inspecting the progress of the defences before the Duke retired for the night to his headquarters. Seeing him coming, the Inniskillings pretended not to notice him, working with an innocence and industry that would have amused a man with less humour than Wellington. In the silence that fell his dry comment to de Lancey could be heard clearly.

'Here they are – my old friends, the Inniskillings. I hang and flog more of them then the rest of my army put together.' His voice rose, full of mock friendliness. 'Good evening, Inniskillings.'

There was a shuffle of embarrassment, then a few doubtful acknowledgements. 'Good evenin', sir.'

As the horsemen pushed past, one of the younger officers noticed O'Connor's pack and halted. 'You! The man with

92

the pack! Do you usually do fatigue in full kit? Turn around!'

Eyes tightly closed, O'Connor obeyed. Wellington, who had heard the officer's sharp complaint, recognized O'Connor and reined his horse. The officer's voice barked out again. 'What do you have in that pack, man? Answer me.'

Wellington came level with the young officer and indicated he would take over. Moving into the light of a hissing flare, he waved the dismayed O'Connor towards him.

O'Connor trudged forward. Wellington made a curt circle with his finger. 'Turn round.'

O'Connor's gyration was as fast as Wellington's gesture. 'Don't humbug me, man! Turn slowly.'

Knowing now that he was lost, O'Connor obeyed. As the bulging pack faced Wellington, the Duke saw it wriggle. His voice made the Irishman flinch.

'You are aware of the punishment for plundering?'

'Yes, sir.'

'What is it?'

O'Connor knew he had one chance left, to survive by his wits. Bracing himself, he made his reply sound like the last word in punishments.

''Tis the stoppage of gin, sir.'

'Damn you, it is death. Take off your pack!'

O'Connor laid his pack on the road and as Wellington jerked an angry finger, undid the straps. As the delighted pig poked out its snout, Wellington stared at the Irishman. 'You have no complaints, sir, against your punishment?'

Gulping, O'Connor did not answer.

'Where did you acquire this plunder?'

O'Connor realized it was a moment for very fast talk indeed. 'That's the very point I was tryin' to make, sir – that plunder acquired me. I found the poor crathur straying in the fields and she looked as lost and hungry as meself. Orphaned and weeping, a pig in tears, you might say.' Pausing a split-second, O'Connor played his trump card. '*You* know what I mean, sir – you was born in Ireland yourself.'

Wellington shot a glance at de Lancey. 'Not everyone born in a stable is a horse.'

'Ah, yes, sir. But it's only an Irishman that would have the wit to say it.'

Wellington was looking fascinated now. 'Go on.'

Picking up the pig affectionately, O'Connor made his last defiant stand. 'The truth is, Your Honour, this little pig has lost her way and I'm carryin' her home to her relations.'

With his last card played, O'Connor stood motionless, waiting for the fall of the dice that would decide whether he lived or died. Two things might have saved him: a young officer who could not suppress his laughter and the pig that nuzzled up and licked his chin. Hiding his expression, Wellington turned away.

'The fellow has merit, de Lancey. He knows how to defend a hopeless position.' He motioned to an Inniskilling sergeant who was gaping at O'Connor. 'See the owner gets his property back and dock the fellow three days' pay. We shall have need of him tomorrow.'

The scene behind the two lines of opposing armies was one of chaotic activity most of the night. The French, being the pursuers, took longer to reach their positions than the Allied soldiers and some of the units were not bivouacked until the small hours of the morning. But the roads behind the Allied lines were no less crowded. Supply wagons, many driven by civilians, rumbled up from Brussels in their hundreds. Many carried ammunition and supplies but many also carried useless impedimenta for Allied officers, such as dress uniform, brandy, wine, and books. One even carried an antique sideboard a major had purchased in Brussels. With little or no discipline among the civilian drivers, the roads became choked as wagons tried to pass one another and became bogged in the roadside mud. Men lashed at frantic horses: rivals cut the traces and allowed the animals to stampede. The chain reaction spread down the roads and started the rumour that the French had attacked and broken through. At once the civilian drivers abandoned their wagons and bolted into the darkness. Cursing Allied soldiers and cavalrymen were roused from their sodden blankets on Mont St Jean and sent back to clear up the unholy mess.

Back in Brussels the mood had switched yet again from uneasy calm to panic. With no more British troops to be seen in the city and with the wounded from Quatre Bras and Ligny still pouring in, the rumour that caused the desertion of the wagon drivers spread like wildfire. It was not helped by another rumour that had circulated through the city for days – that as an incentive to his soldiers, Napoleon had promised them twenty-four hours of licence if they captured Brussels. The report had no foundation – Napoleon needed the cooperation of the Belgians far too much to risk antagonizing them – but as rumour piled on rumour, Belgians became fearful at the thoughts of their womenfolk in the hands of drunken, lustful soldiers.

But on that night of cold and fear there were tiny oases where reflection prevailed. One such oasis was a camp fire in the British artillery lines where three captains, Mercer, Ramsay, and Normyle, were sitting beneath the barrel of a cannon over which a sheet of canvas was drawn. Because of the special skills called for in the artillery, the three men were trained professionals, unlike so many of the infantry and cavalry officers. Ironically, unless they were lucky enough to be well born, this put them in a lower social order.

Mercer, commander of the battery, was a good-looking fastidious man who always carried a supply of fresh linen with him. His troop of artillery was his pride and its behaviour during the retreat from Quatre Bras had given sterling evidence of his training and leadership. Thirty-two years old civilized and literate, he always kept a diary and had just taken it out of his pack.

He and Ramsay had finished their soup: Normyle, a somewhat cynical young officer, was about to commence his. Ramsay, small and dark in appearance, rose to take a look at the French camp fires, then seated himself again alongside Mercer.

'What do you think? Will we stand here and fight tomorrow?'

Mercer, pencil in hand, glanced up from his diary. 'I think the odds are on it.'

'But doesn't it depend on the Prussians?'

'I suppose it does. But where else can we make a stand between here and Brussels? It can't go on raining for ever and we'd fend much worse if they caught us in dry and open country.'

Ramsay's eyes were on Mercer's diary. 'How many men do you think they've got?'

'No one knows except that they outnumber us. But a prisoner said they had two hundred and fifty cannon.'

Ramsay whistled. 'A hundred more than us? We'll be kept busy tomorrow.'

Normyle, about to taste his soup, lifted a cynical face. 'So will our surgeons and burial parties.'

Mercer, known as a man for statistics, nodded. 'They will. The average is one casualty to every four soldiers on the field. So even allowing they've no more men than us, there'll be 40,000 dead and wounded tomorrow night if the battle runs its length.'

Normyle, tasting the soup, let it run back into the bowl. His expression suggested he liked neither its consistency nor Mercer's mathematics. Ramsay, who was cook for the evening, looked annoyed at his fastidiousness.

'Drink your soup, Normyle. If Mercer's right, it could be our last supper.'

In other oases words were less necessary. In the army of that time married soldiers were allowed to take their wives on active service, and on both sides of the valley brave women shared the night with husbands or lovers. Here and there, perhaps in a small tent or perhaps under sodden blankets, couples made love with the urgency and tenderness of those who know tomorrow might bring their final separation.

There was such a scene behind the French lines. Under a crude tent of blankets held up by a musket and a stake, Maria, a beautiful girl in the uniform of a *cantinière*, was lying in the arms of her lover, a prematurely-grey Guardsman called Chactas. The two woke, loved, and slept again while outside the preparation for Armageddon went on apace. Hundreds of cannon were drawn into position and thousands of rounds of shot, canister, and grape were piled in dumps. Cavalrymen queued in long lines outside armourers' tents to have their sabres 'rough-sharpened' so that a slash would inflict dreadful wounds. Officers schemed both awake and in their dreams at the best ways of killing their fellow men. But in that small makeshift tent a sleeping girl's hair moved gently to the breath of her lover.

CHAPTER ELEVEN

While over 130,000 men muttered, cursed, and shivered out in the open, their respective commanders retired to dry quarters: Wellington to his inn at Waterloo and Napoleon to Le Caillou, a farmhouse on the Genappe Road.

Neither man was relaxed mentally. Wellington desperately needed news of Blücher's intentions before he could commit himself to stand and fight. Napoleon, although welcoming the chance to engage the Englishman at last, was uneasy in his mind why Wellington had put himself into a position to be engaged. After the Corsican had eaten – on the Imperial plate that accompanied him on all his military expeditions – he dealt with his civil dispatches to Paris and then joined his unit commanders in the farmhouse dining-room which had been converted for the night into an operations room.

Ney, Soult, Drouot, La Bédoyère, and Kellermann were grouped around a large map on the dining-room table. All turned and drew erect as the Emperor entered. Outside there was a tumult of shouted orders and tramping feet that even the thick walls of the farmhouse could not deaden. Napoleon caught Soult's eye.

'It seems my Old Grumblers have arrived at last.'

Soult nodded. 'Yes, Sire. I have given orders for them to bivouac in the grounds outside.'

The Old Grumblers was one of Napoleon's affectionate names for his Imperial Guard. Late to arrive, there had been fears they had lost their way. Now, to everyone's relief, they were settling down outside in their privileged role of the Emperor's bodyguard.

Napoleon moved to the window and drew back the curtain. The officers thought he was gazing at the guardsmen but when he turned back to them they realized his thoughts were elsewhere.

'Why is the Englishman standing there? Has he lost his caution? Or is there something in his reasoning I do not understand?'

As always it was Ney with the courage to say what the others were thinking. 'Could it be he has heard from Blücher, Sire?'

Napoleon's stare was full of dislike. 'Have you forgotten I thrashed the Prussians at Ligny?'

'No, Sire. But we still do not know the way Blücher retreated. If he has fallen back on Wavre, he could still intervene tomorrow.'

'Did I not give Grouchy orders to follow him wherever he goes? And haven't you noticed the condition of the roads and fields after all this rain.' The Emperor gave a disdainful gesture as he approached the table. 'Blücher is an old hussar and an abuse of nature – he has four legs. But Blücher cannot fly.'

As he reached the map and bent over it, he gave a sudden gasp of pain. The officers stared at one another in alarm, then Ney jumped forward and caught his arm.

'What is it, Sire?'

The Emperor pulled away and glanced at his servant, Constant, who ran to pour him a glass of water. Supporting himself on the table Napoleon turned his drawn face to his anxious officers.

'What are you all staring at? It is nothing but a small colic.'

Controlling his pain, he took the glass Constant handed him and drank deeply. Ney was watching him with deep concern. 'Shall I go and call Doctor Larray, Sire?'

He earned only another glance of dislike. 'You will go and do nothing but your duty, sir. The rest of you – go with him. We'll talk again at dawn when we are certain that Wellington intends to fight.'

The men filed out, Ney throwing back a last anxious glance before the door closed. Napoleon, erect until they vanished, now sank into a chair. 'You can call Doctor Larray now, Constant.'

Opening his eyes he stared down at himself, then at his hands which he spread out on his knees. 'My body . . . my body is a mess, Constant. Only my hands are still good.'

Pushing himself with a grimace of pain to his feet, he moved across to the window and drew aside the curtain again. With Constant running out to call the doctor, his anxious question was made to an empty room.

'Hasn't it stopped raining yet?'

A similar scene was being enacted in Wellington's headquarters six miles away. In an oak-timbered room the Duke and his small staff were seated round a table on which a map was resting. A large log fire burned nearby and among others the firelight picked out the faces of Picton, de Lancey, Uxbridge, and Müffling, the German liaison officer. All looked grave and thoughtful except Wellington who, newly-bathed and changed, appeared his imperturbable self. Calling on a servant to fill the officers' glasses, he settled back in his chair.

'The situation, gentlemen, is this. If Blücher can give me the help of even one corps, then I'll stand and give Napoleon battle tomorrow. If he cannot, or will not, then I must retreat yet again. And as things stand at the moment I am ignorant of his intentions.'

The portly Müffling looked embarrassed as men gave him sidelong glances. Picton asked the obvious question. 'This intelligence has been sent to him, sir?'

He received Wellington's cold stare. 'Naturally. Dispatch riders were sent out hours ago to try to locate him. But so far we have heard nothing.'

Wellington's dilemma was complicated. At that time he had no way of knowing Napoleon had sent Grouchy and 33,000 men in pursuit of Blücher and so believed he was facing the entire, superbly-trained French Army. With his doubtful Dutch-Belgian units and his scratch British regiments, the Duke had no doubt that without Prussian support he would be overwhelmed. His only remaining reserves were his 17,000 British troops stationed at Hal, seven miles west of Waterloo, and with his obsession that Napoleon would try to turn his right flank – a move that would undoubtedly have proved disastrous for him – Wellington dared not call on them.

A further problem for him was time. With the roads behind him blocked with supply wagons, and with his men exhausted, it would be difficult enough to re-commence his retreat now. But in a few hours, when dawn was imminent, it would be suicidal. The sun might dry out the fields, which would enable Napoleon to leap forward and pounce on him like a great cat. Moreover, as Wellington had pointed out to Picton, there were no more natural defence positions between Mont St Jean and Brussels.

Outside, the rain could still be heard beating down. Seeing Picton's eyes fixed accusingly on him, Wellington jerked his head at the window.

'We have one ally on our side tonight. The mud will lie thick in the valley and up the hillside. They will not find it easy to slither up to us.'

Like Ney, the burly Infantry Commander was not famous for his tact. 'If Blücher moves to help us, it will also slow him down. And that could mean our defeat.'

Wellington inclined his head. He could read the thoughts of the assembled men. Every order that could be given to strengthen the ridge had been given. The château and the two farmhouses had been heavily garrisoned. Cannon had been sent down to them, ammunition was being stockpiled, trees cut down to improve the field of fire, and holes driven through the walls to provide embrasures for the infantry. On the ridge itself, the lane was being turned into a defence position and every unit commander had been acquainted with his duty should battle be joined the following day. Yet unless Blücher's reinforcements arrived, it seemed certain the Emperor's dedicated army must sweep over Mont St Jean like a wave over a sandbar.

Had any of the assembled men been able to see Blücher at that moment at least some of their fears would have been relieved. His surviving troops were now fully concentrated at Wavre and the old man himself was fast asleep. He had recovered magnificently from his fall at Ligny but the long day of retreat had exhausted him. He had also quarrelled with Gneisenau. The Chief of Staff still opposed his plan to assist Wellington in the morning, arguing that if the British were defeated, the French would then be able to turn on them in strength, cut their supply lines, and destroy them. The gallant old man had refused to listen. He had led his men in retreat: tomorrow he would lead them to Wellington and victory. After copious doses of his favourite medicine, gin and rhubarb, he had taken himself off to bed.

To keep up the morale of his staff during the long hours of waiting, Wellington, a small drinker himself, ordered more wine for them. As a servant entered with a decanter there was a clatter of hooves in the courtyard outside. A moment later a second servant entered and asked for Müffling, who rose and went out. As the staff officers turned curiously towards one another, Müffling burst back into the room like an explosion, dragging a drenched young cavalry officer after him. In his excitement his English had a guttural quality.

'He is from Marshal Blücher, Your Grace. The Marshal is safe and has sent a message for you.'

Only those close to Wellington noticed the flicker of emotion that crossed his face as he took the dispatch from the young hussar. The watching officers moved forward to the edge of their chairs. Wellington read the dispatch calmly, then lifted his eyes.

'Gentlemen, this is good news. At daybreak Marshal Blücher is sending us Bülow's corps, his only major unit that did not fight at Ligny. His 1st and 2nd corps will proceed towards us later when they are rested.'

Picton's fist smashed down on the arm of his chair. 'By God, this changes everything.'

Müffling could not contain his enormous relief. 'You may now fight your battle, Lord Duke.'

Wellington nodded and turned to the young cavalry officer. 'I am sorry, sir. I must ask you to ride back to Wavre tonight.'

The hussar reset his riding cloak and bowed. 'Oblige me with a fresh horse, sir, and I am at your service.'

Wellington signalled to one of the servants to meet the request. 'Bid Marshal Blücher to be at Waterloo not later than 1 PM. I doubt if I shall be able to hold back the French any longer.'

The hussar saluted and went out of the room with Müffling. Picton's hand came down on his chair again. 'By God, we have a trap for him now.'

He received Wellington's dry smile. 'Which might well spring back on us. You forget your own warning about the mud, Picton. If it delays or stops Blücher, it will become a matter of counting our own dead.'

Uxbridge gave an uneasy glance at the door through which Müffling had passed. 'But with that risk, dare we rely on the Prussian?'

Wellington shrugged. 'As I see it, Uxbridge, the game has gone too far for us to withdraw now. We have to rely on him – and he on us.'

The man tossed in the bed, opened his eyes, and sat up listening. Although the room was quiet, he appeared unsatisfied and walked across to the window. Drawing back the curtain he put his face near the glass to stare out.

In the farmyard a company of lancers on horseback were asleep in their saddles. Enveloped in their white cloaks they looked like petrified corpses – an army of giants struck by lightning.

The Corsican's eyes, however, were on the rain splashing down into the dark puddles. He muttered something in agitation and shook his head. As he moved back across the room, a spasm of pain made him gasp. He sank slowly back on to the bed and lay staring at the dark ceiling.

CHAPTER TWELVE

Dawn came grey and dirty that June 18th. The rain had eased but was still falling. As far as the eye could see, grey mounds in the mud showed where men lay huddled under sodden blankets. Steam, rising from them, mingled with the haze of smoke from dead fires. Sleeping horses stood in pools of shadow or in silhouette against the lightening sky. Somewhere far away a dog was barking.

The first sound of the trumpets brought only a harsh outcry from the woods followed by a loud clatter of wings. Then, low at first like a grumble and then louder like the murmur of the sea, came the sound of two armies awakening. Men lifted their heads from their knapsacks and with tightening stomachs remembered where they were. Filthy, unshaven, shivering, and drenched, they stared across the valley at the lines opposite.

The strident British and French trumpets sounded like echoes of one another. NCOs walked down the lines of prostrate bodies, prodding with their musket butts at men still sleeping. Others yawned, shivered in the cold breeze, and stretched their aching limbs. Some urinated where they stood. There was an all-pervading smell of stale sweat, wet clothes, and dank leather.

Up on the top of the ridge O'Connor's first job was to scratch himself. Then he lit his pipe, put on a dry pair of socks, and began checking his powder cartridges for dryness. In the orchard of La Haye Sainte, among their battery of nine-pounders, Mercer, Ramsay, and Normyle gave the fire their first attention. When it was burning and a kettle suspended over it, the three men had a shave. Afterwards Mercer pulled a clean shirt from a chest in an ammunition wagon and changed into it. Beyond the hillcrest opposite, Sauret, knowing the Old Guard would not be called on until the English were set up for the *coup de grâce*, was enjoying an early-morning pipeful of O'Connor's tobacco while his two younger comrades prepared breakfast. Down the lines a French gunner, who had kept out of the mud by sleeping straddle-legged over his cannon barrel, woke with a start as a corporal prodded him and, ironically, fell straight into a puddle.

All was movement now as chilled men arose from the mud and tried to find fuel to re-light their drenched fires. Cavalrymen rode their horses up and down to restore their circulation. The smell of cooking began to mingle with the smell of stale sweat and urine. As they waited to eat, infantrymen began to dry their muskets and to renew the flints in the locks. As more [and more of them fired practice shots, it began to sound as if skirmishers were already in action. Like two awakening monsters, the Armies were ponderously rising out of the mud to do battle.

At Le Caillou the mood was different from the previous night. As he entered the breakfast room, crowded with his marshals and generals, Napoleon appeared refreshed and in good humour. 'Good morning, gentlemen. Today is a day that we shall all remember.'

He walked towards the breakfast table. It was laid with silver Imperial plate, covered dishes, and crystal. As he reached his chair his staff took their allotted places: Ney to his right, La Bédoyère to his left, Soult at the far end of the table facing the Emperor. A few faces were absent, in particular Prince Jerome, Napoleon's brother, who was out reviewing his cavalry.

Seating himself, Napoleon began to eat quickly. After a couple of minutes he pulled a map from inside his tunic, laid it on the table, and began studying it. He glanced down the table at Soult.

'I shall attack the Duke of Wellington at nine o'clock. What is the state of the ground?'

'It will not dry before noon, Sire.'

'We've charged with mud on our boots before.' It was the red-headed Ney.

In the distance a bell could be heard chiming. Napoleon looked curious. 'What is that?'

'It's Sunday morning, Sire,' La Bédoyère reminded him. 'The priest in Plancenoit won't give up his mass.'

The Corsican took another mouthful of food. 'He won't have much of a congregation.'

A heavy silence fell as Napoleon examined the map. He seemed abstracted and no one dared to speak. After a minute he threw his serviette down and motioned Constant to come forward with two other maps. His staff rose with him, although some had not yet finished eating. As they gathered around him, Drouot, his artillery expert, entered the room. Napoleon addressed him without lifting his eyes from the map.

'Yes, Drouot?'

The Artillery Commander was clearly hesitant. 'Sire, we need four hours. The ground is too soft for me to move my cannon quickly, which I must do to drive him off the ridge.'

Still Napoleon did not look up. 'If I had waited four hours I should have lost Austerlitz.'

Ney gave Drouot a scornful glance. 'Wellington won't hold us for an hour with his bouillabaisse of English, Scots, Dutch, Irish, Belgians, and Brunswickers.'

Drouot ignored him. 'I cannot answer for my cannon, Sire.'

Napoleon shifted indecisively. 'You are the very cannon itself, Drouot. But battles are won or lost in a quarter of an hour.'

'If Wellington were on the move, then I'd say "Go now". But he's sitting, Sire, with the mud in his favour.'

Soult was quick to support Drouot. 'Caution is required, Sire, before we commit ourselves. The British infantry is stubborn and will not give ground easily.'

A rumble of assent went round the table. Many of the officers present had fought against Wellington in Spain and held a high opinion of his leadership and the toughness of his troops. It was an opinion that Napoleon, who had yet to meet Wellington face to face, did not share and it is possible that he might have over-ruled Drouot had not Ney intervened again. The red-headed Marshal, who had served in Spain himself, ought to have supported the artilleryman but eagerness to please his Emperor overcame his judgement.

'Do as you feel right, Sire. Attack the Englishman quickly in case the rumour your brother heard is right and Blücher is on his way.'

The rumour to which Ney alluded came from a conversation Prince Jerome had had with a waiter in a Genappe inn the previous evening. Earlier in the day the waiter had served Wellington's staff and overheard one of the aides saying the British would stand and wait for the Prussians. The waiter had also heard a report that the Prussians had retreated to Wavre. Jerome had brought these rumours to Le Caillou that morning.

It was as unfortunate a remark as Ney had ever made to his chief. At every hint by his staff that Blücher could still be a threat Napoleon, convinced that his defeat of the old man had been a crushing one, had shown anger. Now, with the ambivalence that existed between himself and Ney, the Marshal's remark almost guaranteed a contrary decision. The Emperor turned curtly to Drouot.

'You persuade me. I'll give you a delay but only three hours. We must dine in Brussels tonight.' As he walked back to the table round which his staff were assembled, his earlier, optimistic mood returned. 'A three hours' reprieve for them, gentlemen. But we won't waste those three hours. Before the English die we will dazzle them.'

The parade began late in the morning when the rain finally stopped. The dark clouds moved away and soon the sun was shining on the sodden fields and the glistening mud. It was then observers on the British ridge, a mere 1,500 yards away, saw the French regiments deploying in parade on the opposite rise as their Emperor inspected them.

It was a scene without parallel in military history. First came the chasseurs in their bright green jackets with facings of yellow or scarlet. The hussars followed in their dolmans and pelisses, the plumes in their shakos, red, green, blue, or yellow according to their regiments. Then it was the turn of the dragoons in their helmets of tiger-skin and brass, their green coats criss-crossed by white shoulder belts, their long guns beside the saddle bumping against their high boots. All deployed and gave the salute as the small figure of their Emperor inspected them.

The mighty cuirassiers were next to appear. Wearing short coats with Imperial blue collars, with white breeches, high boots, and steel breastplates, their fearsome appearance was enhanced by great crested steel helmets. The giant carabiniers followed, all over six feet tall and clad in white, with glinting breastplates and tall helmets. All stood proudly to attention as Napoleon passed by and shouted 'Vive l'Empereur' so that the sound rolled like a great wave towards the Allied lines.

Lancers appeared in red kurtkas and blue plastrons; grenadiers in blue coats and tall bearskins; chasseurs in green dolmans wearing huge plumes of red and green on their scarlet kalpaks. The psychology was to awe and daunt and it had worked on many a battlefield before this. Gold and polished metal sparkled like sunlight on water as still more units came to pack the hillside. Now it was the turn of the Emperor's 'beautiful daughters' – his field artillery. Superbly-trained teams swept the cannon into line, row after row of them. To the men watching from the opposite ridge, their numbers seemed endless.

Parading past Napoleon, eagle bearers were inclining the new standards he had presented after the battle of Ligny. Bands crashed out 'Veillons au Salut de l'Empereur', trumpets blared triumphantly, cavalrymen brandished their sabres and lances, and great cheers reverberated across the valley as the last of the regiments, the élite of them all, marched into sight. It was the Emperor's Old Guard and there was no gaudy plumage here. The Old Grumblers wore their campaigning uniform, a plain tunic, blue trousers and gaiters. With their fierce moustaches and side whiskers, their great bearskins that made each man look nine feet tall, with their legend of invincibility that walked alongside them, they gave the parade its last dramatic touch. Intoxicated by the martial bands and the pomp and splendour, men shouted themselves hoarse and laughed their contempt at the drab, silent lines opposite. Their godlike Emperor was in command, what army on earth could check them? With adrenalin running through their veins like fire, men shivered in their eagerness to fight.

Alongside the elm tree on the ridge, near the junction of the lane and the Genappe road, Wellington was watching the display. He was wearing his habitual dark-blue coat, white breeches, white cravat, and hat bearing the cockades of England, Portugal, Spain, and the Netherlands. He had decided to make the spot his observation post and a table and chairs stood beneath the tree. His small staff were present, among them Picton. The tough Welshman, sitting on horseback alongside the Duke, let out a snort of disdain.

'I've never seen a more foolish performance, Wellington.'

Wellington turned to young Lord Hay. Beside the boy's stirrup was a beautiful Dalmatian hound that accompanied the young officer everywhere. Seeing Wellington's movement, Hay gave a nervous laugh. 'I don't think they can do much harm to us, can they, Your Grace?'

Wellington was looking amused. 'Music and flags and uniforms. It's quite beautiful, Hay. You're lucky to see such a wonder in your first battle.'

The entire hillside opposite was now packed with phalanxes of soldiers, cavalry, and artillery. Breastplates, sabres, helmets, polished cannon, glinting martially in the sunlight, were secretly turning the blood of many a young Allied soldier cold.

De Lancey, a handsome, virile figure on a fiery roan, was looking reflective. 'He has filled his stage. As near as I can estimate there will be twenty men to every yard of ground.'

Wellington inclined his head. 'I'm afraid the slaughter will be heavy.'

At that moment the Dalmatian hound let out a bark as young Lord Hay spurred his horse forward. Pointing across the valley he stared excitedly back at Wellington.

'Look, Your Grace! Over there!'

Wellington frowned. 'What is it, Hay?'

'There! Near the road, Your Grace. His white horse. The monster!'

With a glance at Picton, Wellington lifted his telescope and focused it. He smiled. 'So there he is. The great thief of Europe himself.'

Riding Marengo, his white Arab, Napoleon was parading across the French forward slope in front of his massed troops. As their cheering rose to a great crescendo, there was the rapid thud of hooves and a moment later Mercer's horse came scrambling up the bank behind the elm tree. The Duke nodded as the excited artillery officer gave him a salute.

'What is it, Captain?'

'Bonaparte has ridden within range, Your Grace. My portfires are lit and the crews ready. Have I your permission to try a shot or two.'

Excitement at the sight of Napoleon was spreading along the Allied lines. Soldiers had the same kind of perverse admiration for him that the English were to have for Rommel 150 years later. Someone started the satirical song that was in vogue at that moment and it spread rapidly along the ridge.

> *Boney was a warrior, Oh-i-Oh,*
> *Boney was a warrior, John François,*
> *Boney beat the Prussians, Oh-i-Oh,*
> *Boney beat the Prussians, John François.*

Wellington gave de Lancey his dry smile. 'Quite a brotherly business this killing, isn't it, de Lancey?' He turned back to Mercer with some curtness.

'Certainly not, Captain. Commanders of armies have something better to do than shoot at one another.'

The puzzled Mercer retired discomfited. The singing had now spread almost the whole length of the Allied line. De Lancey looked anxious. 'Shall I shut them up, Sire?'

Wellington shook his head. 'No. No. Indulge it. Anything

that distracts or wastes time this morning we must indulge.'

A sweep of wind brought the martial clash of the French bands nearer. As the singing of his troops mingled with it Wellington suddenly appeared anxious. Laying a hand on de Lancey's saddle, he leaned towards him.

'Normally I don't like the men cheering, de Lancey. It encourages insolence – the mob that cheer us today will jeer at us tomorrow if we give them the chance. But like everything else, there is a time for it. Will you kindly announce me, de Lancey?'

De Lancey slapped his horse into a run and waving his hat, galloped along the ridge in front of the assembled troops. 'Three cheers for the Duke!'

The singing faltered, to be replaced by desultory cheers. Spurring his horse towards the edge of the ridge so that he could be better seen, Wellington lifted two fingers to his cocked hat. As the cheering grew louder he hesitated, then, looking amused, raised his two fingers again before withdrawing to the elm.

His parade over, Napoleon rode back to a small inn called Rossomme, three-quarters of a mile back from the hillrise. His servants had brought out an armchair and a table from the inn and put them on a small knoll by the roadside after spreading straw over the muddy ground. The officers present thought the Emperor in pain as he dismounted and sank into the armchair, and, as he sat there, head in hands without speaking, they began to fear he had fallen into another of his lethargic depressions.

After two minutes had passed without a word or movement, Soult cleared his throat and approached with a sheaf of papers. 'These are the Battle Orders, Sire. Do you approve them?'

Stirring himself, the drawn-faced Emperor slipped through the pages and then tossed them back at Soult. 'Battle orders of six pages would be too long for the Siege of Troy! This is how we proceed. Wellington has deployed his main strength on his right: that means he fears for that flank. So we begin by teasing him there. Once we have drawn more men from his centre, we make straight for it. And in less than an hour we'll know the length of this English aristocrat.'

Reille, an excellent tactician who had fought in Spain, threw Soult an alarmed glance. 'Do you think a frontal attack is wise, Sire? I agree with Soult – the British infantry is stubborn. And Wellington has stood his British regiments alternately between his Allied units to stiffen them. Our advantage is our greater flexibility. If we outflank the English, we can draw them away from their allies and cut them up piecemeal.'

The ability to take advice, once Napoleon's greatest strength, appeared to have deserted him. 'There is no time to outflank and in any case the mud is too thick. We attack his centre. I tell you the English are bad troops and the odds are nine to one in our favour.'

The unsubtlety of the tactics alarmed other generals besides Reille, for whether success attended them or not, the cost of such a direct onslaught was certain to be excessive. Throughout his military career Napoleon had won battles by taking risks but these had always been carefully calculated. His sense of strategy remained sound – his move to split Blücher and Wellington had been brilliant. But now he was acting like a deluded gambler. His experienced officers had warned him time and again that the British infantry were tough and unshakable: he held to his opinion that a massive frontal attack would prove them brittle reeds. In addition, although by this time at least three rumours had reached him that Blücher intended to help Wellington, he refused to believe the Prussians could recover so quickly from their defeat at Ligny.

A more rational gambler would have hedged his bets. Reille was right in saying the French had more experience than the British in agile field manoeuvres. An attack down their right flank would not only have made victory more likely, it would also have ensured that the British forces were kept between the French and the Prussians should Blücher arrive at Mont St Jean. A frontal attack, on the other hand, contained the built-in danger that if the Prussians did come the French might be outflanked themselves.

Realizing Napoleon was adamant, Reille attempted to make the best of the situation. 'If you feel certain Blücher is no longer a threat, Sire, then will you not recall Grouchy? If we are to make a frontal attack we shall need more men than those that defend the ridge.'

Unwisely, Ney nodded his agreement at the suggestion the attacking force would suffer heavy casualties in a frontal assault. Seeing it, Napoleon gave him a look of dislike before turning irritably to Soult.

'Send a message to Grouchy that he is to keep in close touch with us but is to continue towards Wavre, driving the Prussians before him.'

There was a hint of despair in the shrug Soult gave Reille as he walked away. If their once-great leader had lost his judgement, one could only pray his luck had not forsaken him too.

The sun climbed higher as the morning began to slip away. The French troops, primed and thirsting to fight, began to suffer from reaction and an uneasy silence settled over the valley. Wellington, conscious that every wasted minute was to his favour, made no move that would provoke an attack but instead spent the time riding up and down the ridge organizing his defences.

It was behaviour that showed the difference between the two leaders and the armies they commanded. All through his military career, first in India and then in Spain, Wellington had been forced to operate with numerically inferior forces. This experience had taught him to use his men economically – at Waterloo it showed in the way he stationed the majority of his forces on the reverse slope of the ridge and in the sunken lane to protect them from the French artillery. Moreover, it had taught him how to win defensive victories – tactics ideally suited to the character of his British soldiers. But the exercise of such a difficult art required much individual supervision and as a consequence Wellington's personal staff was always small and trained to carry out his orders rather than make decisions of their own.

In his early days Napoleon, a supreme opportunist, had shown the same dedicated application and skill, but once he became head of a great empire his need for economy in manpower had gone. Also, once he had the multitudinous affairs of State to attend to, even his colossal energy had not run to giving his armies the close attention they had once enjoyed. Entire campaigns were carried out by subordinates who, lacking his military genius, made mistakes that could only be rectified by pouring in more troops. As a result, in later years, Napoleonic battles tended to be killing matches in which brute force counted far more than skill. While the French retained numerical superiority because of conscription, all had been well, but once her enemies had overcome their jealousies the end had been near. At Waterloo he was back at the head of his army again but, because the only generals he could assemble were those who had served during his first reign, it was proving difficult to wrench from them the authority they had grown to expect. The result was to have no small effect on the battle ahead.

Noon was approaching fast but still Napoleon gave no order for hostilities to commence. Men talked in whispers, in loud voices, men smoked their pipes, became bored, or grew progressively more nervous according to their natures. Those with premonitions of death – and every army has those before a battle – accepted every minute as a bonus and found an extra sweetness in the singing of the birds and the sunlit castles of cloud that drifted overhead.

Historians have argued for 150 years about Napoleon's behaviour that day and during the two days that preceded it. At Ligny he had shown irresolution that had allowed Blücher to escape. Now he was using the mud as an excuse for delay. The old Napoleon scorned excuses and would have taken the weather conditions in his stride.

Jerome, his brother, let it be known years later that Napoleon had suffered an acute attack of piles the previous evening. There is also a suspicion he had a re-occurence of cystitis, a painful complaint brought on by cold and wet that had put him out of action at the battle of Borodino.

If this were true, his inability to concentrate and make positive decisions is easily understood, for cystitis not only produces crippling pain but brings with it fever. That either complaint should have struck him on the eve of the most important battle of his life must have caused him intense bitterness, and sympathy can be felt for his occasional outbursts of irritation.

The possibility also exists that his brain was less active than during his earlier campaigning days but, as he was only forty-five at Waterloo, this seems unlikely. Another theory for his uncharacteristic irresolution is that he suffered a disease of the pituitary gland, which would account for his increased weight and attacks of lethargy. Whatever the reason, even his most loyal marshals and generals saw the change in him and their loss of confidence in his leadership not only worried them but perhaps strengthened secret resolutions to act on their own initiative.

While the uneasy silence lay over the battlefield, an event was happening at Wavre that would have disturbed the calm of even Wellington. Although Blücher had kept his word and sent Bülow's corps marching towards Mont St Jean, a large fire had broken out in Wavre as the troops were passing through it. Spreading rapidly, it had blocked the road and the Prussians were forced to delay their advance while they saved the village. Thus, hours were lost and another factor introduced that could swing the battle either way.

It was well past eleven o'clock when Napoleon finally aroused himself and called for his horse. A quarter of an hour later observers on the opposite ridge saw a cloud of skirmishers followed by four regiments of infantry start moving down the slopes in the direction of Hougoumont wood. At the same time there was intense activity as batteries of cannon moved up to support them. Under the elm tree Wellington lowered his telescope and turned to his tense staff. On the table before him was a tray of glasses and a bottle.

'Gentlemen, it is about to commence. So before we go to work – a little sporting ritual.'

He made a signal to an orderly who filled the glasses with cherry brandy and handed them round. Smiling wryly, Wellington lifted his glass and offered his toast. 'Gentlemen – today's fox!'

As his staff followed suit and drank, a great cheer swelled from the glittering phalanxes opposite. De Lancey glanced down at his watch. 'Eleven thirty-five, Your Grace.'

As if in answer there was a rolling clap of thunder as Jerome's divisional batteries before Hougoumont opened fire. The battle had begun.

CHAPTER THIRTEEN

The French division that led the attack on Hougoumont was commanded by Jerome, Napoleon's brother. Their first objective was the wood that lay between them and the château. After an initial barrage that hurled huge blocks of stone and bricks from the buildings, they began marching down the slopes towards the wood. British troops stationed on the ridge behind Hougoumont could see their flowing pennants and hear their bugles sound the attack.

Their objective, the château, was a complex of buildings that comprised the château itself, granaries, cowsheds, barns, and two small houses that belonged to a farmer and a gardener. These buildings enclosed two yards which were separated from one another by a low wall and a chapel. On the east side of the house (which faced La Haye Sainte) there was a flower garden enclosed by a six-foot wall. Beyond was an orchard. The wood that stood to the south was densely planted. The entire grounds were surrounded by a hedge and ditch.

The colonel in charge of the garrison was James Macdonell, a huge dependable Highlander, and his responsibility that day was immense. The château overlooked a narrow valley deep enough to hide French troops from the British artillery should they be allowed to make their way along it. Once past they could outflank Wellington and make the ridge untenable. Macdonell's command for this post of high responsibility consisted of light companies of Scots and Coldstream Guards and German troops from Nassau and Hanover. The Germans were given the woods to defend: the British the buildings, the garden, and the orchard.

As the advancing French drew within range, the British artillery on the ridge opened fire. Shells screamed down on the skirmishers, burying them in geysers of water and mud. Soon it was the turn of the marching regiments to come into range. Musket fire from the hidden Germans cut them down and cannonballs slashed bloody swathes through their ranks. Still they came on and, cheering and shouting, they swept into the woods. Foot by foot, with musket ball and bayonet, they drove back the dogged Germans until the grey walls of the château appeared before them.

Back on the ridge de Lancey was galloping anxiously towards Wellington's observation post. The Duke was seated and staring at a battle plan on a table before him. Across the valley new units of French troops could be seen flooding down the hillside towards Hougoumont. De Lancey dismounted and pointed back along the ridge with his telescope.

'He's sending in reinforcements, sir. He intends to turn us on our right.'

Wellington turned to him with a slight frown. 'What Bonaparte intends to do and what he does are as different as hare and hounds.'

'I know, sir, but it will be fatal if our flank is turned.' De Lancey pointed down at the battle plan. 'The 95th is ready. We could move it across immediately.'

The Duke sat coldly back in his chair. 'I do not intend to run about like a wet hen, de Lancey. In any case there'll be plenty of opportunity today to throw living men in after dead ones. Macdonell will have to manage with the men I have given him.'

An unnatural quiet lay over the rest of the valley as

soldiers on both sides watched, or tried to watch, the action at Hougoumont. As the French emerged from the northern end of the wood they discovered the château had been turned overnight into a fortress. Loopholes had been made in the massive walls at different levels, with the British infantrymen standing on specially-built platforms to man them. Other defenders were hidden behind windows and terraces. As the French started forward a withering fire hit them. A young drummer boy, beating the charge, had his face blown away. Gritting their teeth, men scrambled over the dying bodies of their comrades, only to scream and die in their turn. Others, with gaping wounds, tried to crawl back to the sanctuary of the woods. Bodies began to pile in mounds in the thick mud of the courtyard.

Retreat was ordered. Women were now seen in the woods, attending to the wounded. Maria was among them, holding a dying man's head in her arms and giving him water from her canteen. Other *cantinières*, helped by drummer boys, were trying to drag wounded Frenchmen back to their lines.

Reille, conscious that the assault had been intended only as a diversion, sent orders that the action should cease with the taking of the wood. Jerome, however, perhaps wishing to prove to his sceptical brother that he knew how to fight, called in more units and ordered a death or glory attack on the château.

This time the sappers led the assault. One was Legros, a massive man nicknamed 'L'enfonceur' by his comrades because of his strength and courage. He was swinging a grappling hook, and ignoring the men who fell around him he got within ten yards of the wall and hurled the hook upwards. It caught, and pulling tight on the rope he swung himself upwards, his very nearness to the wall making it impossible for musket fire to reach him. Other sappers followed his example and also reached the top of the wall. There they were met by British infantrymen wielding bayonets and one after the other their transfixed bodies fell to the mud below.

More courageous Frenchmen followed. As they also fell, their bodies began to pile against the wall like some hideous ladder that their comrades could use instead of the ropes.

The fight was equally fierce around the other strong-points. The British inside the walled garden were resisting every effort to dislodge them. The concentration of French outside was so great that a man had no need to aim his musket: as soon as it was loaded he had only to thrust it through a loophole and pull the trigger for a man to fall. Officers on both sides, abandoning their horses, were fighting side by side with their men. The wounded tried to crawl into the barns, the cowsheds, and the chapel.

The crisis came when a company of French infantrymen, hidden by gunsmoke, managed to reach the other side of the château. Here they found the main gate to the court-yard open and, although its defenders put up a desperate fight, killing the general leading the French, they were overpowered and enemy soldiers streamed into the court-yard.

Colonel Macdonell was in the garden when he heard the triumphant cries of the French. Running back into the courtyard he saw his men fighting a desperate hand-to-hand battle with musket butts, bayonets, and axes. Already some of his guardsmen had been driven up the steps to the door-way of the château. Calling to four of his men, Macdonell fought his way through the struggling mass to the entrance where the five of them put their shoulders to the gate. The French outside tried to fling them back but their reinforce-ments had not yet arrived and Macdonell was able to close the gate and drop the massive locking-bar into place. Although the battle raged on and off most of the day, the French were never closer than this to victory, and after-wards Wellington was to say that the entire success of Waterloo had rested on the closing of those gates.

It was by no means the end of the slaughter at Hougou-mont, however. Desperate now in their efforts to dislodge the garrison, the French threw bunches of burning sticks over the walls of the buildings and through the windows. Wounded men, still firing through the embrasures, were unable to drag themselves away and died in agony. Inside the chapel the head of the Holy Child was struck off by a bullet and a wooden statue of St Anne caught fire. But, defying the heat and horror, the garrison fought on for another hour and a half, when Jerome was forced to withdraw his men temporarily into the wood. The heroism displayed at Hougoumont on both sides was astonishing; the slaughter a portent of what was to come when the main battle commenced.

Napoleon was still at Rossomme, intermittently rising from his chair and using his telescope to see how events were progressing at Hougoumont. From the knoll he could see across the wood to the château and the top of the ridge that Wellington was defending, but little of the valley in between. After the second assault on the château commenced he traversed the ridge with his telescope and then turned to Ney and Soult who were watching alongside him.

'It appears he has not moved a single man.'

The serious-faced Soult inclined his head in an I-told-you-so fashion. 'He is a shrewd commander, Sire, and not easily stampeded.'

This time Ney was wise enough not to add his comment. The Corsican closed his telescope and moved painfully towards the table where red-topped pins were stuck in a map. 'If he has nailed himself to the ridge, we must unloosen him.' Glancing at Ney who was to lead the frontal assault, he pointed down at the map. 'How many cannon are assembled there now?'

'Fifty-six, Sire. And eighteen thousand of my infantry are waiting in columns behind.'

The Corsican leaned over the map and shifted pins. 'It isn't enough. Line Vincent's battery on the eastern flank.'

An aide rode off and a moment later a trumpet sounded. While he waited Napoleon moved to the edge of the knoll again and sighted his telescope on the far right of the valley. A few seconds later he stiffened, then swung round. 'Come and train your telescopes on that wood to the east – the one on the heights of St Lambert!'

Soult, Ney, Drouot, and La Bédoyère hurried over and obeyed him. Soult, the first to focus his telescope, gave a start. 'It's a herd of cattle, surely, Sire. Black cattle.'

Drouot shook his head. 'No; it is moving. It is the shadow of a cloud.'

Napoleon's eyes turned to La Bédoyère, who shook his head. 'I think it is a body of men. Moving in columns.'

The Corsican's voice was ironic. 'Not just the sun shining on wet rocks.'

'No, Sire. I believe it is the sun shining on steel.'

Soult was now showing doubt. 'You could be right. But then who is it? Grouchy? Or Blücher?'

Napoleon closed his telescope with a snap. 'Blue is blue and black is black. Whoever they are, they are nothing as yet but a shadow on a hill.'

Ney, the only one who had not spoken, was watching the shadow intently. Napoleon reached out impatiently and pulled down his arm. 'They are miles away and the ground is a morass. So for the next few hours, for all they will concern us, they might as well be on the moon.'

On the ridge opposite, Wellington and his staff were also giving the far-off shadow their closest attention. Although Bülow had sent word to Wellington he would reach him by four o'clock, the Duke's patrols had established that the flooded fields and roads were in such an appalling condition that Bülow would do well to make contact by the early evening. Moreover, the possibility existed that Grouchy might have struck due west to cut Bülow off and it might be his troops they were watching.

De Lancey, dismounted, was resting his telescope on his horse's saddle to steady it. 'What do you think is the colour of their coats?' Wellington asked him.

De Lancey was trying to adjust his telescope to a finer focus. 'It could be Grouchy's blue, Your Grace.'

Uxbridge expressed all their fears. 'Has he heard the sound of the cannon and come straight across?'

Wellington reached out for Uxbridge's telescope and stared again at the shadow. 'Damn it, it could also be Prussian black.' He frowned at young Lord Hay who was alongside Uxbridge. 'Your eyes are young, Hay. Aren't even you able to tell me the colour?'

The seventeen-year-old boy, who had been asked the same question a minute earlier, looked almost in tears at his failure to help. 'It could be black, Your Grace. But I can't be sure.'

While the agonized guessing continued on both sides of the battlefield, the truth would have brought neither commander much comfort. Although it was the advance guard of Bülow's corps that could be seen, their advance across the rain-flooded fields was proving a murderous ordeal. In places men were sinking up to their knees in glutinous mud and being called on every few minutes to heave caissons and supply wagons out of flooded craters. Suffering agonies from exhaustion, it is doubtful if they could have continued had not the iron will of Blücher been urging them on.

Meanwhile, just over fourteen miles to the south-east, Grouchy was finishing lunch at a summer house outside the village of Walhain. Lying on the lawn before him was an old favourite, Commandant Rumigus, a many-times wounded Napoleonic veteran who had only one arm. A group of Grouchy's officers were standing near the garden entrance and as one raised his hand sharply, the others froze into listening postures. A moment later, General Gérard hurried across the lawn to Grouchy's table.

'Sir, we can hear cannon. And smoke can be seen over to the west.'

Grouchy, about to eat a plate of strawberries, put the plate down and hurried out of the garden with Gérard. Rumigus followed them. Outside, the fields were littered with thousands of French infantrymen who were resting with their heads on their packs. Gérard pointed to the west where faint smudges of smoke could be seen on the horizon. As the wind shifted, a low rumbling could be heard.

A peasant leading a mule down the roadside informed the officers the gunfire was coming from Mont St Jean. Gérard turned in some urgency to Grouchy.

'We must march towards the cannon at once, sir. We have a third of the Emperor's army with us.'

His tone clearly irritated Grouchy. 'Do not presume to teach me my duty, General Gérard. My orders were precise – to keep my sword in Blücher's back.' He swung round and pointed up the road. 'And that is the direction Blücher is running.'

Gérard moved a step closer. 'But if we march towards the battle, we will cut Blücher off.'

As Grouchy hesitated, a gruff voice made both men turn. Two officers, Rumigus and General Valazé, an engineering officer, had now joined them and it was the blunt one-armed veteran who was speaking.

'You forget the condition of the fields, Gérard. If we march west we'll sink up to our arses in mud.'

Valazé sided with Gérard. 'We must join the battle. Once Wellington is defeated we can deal with Blücher as we will.'

The argument grew more heated. Although secretly beset by doubts, Grouchy disliked his lieutenants questioning his judgements and the more they argued the more his decision hardened.

'The Emperor told me he intended to attack the English and that I must follow the Prussians. You have all read his dispatches.'

Gérard's cheeks were flushed with dismay and anger. 'But what can be lost by marching towards the cannon? If Blücher tries to help Wellington we can still destroy him.'

Grouchy motioned his servant to bring over his horse. 'If the Emperor had wanted me at Mont St Jean he would not have sent me here. We obey our orders, Gérard, and continue our march.'

Back at Mont St Jean it was not long before both commanders knew the distant troops were Prussians. Wellington received the news via Müffling, and a captive Prussian cavalryman brought to Napoleon admitted the troops were the vanguard of Bülow's corps.

Although the news vindicated the fears of his staff, Napoleon remained oddly unperturbed. 'This morning we had odds of nine to one in our favour,' he told them. 'Now we have six to four.' Dictating a letter to Grouchy to waste no time joining him, he sent off two cavalry divisions to provide a screen in Bülow's path and behind them sent Lobau's 6th Corps to hold the Prussians back until Grouchy fell on them from the rear. For although Grouchy was fifteen miles away and therefore could not receive his message for at least two hours (which meant in the normal course of events he could not arrive before nightfall) Napoleon appeared certain that once Grouchy heard the cannon fire he would march straight towards it. In such a case, his argument ran, the presence of Bülow's corps simply meant its destruction, and he refused to consider any change in his plans to engage Wellington in a head-on collision.

His mood, indeed, seemed inconsistent with the serious-ness of the situation and, as he traversed the ridge with his telescope again, he began humming the old revolutionary song: 'Ah, ça ira, ça ira . . . The aristocrats to the lamp posts.'

There was a rumble and clatter down the road and a moment later three batteries of twelve-pounders came sweeping past. As the artillerymen came to the salute, Napoleon laughed and slapped Soult's shoulder. 'Look at them, Soult. Twenty-four of my beautiful girls!' He turned to Ney. 'Well, Ney, are you ready? You are the man to put glory into the afternoon.'

He had chosen Ney to lead the frontal attack on the ridge, a striking demonstration of the ambivalence he held towards the red-headed Marshal. Ney motioned to a servant who brought his horse over. He swung into the saddle, removed his hat, and tucked it into his belt. As he lifted his sword in salute, his eyes met and held Napoleon's. Then he spurred his horse and galloped down the road.

There was compulsion in the way the Corsican moved to the edge of the knoll to watch him. Following him, La Bédoyère heard his low murmur. 'To Paris in an iron cage . . . Could he ever have said that?'

As if anticipating the massive onslaught about to begin, the musket and cannon fire at Hougoumont momentarily ceased. Down the hill the red head of Ney could be seen shining in the sunlight as he galloped towards his waiting columns. A trumpeter rode ahead of him, sounded the 'Ready'. Drums began to tap. Artillerymen lit their portfires and stood alongside their cannon. A tremendous hush settled over the battlefield. With his eyes still on Ney and strangely bright, Napoleon half turned his head towards La Bédoyère. 'A hundred times that man has given his life to me, La Bédoyère. And now he goes to give it again.'

CHAPTER FOURTEEN

The seventy-four guns massed along the front before La Belle Alliance opened fire simultaneously at one-thirty. The veterans among Wellington's army, who had experienced the deadly accuracy of French gunnery before, said they had never faced a bombardment as destructive. As the cannon fired and erupted great gouts of smoke, watching eyes seemed to turn liverish as they filled with black specks. To others, the very sky seemed to darken as the terrible cannonballs of Waterloo arched over the valley.

Two seconds, perhaps three, passed before they struck. Hitting the ridge just below the crest the great iron balls, eight- and twelve-pounders, bounded upwards in massive frog leaps. At such range their effect on closely-packed men was hideous: cannonballs did not wound, they smashed men to pieces.

It was Bylandt's brigade of Dutch-Belgians who suffered worst from the barrage. For some reason they had been left on the forward slope of the ridge, just left of centre of the Allied line. Some say it was a staff oversight, others that it was deliberate policy of Wellington's to use his weakest troops to soften the initial onslaught before throwing in his battle-seasoned veterans. These were Picton's regiments of Scots, English, and Germans, the 5th Division, and they were sheltered behind the ridge and the cuttings in the lane.

Whatever the reason, Bylandt's men were brutally savaged. Men saw their comrades smashed into bloody meat as the cannonballs cut swathes through their stationary ranks. Horses were hit, some disembowelled, and fell to join the hideous carnage in the mud. The living, condemned by the traditions of the day to stand motionless, became drenched in the blood of their comrades. With the cannonballs and shells screaming among them, they were in a hell that seemed to stretch into eternity.

After the bombardment had lasted fifteen minutes, Wellington, accompanied by a few members of his staff, rode along the ridge to Picton. He found the eccentric Welshman, who was wearing a civilian top hat and smoking a short pipe, standing on the crest of the ridge. Behind him only his officers were on their feet: his troops, under orders from Wellington, were all lying prone in the long grass or sheltering behind the cutting. The British artillery had been giving counter-fire for some time and the sky was full of smoke and ash.

Wellington reigned his horse beside the tough Infantry Commander. 'It appears he is throwing his weight on you, Picton.'

Both men were watching d'Erlon's corps that, led by Ney, was marching in three massive columns across the valley towards Picton's position just east of the Genappe–Brussels road. Two batteries of French artillery swept down to deploy along their flank and Picton pointed to them.

'I've never seen guns moved about so quickly.'

Wellington nodded. 'It seems he can use a hundred cannon with the lightness of a pistol.'

Led by a cloud of skirmishers who kept up a sustained, harassing fire, the three great columns, two hundred men wide and at least twenty-five ranks deep, drew nearer. Young soldiers whispered their awe. Trained to advance in line of battle so that each man was free to fire ahead, they could not understand such tactics. To them it seemed the enormous phalanxes were indestructible and they must break through the Allied lines by their very weight and momentum.

It was not the first time Napoleon's army had been used in such a way. Originally the method had been devised to protect hastily-trained conscripts, who found comfort and guidance in the centre of such a formation. Later, the French had discovered the sight of such massed power often over-awed troops lined up against it. Seasoned infantrymen, however, knew the formation's defects. Only its first three ranks could fire ahead: the soldiers behind were as helpless as if they were unarmed. As a consequence a smaller enemy force, deployed in line, could often muster greater firepower. And when the column tried to deploy more efficiently, its movements were clumsy and costly.

Yet the psychological effects could not be ignored. The columns were now close enough for every detail to be visible. Although British cannonballs were smashing into the massed ranks, the scene was almost gay with flags and eagles held high in the sunlight. Leading each column was a line of drummer boys tapping out the attack. Ahead of them was a sixty-year-old sergeant drummer nicknamed Rata. Ignoring the musket fire from the British skirmishers who were trying to harass the oncoming juggernauts, he was dancing, clowning, and mock-marching as if leading some high-school jamboree. Dancing forward, then backward, he ran right along the line of drums tapping each one in turn. Behind him the troops roared out their admiration.

As the columns neared the ridge, the heavy French shelling abruptly eased. In the silence that fell, Allied soldiers both on and behind the ridge heard a new sound they would remember to their dying breath: the quickening drum beat of the '*pas de charge*'. Even those who could not see the massive force advancing towards them felt shivers run down their backs at the menacing sound. Louder it grew and louder, and with it great shouts of 'Vive l'Empereur' rolled over the ridge.

Picton's British regiments were lying hidden in the thick rye a hundred paces behind the holly hedges of the lane. They were unable to see what lay over the hill rise and the alarming rhythm of the *pas de charge* and the cheering and ever-increasing tumult of the oncoming hordes put a severe strain on their imaginations. Conscious of their nervousness, NCOs were hurrying along the lines pouring gin into upheld mugs.

O'Connor was lying alongside McKevitt, one of the men who had been on sentry duty at the Duchess of Richmond's ball. He sniffed into his mug of gin and grinned.

'Isn't it nice of a busy man like the King of England to think of us idiots at a time like this?'

McKevitt was looking decidedly frightened. 'How many of them are there, would you say?'

O'Connor took a deep, satisfying swig of gin. 'I'm not God to see through a hill.'

McKevitt's hand moved instinctively to his neck where he wore rosary beads. 'It sounds like the whole of bloody hell is comin' out of the ground.'

O'Connor, as superstitious as the rest of his kind, hid a shudder and took another swig of gin. As he saw McKevitt's fingers counting the beads, he scowled and tugged at a chinstrap that was already too tight. 'Nothin' scares me more than being next to a friend of the Almighty,' he muttered sourly.

On the ridge ahead, Picton turned to Wellington. 'The way they are coming, they can win this battle at a walk.'

Wellington lowered his telescope. 'If we don't time it right they will. If we go in a minute too early they'll swallow us. If we're a minute late, they'll break in and flood us.'

There was sarcasm in Picton's reply. 'I hope you can rely on your watch, Wellington.'

Someone among Wellington's staff let out a titter. The Duke turned round angrily. 'When you're in the presence of so many brave men who are about to cut one another's throats, it is best not to be amused.'

He turned back towards the oncoming French infantry. 'Their cavalry support does not match their numbers, Picton. If you can hold them it could prove their weakness.'

Picton raised his top hat and galloped away. On the slopes below, seeing they were going to be overrun, the 95th British Regiment, who had been left in the gravel pit to provide a salient, were now streaming back. The dazed survivors of Bylandt's brigade, whose position ensured them the first clash with the advancing hordes, were staring at them in hypnotic fascination. They could not see the difficulty the French were having tramping through the tall rye which wound itself around their gaiters and sometimes pulled off their boots. To them the phalanxes seemed irresistible, and suddenly they broke. Throwing aside their muskets they fled back up the ridge and past the British troops waiting beyond it. In retrospect no one could blame them. Pawns in the game of power politics, many of them had served Napoleon in earlier days, and their very presence on the battlefield must have bewildered them. To have been the only troops exposed to the full fury of the French artillery had been the last straw. The Allied soldiers behind the ridge, who had not been exposed to the brutal gunfire, made a great show of indignation as they fled past and many wanted to shoot at them. The Dutch and Belgian officers, in particular Perponcher, who had played such an important part in the Quatre Bras affair, did all they could to halt the flight but for the rest of that day the brigade proved little use as a fighting force.

The retreat opened a great gap in Picton's line that had to be filled and left his remaining troops heavily outnumbered. At the same time it deceived Ney into taking risks he might otherwise have avoided. With most of Picton's troops sheltering behind the ridge and with Bylandt's brigade streaming back over it, it seemed to French officers and men alike that Wellington's line was cracking.

At this point only the artillery and the Rifle Brigade were engaging the French infantry. Far to the left of the line Durette's division had already taken Papelotte. In the centre, the Germans manning the strongpoint of La Haye Sainte doggedly drove back all attacks but the majority of Donzelot's division merely by-passed the farmhouse and continued up the slope. To Napoleon, scanning the smoking ridge with his telescope, it looked as if his divisions had broken through by the very terror of their appearance.

But, in spite of their magnificent *élan* and indifference to the hail of grapeshot pouring down on them, the French infantry were now to pay for their leaders' outdated tactics. The higher they climbed, the more obstacles the natural terrain threw in their way. From the thick mud and the tall rye they now saw the holly hedges of the lane stretching ahead of them as they crested the ridge. A single man would have no problem slipping through the occasional gaps but the hedges presented a formidable obstacle to a dense formation of men. Orders were given for the huge phalanx to halt and deploy into line, a clumsy manoeuvre that occupied precious time. It was the moment Picton chose to strike.

He had brought up his British infantry to the rear of the holly hedges as the French neared the crest. Now, as the formation began its complicated manoeuvre, he yelled an order for his men to fire. Being in double line only, they were able to discharge all their muskets at once whereas the French, although outnumbering them, could bring only the muskets of their three front ranks to bear.

As a consequence, in the exchange of volleys that followed, the French suffered far the more heavily. As they were momentarily checked, Picton spurred his horse and waved his sword forward. His powerful voice roared out like a blast of trumpets.

'At 'em, you drunken rascals! Give 'em the bayonet, you whore's melts. Forward!'

With a cheer his line of men – the only infantry between the French and Brussels at that moment had Napoleon known it – hurled themselves forward. Picton galloped ahead, waving his sword and yelling at the top of his voice. 'At 'em, you thieves. Slit their throats, you blackguards! . . .'

His bloodthirsty exhortations were cut off as he slumped over his horse's neck and then fell to the ground. A musket ball had struck him in the temple and he was dead in seconds. But his men, with kilted Highlanders well in the van, ran on to the hillcrest and fell on the French with their bayonets.

The battle that followed had an almost unnatural savagery. Perhaps it was caused by the hardships and strain the British had suffered during the last two days or perhaps it was an explosion of relief at getting to grips with the huge legions whose studied march across the valley had brought them such secret terror. Whatever the cause the heavily-outnumbered British, hurling themselves forward with sword, bayonet, and musket butt, fought like men possessed. With their rear ranks still moving forward, the French were not able to ride the shock of the attack, and as the half-wild British infantry hacked and slashed their way downhill, cracks began to appear in the massed formations. To those watching from the ridge above, it was like witnessing the slow disintegration of ice packs, first the thin cracks, then the slowly-widening lanes as the pieces threatened to break apart.

Through telescopes on the rise opposite, the kilts and feather bonnets of the half-savage Highlanders could be seen clearly. Napoleon, taken aback by the ferocity of the counter-attack, turned to La Bédoyère with some bitterness.

'When I see those skirts and hear those pipes I could believe I am Caesar in the woods of Germany and we are back in barbaric times.' He lifted his telescope again, his low mutter reaching La Bédoyère. 'The cavalry, Ney! Why were they not in closer support?'

This weakness in Ney's tactics – yet another penalty unfairly inflicted on the French infantrymen – was now being rectified: detachments of cuirassiers were thundering up the ridge past the flanks of the French divisions. Once ahead, they broke left and right, galloping along the rear of the British and sabring them down.

The manoeuvre was classic and full of danger to Wellington. To protect themselves the British would be forced to form squares, the only defence against cavalry attack. But in squares they would be easy targets for the rallied French infantry who would then cut them to pieces with musket fire.

The Highlanders, the first to receive the crushing impact of the cuirassiers, were already forming squares when Uxbridge glanced at Ponsonby, Colonel of the Royal Scots Greys. Ponsonby, ice cool, pulled a silver snuff box from his pocket and offered it to Uxbridge. 'Will you, Uxbridge? Before I go?'

Uxbridge tapped the box on the back of his hand and sniffed. 'It's savage stuff, Ponsonby.'

Ponsonby rubbed a pinch of the snuff between his fingers. 'You don't get its like these days. My father left me a hundredweight. A Jew in Alexandria has the blend.'

Uxbridge sneezed and dabbed at his eyes. 'Blend!'

Ponsonby nodded, his voice turning reflective. 'My father, y' know, was killed by the French. Twenty years ago. Should never have happened, Uxbridge. His horse got bogged in a ploughed field when seven damned lancers were after him. The brute just gave up and the Frenchies had my father like a tiger in a pit.'

Uxbridge nodded his sympathy. 'Damned bad luck.'

'Remarkable bad luck when you consider he had four hundred better horses in his paddocks at Hatton.' As he spoke Ponsonby's eyes were on Wellington on the hillcrest ahead. At the intervention of the cuirassiers the Duke had risen in his stirrups to watch their progress. Suddenly he turned towards the Greys, took off his hat and waved it. Uxbridge nodded at a flushed young trumpeter who was waiting a few yards away. As the shrill notes of the 'Ready' ran out, the hundreds of horsemen lined up in the fields behind Ponsonby executed a swift movement of incline which brought them so close their boot-tops touched. As the last notes of the bugle died away they transferred their sabres from the rest to the ready position.

Nodding to Uxbridge, Ponsonby rode to the head of the horsemen and raised his sword. 'Now, Scots Greys! Now!'

The Greys broke into a walk, then a trot, and then a gallop as they rode up the reverse side of the slope. Fierce cavalrymen, by tradition riding dapple-grey horses, all had rough-sharpened their sabres the previous night to inflict maximum wounds on the enemy. Their bearskin head-dresses and white feathers, their beautiful horses and burnished sabres, invested them with a savage, mythical grandeur. As the first rank was momentarily silhouetted against the sky, it was as if a legion of centaurs had appeared on the battlefield.

Ponsonby, sword held high, was now in full gallop.

Beside him the young trumpeter was blowing the 'Charge' in a kind of ecstasy. Behind them, no more than three feet apart, the huge grey horses were shuddering the ground as they pounded in pursuit.

Because men are never so alive as when courting death, in the few seconds it took them to make that charge – probably the greatest cavalry charge in history – every detail was etched indelibly on their memories: the wind on their cheeks, the skirl of pipes, the writhing blaze of colour, the burst of shells, the proud banners and eagles, the cheers and screams, the blood-stirring pound of hoofbeats. The very horses seemed to share the mad intoxication. Encouraged by name, 'On Rattler', 'Up Foxhunter', the magnificent greys rolled their bloodshot eyes and bared their teeth as they headed down the slope towards a gap in the French columns. As they swept past a unit of Gordon Highlanders the men broke ranks, grabbed hold of the stirrups of the horses, and propelled themselves into battle. The cries of 'Scotland forever' could be heard above the tumult. Ponsonby, leading the charge beside the flag, was yelling as madly as the rest. 'Spurs! Your spurs! Fight them with your spurs!'

A moment later the Greys hit the French left flank. The troops were so tightly packed that the nearest ranks could only wait for the slashing sabres and the crushing impact. But farther back, where lanes had already opened in the formations, the disintegration spread rapidly and a general retreat commenced as the French began to fall back towards their lines.

The battle began to break up now into smaller but equally fierce engagements. In places where the French divisions had completely scattered, British cavalrymen fought to capture regimental colours. Other horsemen were running down and sabring helpless infantrymen. As the French cuirassiers tried to protect their infantry, individual duels between British dragoons and French cuirassiers spread all the way down the forward slopes of the ridge. Artillery fire killed friend and foe alike.

Although there was little to choose in numbers between the cuirassiers and the British cavalry, the British had the advantage of the slope and the French were forced to give way. As the exultant Greys got once more among the fleeing infantrymen, the slaughter was appalling. Helpless men, unable to run in the thick mud, were slashed to pieces. Even the horses seemed to have joined in the ecstasy of killing, biting and kicking at everyone within range.

Seeing the French retreat was now complete, Wellington ordered his trumpeters to sound the 'Recall' and the British regiments began moving back to their original positions. Farther down the ridge, however, the British cavalry seemed to have lost all sense of caution and were still in full pursuit of the French. A standard, with the golden eagle of the 35th French Regiment inscribed with the victories of Austerlitz and Jena, was captured. The floor of the valley was strewn with French bodies but still the exultant, blood-thirsty cavalrymen were not satisfied. As they paused, looking for more victims, Ponsonby rode towards them and some heard him say: 'Wipe your blades, boys. You have killed enough.'

But only a few heard his order and at that moment the hated French batteries opened fire again. As canister and shells burst among the horses, the cavalrymen went berserk. Officers rose in their stirrups, waved their swords, and yelled at the men to charge the guns. A few seconds later Scots Greys, Life Guards, First Royal Dragoons; almost all the British cavalry that had been thrown into the attack was sweeping like a frenzied mob up towards the lines of the French artillery.

It was a moment of pure madness. Ponsonby saw the danger and yelled at his trumpeter to blow the 'Recall' but the yelling, cheering horsemen either did not hear or took no notice. The wind was on their cheeks, the smell of gunpowder in their nostrils, and the French guns little more than three hundred yards away. Ponsonby, half-frantic, rode among them and tried to beat them back with his sabre. His voice was hoarse with his frantic protests.

'You're killing yourselves! They'll cut you off. Back. Get back. Obey the trumpet!'

His exhortations and curses were ignored. Ahead, the sight of the screaming horde caused some of the French infantry and artillerymen to turn and run. Others, tough and reliable, held their ground and fired volley after volley at the oncoming horses. At such range canister and grape-shot did fearful damage, sweeping away men and horses like leaves in a wind. But it seemed nothing could stop that wild charge.

Uxbridge had joined Wellington beside the elm tree on the ridge. He had been involved in an action farther down the line that had denied the charge his leadership, a conse-quence he was to regret for the rest of his life. Horrified at his cavalry's suicidal recklessness, he was urging his young trumpeter to greater efforts. 'The Recall! Give it more, boy! Again!'

The red-faced boy's eyes were bulging with the effort of blowing. As Uxbridge saw the horsemen racing on to the very barrels of the French guns his voice turned more urgent. 'Blow, boy! Blow!'

Wellington reached out and pushed the trumpet away from the distressed boy's mouth. 'Enough, boy. You'll only hurt yourself and they cannot hear you.' He gazed back across the valley with some bitterness. 'But why can't they hear the cannon that are destroying them?'

At point-blank range the French artillery was doing mas-sive slaughter. Men were being blasted from their saddles like rag dolls and horses were cartwheeling in the mud. But their very momentum took the rest of the horsemen up the slope and a moment later they were among the guns. Yel-ling their hate, they rode down the line, slashing and thrus-ting at the helpless French gunners. Traces were slashed, ramrods broken, young drivers killed, and even the French horses cut down in the orgy of destruction.

On the rise above, Kellermann had joined Napoleon for his orders. The Corsican was shaking his head in disbelief. 'Those terrible grey horses. They have kicked three divisions into the ground.'

Kellermann nodded. 'They are the noblest cavalry in Europe and the worst led, Sire.'

Napoleon turned to him, his voice soft with menace. 'Cut them off with Jacquinot's lancers.'

CHAPTER FIFTEEN

The lancers seemed to appear from nowhere, their polished breastplates and helmets glinting in the sunlight, their lances held erect. In line of column, their strong black horses trotted across the valley, interposing themselves between the British cavalry and the Allied heights. At the sound of a bugle they wheeled in a single graceful movement to face the Greys and Dragoons.

Up on the French slopes the British cavalry were beginning to regain their sanity. With their horses winded or wounded, and with fresh French infantry pouring down the slopes, it was suddenly obvious to the most warlike that they would be lucky to regain their lines alive.

The long line of French cavalry had now slung forward the arrow-sharp heads of their lances. For a few menacing seconds the only movement came from their horses, pawing the ground in impatience. Then a bugle sounded the charge and the line broke into a trot and then a gallop. As they swept forward, the line curved into a crescent to flank and envelop the enemy horsemen.

Conscious at last of their peril, the British cavalry rallied to the shouts of their officers, wheeled their horses and made a desperate counter-charge. The collison when it came was frightful. Horses crashed to the ground, breaking the legs and backs of their riders. Half-stunned men lifted their hands to fend off the deadly lances, only to be pinned to the ground like insects to a board. Other British cavalrymen found their exhausted horses could take no more. Sliding down on their haunches like dogs, they left their riders to the mercy of the vengeful French lancers. The air was a bedlam of clashing sabres, snorting horses, and the curses and screams of dying men.

The trap drew tighter as Kellermann threw in units of cuirassiers on the British flanks. Noticing the move, Uxbridge ordered out Vandeleur's 12th and 16th Dragoons in a desperate attempt to prise the trap open. The gaps they drove at some cost into the line of lancers enabled the majority of the survivors to break out and escape to their lines.

But not all were so lucky. Sir William Ponsonby and his youthful trumpeter had been cut off from the main body of the Greys and were in full flight across the valley with seven lancers in pursuit. As they galloped past a freshly-ploughed field Ponsonby felt his horse stumble from weariness and tried to give it encouragement.

'Keep up, boy. Stay, stay!'

The horse faltered again and bore to the right. Seeing the ploughed field approaching Ponsonby pulled at the horse and then struck it across the jaw with the flat of his sword. 'Keep straight, dammit.'

The terrified horse was too exhausted to respond. Ponsonby gazed back at the seven pursuing Frenchmen whose lances were poised and ready. 'Oh, God, keep me out of the muck!'

The horse cleared a small mound and landed in the wet, sticky clay. Ponsonby's spurs dug into its sides as it paused, shivering. 'Move! Move!'

The French lancers had changed direction and were making across the ploughed field. The young trumpeter, pale to the lips, had reined his horse at the edge of the field. Ponsonby reached inside his jacket and held out his snuff box and watch. 'Take them! For my son.'

The snuff box reached the boy safely but the watch was fumbled and fell into the mud. As the trumpeter hesitated, Ponsonby gestured at him violently.

'Leave it! Get away and save yourself.'

The lancers were close now. As the boy hesitated, Ponsonby reached out with his sword and struck the other horse's haunches. It reared and then stampeded away. Left alone, Ponsonby turned towards the approaching lancers and lifted his sword. It was not an action of defence, it was to uncover his body to the lances that a moment later drove through his chest. By a coincidence in a million Ponsonby died precisely the same death as his father twenty years earlier.

Three of the lancers wheeled away and followed the fleeing trumpeter. Glancing back, the boy saw the foremost lancer was overtaking his tired horse. As the blood-stained lance drew nearer his back, the boy began sobbing in terror.

Behind him the lancer was steadying himself for the kill. His chance came as the exhausted horse stumbled. His lance went forward like a snake's tongue into the boy's kidneys. The boy screamed, then fell sideways into the mud. As the lance was driven down again, this time through his lungs, Ponsonby's snuff box could be seen lying in the mud near him.

By 3 PM the battle died down except at Hougoumont where the fighting was as fierce and bloody as ever. The slopes in front of the British ridge were cleared of the enemy and the no-man's-land between the two Armies was occupied only by the corpses of men and horses and a few brave women who were trying to succour the wounded. Riderless horses were galloping about or grazing in the trampled fields. A few horse-drawn carts were also seen, among them a few of Baron Larray's famous flying ambulances that were trying to clear the French wounded. The two Armies were counting their losses and preparing for the next collision.

Napoleon's three divisions belonging to d'Erlon had been badly mauled, suffering 5,000 casualties of whom 3,000 had been taken prisoner. Wellington's Dutch-Belgian brigade under Bylandt had been virtually destroyed and in addition the Duke had lost about 2,500 of his cavalry. Neither side could be certain how many men in the line had been killed by artillery – shattered bodies were being found all the time in the wheat fields and among the tall rye.

On paper the losses seemed to balance out but the figures were deceptive. The recklessness of Ponsonby's brigade had cost Wellington a quarter of his entire cavalry, and as he had begun the battle with a numerical inferiority in mounted troops, the heavy loss, due entirely to disobedience, could cost him dear before the day was over.

Yet there was a credit side to Wellington's balance sheet. His line remained intact. Hougoumont still held out gallantly although the French were now employing howitzers against it, and La Haye Sainte remained a vital bastion a few hundred yards in front of the British centre. In addition, the earlier, questionable morale of some of his units had been improved by the sight of Napoleon's legions being thrown back to their lines. Perhaps most valuable of all, with Bülow's corps making its painful foot-by-foot advance, two hours of priceless time had been won.

In personal terms the sights behind both lines were harrowing. The drivers of the French artillery caissons were mostly youngsters and many of them had been trapped by Ponsonby's cavalrymen. Men wept as their slim, mutilated bodies were dragged away. Back of the British ridge the scene was equally heart-rending as the remnants of the Greys and Dragoons lined up for inspection. Of one regiment only fifty of three hundred men had returned. Nearly all wounded, their bandages bloody, they could barely stay in their saddles while the horses, many bearing terrible slashes from bayonets and sabres, stood shivering with drooping heads. Other riderless horses, who had faithfully returned to the lines, were nuzzling about and whimpering for their dead masters. Men who had seen death in many guises had to turn away to hide their distress.

To the left of the pitiful assemblage a small party of soldiers was carrying away Picton's body on a rough stretcher. Colonel Taylor, his aide, was walking alongside the stretcher carrying the Welshman's top hat and sword. Picton's young trumpeter, leading the General's horse, was following behind, tears streaming down his grimy cheeks. As a lull came in the cannonade it seemed as if both sides were observing an armistice for their dead.

Beneath the elm tree Wellington was studying a map pinned to the table. His aides-de-camp were grouped around, waiting to carry away his orders. Hearing an exclamation from de Lancey, the Duke glanced up and saw that the young American had his telescope trained on a solitary horseman who was galloping across the valley towards the Allied lines. As Wellington raised his own telescope he saw the horseman was a French hussar.

De Lancey showed his surprise. 'Who can he be? A deserter? A traitor?'

Wellington shook his head. 'He sits too straight in the saddle.' Seeing a gun crew lining up a nine-pounder, he motioned at them curtly. 'Leave him be! Pass the word, de Lancey. He might be a courier.'

'Perhaps our little Corsican has had enough and wants to know your terms, Wellington.' The comment came from Uxbridge, who laughed at the look the Duke threw him.

The fast-riding hussar was causing a commotion along the ridge as Allied troops pointed him out to their comrades. His white breeches, gold-faced green dolman, and plumed kalpak showed him to be an officer. His horse, a magnificent bay, was hurling clods of mud behind it as it began the final gallop to the hillcrest. Halfway up, the hussar shouted something, and drawing his sword he held it forward as if making a lone charge. Exchanging startled looks, Uxbridge, de Lancey, and two aides rode forward to put a screen in front of the Duke.

The Frenchman was less than twelve yards from the elm tree when he reined back. His foaming horse reared high, then dropped back to face Wellington. Lifting his sword high, the hussar shouted 'Vive l'Empereur!' Then, with a final contemptuous sweep of his sword, designed to embrace the entire Allied line, he turned and galloped back down the slope.

The yell that rose from the Allied troops was a mixture of anger and admiration. A few musket shots were fired but only half-heartedly and the hussar reached the floor of the valley safely. Uxbridge turned towards the duke with a laugh. 'A romantic lunatic, Wellington.'

There was a grimness in Wellington's smile. 'Yet a lunatic that emphasizes their morale, Uxbridge. It may be an even harder day than we feared.'

During the next half-hour the busiest officers were the army surgeons on both sides of the lines. Sixty per cent of the wounded remained where they had fallen but enough had been carried away to overwhelm the crude medical services that had been established in barns and cottages.

In transporting the wounded from the battlefield the French were better served than the English. Baron Larray's flying ambulances, two-wheeled carts with springs, were a speedier and more humane method than the haphazard English one of carrying men away in army blankets. But, once they arrived at the makeshift hospitals, there was little to choose between the suffering of the French and the Allied wounded. At the time of Waterloo there were no antiseptics and no anaesthetics. A wounded soldier lucky enough to reach a surgeon knew exactly what to expect. If his wound was in the chest or abdomen, the surface flesh would be stitched together and he would be put aside to see what happened. If his wound was in a limb, and it was anything more than a simple fracture or flesh wound, the limb would be amputated. The practice was not as inhuman as it sounds. The surgery of the day was incapable of saving bones shattered to splinters by leaden musket balls and jagged grapeshot.

The procedure varied little from surgery to surgery. When his turn came the soldier would be carried inside the barn, tent, or cottage and laid on a makeshift operating table. The shadows inside would be relieved by the red glare of fires on which vats of oil and pitch were simmering. If the battle had been under way for any length of time, hundreds of men might already have been operated on, and the conditions of hygiene prevailing can best be imagined. If the soldier were lucky he would be given a glass of wine or gin to fortify him for the ordeal; if the battle had long begun the liquor supplies were almost certain to be exhausted. The surgeon's untrained assistants – often band musicians who, in the British Army at least, were considered redundant once the battle was joined – would then hold him down while the surgeon in his blood-soaked apron would apply a saw to the shattered limb. When it was removed, to be thrown on a pile of similar remains on a cart outside, boiling oil and pitch would be applied to the bleeding stump to cauterize it.

A further shock to the soldier was the bleeding the surgeons frequently practised as a precaution against sepsis. If he survived all this abuse – and a surprising number of men did – he might then have to wait a day or longer before being carried to the nearest town in a crowded and un-sprung wagon.

To later generations, insulated to a degree against pain by anaesthetics, the stoicism exhibited by these soldiers seems almost superhuman. Their suffering, however, poses an inevitable question. At a time when even a minor wound could lead a man into one of those cockpits of horror, what dark instinct induced so many to plunge into battle with such self-destructive enthusiasm?

Although the truce was of short duration and cannonballs were soon criss-crossing the valley again, some men found time to watch the great column of smoke rising from the end of the ridge. No truce had been observed at Hougoumont and Wellington had been forced to send the garrison three fresh companies. Jerome, wounded by a spent musket ball, had been ordered by Napoleon to retire and Reille had assumed direct command. A howitzer bombardment had set fire to most of the outer walls but although wounded men were being burned alive, the Allied survivors in the court-yards were resisting as fiercely as ever. The action that had started as a feint had now turned into a major battle in its own right.

There was at this time a marked contrast in the mood and behaviour of the two commanders. Wellington, who on Copenhagen was riding unceasingly up and down the ridge from Hougoumont to Papelotte, appeared calmness itself and was always available when any of his staff wanted advice. With no one to replace him if he were hit, his staff were acutely concerned for his safety, but in spite of the shot and shell raging over the hillcrest none of them dared to suggest he took cover.

At Rossomme, perhaps understandably, Napoleon was in a less composed state of mind. With his first heavy assault hurled back, and with the Prussians drawing slowly but inexorably nearer, he might in other circumstances have withdrawn until conditions were more favourable. But this was impossible: from the outset his strategy had been to divide Wellington and Blücher and destroy them separately, and if he withdrew now his chance would have gone for ever. And to retreat back into France without a victory would be political suicide.

Committed as he was, his only chance lay in defeating Wellington quickly, whatever the cost. Then the advancing Prussians would become a sacrifice instead of a threat and Northern Europe would be his once again.

Although he could ill be spared, the battle-stained Ney had stolen a few minutes to ride back to Rossomme after d'Erlon's divisions had been defeated. He found the Emperor moody and bitter.

'Wellington has found a new way of waging war unknown even to Quintus Fabius Maximus – he fights sitting on his backside.' Pulling Ney over to the edge of the knoll he pointed accusingly at La Haye Sainte across the valley. 'You neglected that farmhouse – the key to Wellington's position. Take it and you have cut the Englishman's throat. Allez! Allez vite!'

As Ney galloped away the Corsican gave a violent cry and hurled his hat to the ground. 'Where is Grouchy? God in heaven, where is Grouchy?'

A second later he grimaced with pain and his hand slipped inside his tunic. La Bédoyère gave Larray, who attended Napoleon all that day, a glance of concern. The Emperor's display of anger was not uncharacteristic to those who knew him but the pain that accompanied it was another matter. The Corsican closed his eyes for a moment, then shouted his frustration at the watching men. 'What's the matter? Can none of you do anything without me?'

Larray came quickly forward. 'Sire, I advise you to come off the field. You should take to your bed for an hour.'

He received a look of dislike. 'Take to my bed – with my name rattling in the breath of dying men! It is indecent.'

Larray stood his ground. 'It is necessary, Sire. Otherwise you might not see the day through.'

As another spasm of pain made the Corsican wince, Larray motioned to a servant who brought up a horse. La Bédoyère and the surgeon helped the sick man to mount it. As La Bédoyère took the rein and led the horse down the road Napoleon stared at him bitterly.

'After Austerlitz I said I'd be good for six more years. Now ten years have gone and nine more campaigns. A man has his duty in war as in everything else.' He paused. 'You are not listening, La Bédoyère.'

La Bédoyère's pale face lifted. 'You are wrong, Sire. I am listening to every word.'

The Corsican's eyes were bloodshot with bitterness. 'Does age increase a man's wisdom or just spoil his ability to gamble?'

La Bédoyère walked faster without speaking. Napoleon glanced back and hunched his shoulders in distaste. The sun was hidden behind a cloud and the heavy smoke was turning the sky leaden. He suppressed a shudder.

'The very clouds and air seem oppressive here – to hold a threat. What will men say of me in the future, La Bédoyère?'

'They will say what men say now, Sire: that you have extended the limits of glory.'

La Bédoyère's loyalty appeared to change the sick man's mood from bitterness to irony. 'That thought at least my son can safely inherit. Even if he cannot count on forty thousand francs a year.'

CHAPTER SIXTEEN

Less than fifteen minutes later the storm from the terrible French artillery, concentrated now on the centre of the Allied line, broke with even greater fury. Great cannonballs bounded forward, crushing wagons and gun carriages as if they were matchwood. Others burst and their lethal shrapnel scythed out in all directions. An ammunition dump was hit and exploded in a great sheet of smoke and flame. Terrified horses screamed, kicked, and stampeded.

The air grew hot as an oven and a great pall of smoke thickened over the ridge. To some the hail of grapeshot and musket balls that swept through it sounded like the hum of a million beetles. To others it was like the howl of a hurricane. As the haze of death shimmered and danced along the ridge, the men hugging the ground cursed or prayed according to their natures.

At this time Wellington was assembled with his staff beneath the elm tree at the crossroads. With lethal metal slashing through the branches, their horses were almost uncontrollable. As a grenade burst less than thirty yards away and the smoke rolled over them, Wellington turned wryly to de Lancey.

'By God, it's blowing strong now.'

As de Lancey nodded the Duke's eyes fell on the pale, slim figure of Lord Hay. He called him alongside. 'Tell General Alten to retire his troops a hundred paces from the ridge and to find them shelter. Hurry, boy.'

The seventeen-year-old officer saluted and rode away. Wellington watched him anxiously, relaxing only when he reached the lee of the ridge. Turning, he surveyed the battle-field for a moment, then nodded curtly to his uneasy staff.

'Gentlemen, we will make that a general order. The whole army will retire one hundred paces.'

With the exception of de Lancey, his relieved staff galloped off helter-skelter in all directions. Orders were shouted, trumpets blew, and crouching infantrymen scuttled back from the hill crest. Cannon were limbered up and, with sweating drivers cracking whips, were hauled away from their exposed positions. In a few minutes the ridge crest was empty.

Seemingly unaware of his danger Wellington remained gazing down into the smoke-filled valley. Hesitating, de Lancey took Copenhagen's bridle and led the Duke away. Deep in thought at his next move, Wellington offered no resistance.

*   *   *

Under cover of the tremendous bombardment Ney had made his attack on La Haye Sainte. Napoleon had instructed him to use d'Erlon's and Reille's infantry, but with d'Erlon's divisions still shaken after their reverse and Reille's units fully committed at Hougoumont, he had managed to raise only two battalions from these commands and they had proved inadequate to drive out the tough German troops who were defending the farmhouse. However, it was a reverse that did not worry Ney over-much for while leading the attack he had caught sight of Wellington's order being executed. As thousands of prisoners and wounded men could also be seen streaming back towards Brussels, the impression Ney and his fellow officers received was that Wellington had ordered a general withdrawal.

Impulsive as ever, Ney decided on an immediate cavalry attack on that part of Wellington's front that he believed was disintegrating: the 1,000 yards between Hougoumont and La Haye Sainte that was largely manned by British troops. Leaving the attack on the farmhouse in the hands of subordinates, Ney raced back to his lines with the news that he only needed a large enough force of cavalry and he could punch a hole straight through the Allied lines. In normal circumstances cavalrymen did not attack infantrymen without support because foot soldiers could form squares which it was extremely difficult for horsemen to break. The conditions that had to exist were that they were either deployed in line – in which case cavalrymen could easily cut them down – or previously softened up and scattered. Convinced by Ney that the artillery barrage had achieved this softening up, cavalry commanders rushed orders to their regiments to deploy immediately behind him. No infantry support was thought necessary and little field artillery: the theory being that the attack must be made swiftly before Wellington's troops had time to rally and reorganize a new line of defence.

The first squadrons in the field were Milhaud's cuirassiers, their helmets and breastplates glinting ominously. Lancers of the Guard moved in on either side of them, their gay, fluttering lanceheads a contrast to the grim stillness of the cuirassiers. Over the hill rise behind them the Chasseurs à

Cheval of the Guard appeared at a fast trot, a splendid sight in their bearskin shakos and scarlet pelisses. They massed in formation at the rear.

Warned by his observers of the move, Wellington returned with de Lancey to the hillcrest. The Duke was frowning as he swept the parade with his telescope. 'He's concentrating most of his cavalry and yet his infantry are still sitting on the slopes. What has he in mind this time?'

The bombardment, which had slackened for a few minutes, started up again. Wellington turned his horse and rode along the ridge giving instructions to his gun crews whose cannon were now inclined up the ridge crest. One of the batteries he rode towards was Mercer's whose cannon were not pointing ahead but thirty degrees to the right.

Mercer and Normyle, faces and uniforms blackened by powder smoke, were on horseback beside one of the cannon when Wellington came galloping up, his horse in a lather. As always his orders were sharp and laconic. 'Give them grape until the last second. Then leave your guns and get into the nearest square.'

The order was given from experience. Wellington's courageous artillerymen had stood by their guns on other battlefields and as a reward been cut to pieces by storming cavalry. And without artillerymen, the Duke knew he could not long face repeated cavalry charges.

As Mercer acknowledged the order Wellington noticed the curious angle of his guns. He jabbed an impatient finger forward. 'What do you mean, sir? There is your line of fire.'

Mercer shook his head. 'The cutting down to the lane is very deep here, Your Grace. To reach us they must go round it.'

Wellington saw he was right and galloped on. By this time the French had started their advance. To watchers from the British ridge it looked as if part of the brightly-coloured hillside opposite were sliding down in a great avalanche into the valley.

The red-headed Ney, who had already had three horses shot from beneath him that day, was leading the attack. As his horse increased its stride the trumpeter alongside him took his cue and sounded the 'Gallop'.

The great horses lengthened their stride. The cuirassiers crouched forward in their saddles as if riding into a wind. The lancers of the Imperial Guard and the hussars rode with upright elegance. The sun, penetrating the dark clouds and the hanging smoke, glinted on breastplates and burnished swords. Flags and pennants streamed out proudly.

The concentration as the horde crossed the valley was at least 5,000 men to 1,000 yards of British front. As the ridge drew nearer the field officers, realizing the flanks would pass too closely to the defiant fortresses of Hougoumont and La Haye Sainte, ordered the ranks to close in. As the mass compressed, horses in the centre were lifted from the ground by the pressure. Before the van reached the foot of the ridge the concentration was ten horsemen to every yard of allied front – a concentration probably unequalled in military history.

The tall rye grass that clothed much of the valley was crushed down as if the ocean itself were sweeping forward. The ground trembled under the pounding of 5,000 galloping horses. With the French artillery covering the attack with a heavy barrage, the noise was deafening, and to waiting regiments behind the ridge it seemed that all hell was rising from the valley to pour over them.

By this time the order had been shouted down the full length of the line 'Prepare to receive cavalry', and the infantry had run into squares. With two lines of men, the front rank kneeling, forming each wall and with all bayonets thrust forward, a square of bristling steel was created that horsemen found difficulty in breaching.

A square, however, was only impregnable as long as the infantrymen held fast or the casualties were not too high. If men faltered or if the pounding artillery could blast a large enough gap in their living flesh, the enemy horsemen were inside like a flash and the square became a death trap. To watch for danger points and to give their men encouragement, infantry officers on horseback patrolled the inner courtyard of the squares.

The problem with squares was their vulnerability to artillery fire and in the time it took the French to cross the valley their artillery took full advantage of this weakness. Jammed shoulder to shoulder in the tightly-packed formations, the British and Allied infantrymen could do nothing but kneel and wait as the great cannonballs streaked towards them and the grenades flung out murderous shrapnel. Men saw their friends beheaded or crushed into unrecognizable carcasses of meat. The slaughter was so severe on Halkett's brigade, on Wellington's right centre, that the remnants of the 30th Regiment were forced to join with the survivors of the 73rd to complete one whole square. A similar union had to be made between the 33rd and the 69th. Most of Wellington's infantrymen were now praying for a sight of the French cavalry. While it would herald a ferocious onslaught of sabre and lance, it would at least bring an end to the hail of steel.

Mercer discovered his artillery battery was situated just in front of two squares of Brunswickers. They were a very young regiment whose average age appeared no more than eighteen and were receiving a brutal mauling from the French barrage. As cannonballs hurled boys aside, officers and NCOs could be seen thumping other ashen-faced youngsters forward to fill the gaps. Although Mercer's orders were to fall back into the squares as soon as it looked as if the French cavalry might overrun his guns, he decided there and then to ignore the order. If his gunners ran back, the chances were great that the terrified young infantrymen would panic and leave a gaping hole in the centre of the Allied line.

The bombardment ceased when the vanguard of the cavalry was halfway up the slope. Now the air was filled with the jingle of bits, the tremendous pounding of hooves, and the blast of trumpets. Officers and NCOs steadied their men and all eyes turned on the hillcrest ahead.

One moment it was an empty skyline. Then a line of upraised swords appeared, followed by crested helmets and the gaping jaws of horses. It was the dreaded cuirassiers who, with their heads bent forward so that the peaks of their helmets looked like visors, appeared men of steel from helmet to saddle.

They looked invincible but there was already confusion among them. Believing they were riding after disintegrating British infantry, they had a shock to see the disciplined red squares drawn up with chessboard neatness in the fields behind the lane. No one was more horrified than Ney who came over the ridge sixty yards to Mercer's right. Thrusting his legs right forward in the stirrups, he dragged hard on the bit in an attempt to halt his horse. All along the line horses reared up wildly on their hind legs, only to crash forward again as the onrush behind drove them forward. British gunners, standing with lighted portfires, were watching their officers. As the leading horsemen closed to within a hundred yards, the officers dropped their swords. Smoke belched out from over a hundred cannon with a thunderclap that deadened the senses.

The effect on the close ranks was devastating. Men were hurled bodily from their saddles. Canisters and grapeshot sliced through the shoulders and hindquarters of the magnificent horses and dropped them like slaughtered cattle. Survivors left to face the cannon tried to turn but were thrown forward by those behind. Sweating British gunners swabbed out gun barrels and rammed in more grapeshot, while behind them the infantry squares kept up a rolling, rhythmical fire. Thousands of faces, showing strain, hatred, agony, or terror appeared and vanished nightmarishly as acrid smoke swept over the ridge.

As the tide of horses and slashing steel drew nearer, the British gunners fired a last round and then, obeying orders, ran back into the squares for protection. Mercer, with one eye on the square of young Brunswickers, held his ground. To the right, his battery had piled up a barricade of dead horses. Ahead, at the foot of the bank, there was a carnage of kicking animals and feebly struggling men where cuirassiers, unable to halt, had been hurled down to the lane and crushed by the second rank of horses falling on top of them. In their efforts to escape, cavalrymen had used the pommels of their swords on one another. Now other cuirassiers were sliding down the muddy cutting and finding a footing on the living flesh below. Seeing the danger Mercer ordered two of his cannon to be swung round and double-loaded with ball and case-shot, the most lethal short-range charge possible. When the black smoke cleared away, the cuirassiers had vanished like leaves in a wind.

But along the rest of the line, with the terrible cannon silenced, the cuirassiers were able to hurl themselves at the infantry squares. To Uxbridge's cavalry, waiting in the fields behind for their chance to counter attack, it seemed impossible that the great tide of horsemen would not overwhelm the squares and destroy every man in them.

O'Connor was at that moment kneeling in the front rank of the Inniskillings with the butt of his musket jammed into the mud and the muzzles and bayonets of the rear rank bristling over his head. His view of the battle was the infantryman's view: a few yards of smoke and trampled mud. Through the smoke a horde of cuirassiers were charging straight at his square. On their gigantic horses, with their helmets lowered and huge sabres upraised, they looked like horsemen from the Devil and froze the blood of younger soldiers. But old sweats like O'Connor muttered encouragement, shifted their plugs of tobacco from one cheek to another, and waited.

The rear line fired the first volley when the raging horsemen were no more than two dozen yards away. Horses crashed down and cuirassiers rolled dead or dying into the mud. Others reached the wall of bayonets only for their horses to shy away. Some managed to slash downwards and split the skulls of kneeling soldiers before the cold steel of bayonets pierced them. The majority broke round the squares like a wave around rocks and galloped past on either side.

NCOs ran round the inside of the squares, pushing reserve soldiers in to fill the gaps and dress up the lines. The sides and rear of the squares were now in action, firing at the backs of the French as they galloped past. Impressions registered on men's minds that were to last with the survivors all their lives: the smell of burnt cartridges, the peculiar rattling of musketballs on cuirassiers' breastplates, the wounded horses raising their heads as if soliciting help.

From Rossomme, where the French cavalry could be seen milling around Wellington's squares, some staff officers were jubilant, believing the charge had been successful. Napoleon, who had returned after his short rest, was less convinced: he felt the ridge was too shrouded in smoke for an accurate assessment.

His doubts would have been greater had he known the blunder that was being made. Waterloo is known as the battle of squandered opportunities but this was surely the most monumental of them all. At that time it was standard practice for captured guns to be spiked if they could not be drawn away. This was the simple operation of driving a headless nail into the touch-hole of the cannon which rendered it useless. Or, if nails were not on hand, the smashing of sponge-staves would soon make the guns impossible to operate. As Ney's cuirassiers had suffered such terrible losses in overrunning the British guns, it would have seemed an automatic response to ensure those cannon could not inflict such damage twice. Yet, although the French were to over-run those batteries time and again that day, when each cavalry wave receded the guns were found to be undamaged.

By this time the cuirassiers who had been driven round the squares were turning their horses back to the ridge. It was the moment Uxbridge had been waiting for and he struck with his cavalry all along the line. The counter-attack took the weight off the hard-pressed infantry and they were able to watch the fierce hand-to-hand fights that developed between the horsemen. Before O'Connor's eyes a Life Guard countered the sabre slash of a cuirassier, and with a backward slash of his own sent the Frenchman's head flying from his shoulders. The terrified horse, with the headless body still erect in the saddle, dashed off into the mêlée.

It was 4.20 PM when the first French cavalry charge was finally repulsed. It was a mixed blessing for the powder-stained Allied infantry, for the moment the French disappeared behind the ridge the French artillery began firing at them again. This time slow-burning grenades fell into the squares and men could only watch the spluttering fuses and hope they would not die in the forthcoming blast.

Meanwhile, Wellington's gunners had run back to their cannon and found them serviceable. On the opposite side of the ridge Ney was organizing his cavalry for another charge.

When it came a few minutes later, skirmishers preceded it and poured a harassing fire on the British gunners who knew that to fire back would give the cavalry a chance to break through before they could reload. To pacify his men Mercer leapt on his horse and paraded calmly in front of his battery while the skirmishers fired at him from less than fifty paces. He was not hit but a few of his gunners were killed or wounded. A minute later the French cavalry appeared again over the ridge.

This time their advance was slow and deliberate. The sweating British gunners poured salvo after salvo of grapeshot into them. Men and horses fell in heaps but those following rode unflinchingly over them. A final salvo and then the gunners were forced to run back again into the shelter of the squares.

This time Ney had shown the sense to bring up a few field guns on the flanks of his cavalry. They were inadequate in number for their task, but the damage they did to the 2nd Battalion of the 73rd Foot showed the influence they might have had on the course of the battle had Ney employed them sooner.

As the hurricane of shot from the British batteries ceased, the cuirassiers and lancers gathered themselves and then charged full tilt at the squares. Seeing the danger to his regiment Lieutenant-Colonel Colborne, in whose square Wellington and his staff had taken temporary shelter, rode round its inner walls shouting: 'Shoot the horses! Pile them up!'

The long volleys rang out. Horses stumbled and dived nose first into the mud. Picking themselves up, cuirassiers flung themselves bodily at the walls of bayonets in an effort to break through. Others tried to back their terrified horses at the kneeling men, only to fall from musket fire or bayonet thrust. Yet others drove their horses into gaps and slashed their way through reeling infantrymen until they in turn were cut down by horsemen defending the inside of the squares. Yells, screams, orders, musket fire, and the clash of steel turned the ridge into bedlam.

Ney was leading the attack. He pulled the heroic cuirassiers back a short distance, then drove them forward again at Colborne's square. The massive horses reared up against the human wall, sabres hacked down at unprotected heads, and for a moment it seemed the square would break. Colborne's urgent voice rang out again over the tumult.

'You're wasting ammunition! Fire at the horses!'

Ney's horse was shot from beneath him. Cursing, he ran towards one of the many riderless animals that were running about the ridge in loose packs. Catching its bridle, he swung himself into the saddle. His face was black with powder and filth, his white culotte stained with horse's blood. Spurring forward, he yelled at the cuirassiers like a madman.

'Forward! Forward! Again.'

CHAPTER SEVENTEEN

Spurts of red flame lanced out from the murk of smoke that overhung the ridge. From Rossomme, retreating cavalrymen looked like toppling toy soldiers as grapeshot hurled them into the mud. Pale and tense, Napoleon lowered his telescope and turned to Soult. 'His second attack and it is thrown back too. The madman. He committed the cavalry an hour too soon.'

Soult looked equally dismayed. 'He has compromised us as he did at Jena.'

'Why did you let him? Were you asleep?'

'It happened without my knowledge, Sire. He said the English were retreating and Milhaud's cavalry poured after him like one man.'

Agitated, the Corsican paced up and down behind the

table. 'If we do nothing to help him the battle could be lost. Tell Kellermann to give support.'

Soult looked shocked. 'Is that wise, Sire, without first withdrawing Milhaud's divisions? We might overcrowd the ridge with horsemen and it leaves us without cavalry reserves.'

Napoleon's bloodshot eyes swung on him. 'We are committed. Send them.' As Soult sank into a chair and pulled a dispatch pad towards him, Napoleon stared again at the smoking ridge. 'At least Ney has forced their infantry into squares to give our cannon targets. Tell Drouot to hammer them at every opportunity. And send out infantry. We must capture that farmhouse.'

Soult began scribbling frantically on the sheets of paper while dispatch riders formed a queue behind him. As Soult passed the first message over his shoulder, the distraught Corsican shouted at the dispatch rider: 'Run to him and say "the farmhouse". It must be taken.'

But La Haye Sainte, like Hougoumont, was proving a bleeding wound to the French infantry. Mounds of bodies lay around it and grew as each new attack was repulsed. With flesh and blood unable to take any more, dazed French soldiers wandered off, to be shot as they stumbled over the bodies of their dead comrades. The King's German Legion, who were fighting so magnificently behind the shell-pocked farm walls, heard their dying cries. 'Vive l'Empereur! Vive l'Empereur!'

It was four-thirty and Blücher was near enough to see the fighting. His men were nearly collapsing from exhaustion and only the old man's indomitable spirit and his reminder that he had given his word to Wellington kept them going. Although he had hoped to make his initial attack with a stronger force, it looked to him as if Wellington's hard-pressed infantry might break at any moment and so he moved his two advance brigades out of a small wood to attack the French Army's right flank. Although as yet little more than a gesture, it served to bring a precious unit of French cavalry galloping down the valley to meet him.

Back on the ridge no one could remember how many

times Ney led his cavalry against the Allied squares, although officially the number was given as twelve. Reinforced by Kellermann, he now had over 10,000 horsemen at his disposal and as the enormous horde thundered up the slope and over the hillcrest it seemed impossible the thinning squares could withstand them. Between each attack the Allied infantrymen had to endure a tempest of shot and shell from the French batteries, and as the squares shrank in size their courtyards became filled with wounded and dying comrades. Hardly a man holding a musket did not have a wound of some kind, and when they fell other wounded men crawled back to take their place. Never did soldiers serve their country better than on that bloody day at Mont St Jean.

Before his eyes, Wellington was seeing his army melting away into the Belgian mud. But neither the slaughter nor the bravery was one-sided. Each time the French charged over the hill, the Allied guns took revenge with ball and case-shot. With so many of their comrades fallen the French horsemen had at times to find ways through the mounds of bodies, but they still flung themselves at the squares with magnificent courage. Some French officers had broken their scabbards as a pledge they would not return unless the squares were broken, and they whipped their terrified horses right up to the kneeling infantrymen. As the horses fell, their riders would be momentarily suspended on the points of bayonets. Other cavalrymen hurled their lances like spears at the bloody, resolute foot soldiers.

Some of the French were so terribly wounded that they either blew their brains out or begged the Allied infantry-men to kill them. Ney, frantic at his new failure to gain a victory for his Emperor, was here, there, and everywhere. At one moment he was seen frustratingly striking a British cannon with his sword, in the next leading another heroic charge. Like Wellington, who was also in the thick of the battle all that day, he saw most of his staff killed but although he hurled himself at the squares as if courting death, neither shot nor musket ball hit him.

To men on both sides time lost its meaning. They had

been fighting since memory began and they would continue until memory ceased. Waterloo had become a monstrous killing match, a moment in history when an irresistible force ran into an immovable object, and even veterans like O'Connor began wondering if all the combatants had to be killed before the battle was decided.

As the afternoon turned into evening the situation was reached when both the French cavalry and the Allied infantry were glad to be at each other's throats: in such close proximity it meant both were spared the hell of the other's artillery. As cuirassiers milled around the Gordon Highlanders' square, a piper was pacing backwards and forwards over the wounded and dying, the harsh skirl of his pipes bracing the surviving Scotsmen to even greater defiance.

Wellington's small staff was diminishing by the minute. He had pushed young Lord Hay into a square for protection but the youngster did not last long. Seeing a wall of the square being forced back, he rode towards it shouting:

'Hold them, men, hold them! Remember England. Think of your wives, your homes, and your sweethearts!'

What words would have passed between the tough, sweating infantrymen if they had heard his youthful exhortations is best imagined. As it was, a second chance was denied them. A musket ball struck the boy in the breastbone and he fell from the saddle to the ground. The Dalmatian whined and tried to lick his ashen face. A sergeant-major, running up, shooed the animal away.

Wellington, who had been riding from unit to unit, was forced to take cover inside the square of the Inniskillings as a large force of cuirassiers swept along the ridge. Wheeling round the square they tried to break it with pistol and musket fire. To the tough Irishmen, loading and firing with professional skill, the world fined down again to a few yards of mud and smoke and fierce, sanguinary faces.

The inside of the square was like a mortuary as more wounded were dragged back to die. But the lines held and at last the onslaught ceased as the frustrated cuirassiers drew back. The infantrymen, who had discovered it was while they were reloading that the attacks came, held back their fire and there was a momentary truce as the French prowled round the square looking vainly for a point of entry.

The same situation could be seen on other parts of the ridge. Exhausted men who had tried to kill one another in every conceivable way were now staring into each other's faces with an ambivalence of enmity and admiration. Freed momentarily from the urgency of survival, their senses could take in extraneous impressions. They noticed horses with bleeding stumps for legs grazing in open stretches along the ridge. The smell of Waterloo, sodden rye and grain mixed with the fumes of sweat and gunpowder, reached their nostrils. The enemy faces staring at them changed from devil-masks into faces as human and vulnerable as their own. As the entire ridge seemed to quieten, some exhausted soldiers had the illusion the battle had been a nightmare and friend and foe were in reality brothers-in-arms.

Lying in the trampled rye a few yards away from O'Connor was a cuirassier with terrible stomach wounds. He had been repeatedly ridden over by his comrades but instead of bringing him merciful oblivion the trampling hooves had only increased his agony. Three times he had tried to kill himself with his sword but it was too long for the purpose. Now his agonized hands had obtained a bayonet from a dead British soldier who had been thrown out of the square. Watched by French and British alike, he lifted himself up and inserted the bayonet point beneath his cuirass. As his body fell forward and his eyes rolled upwards in his death agony, O'Connor heard a strangled cry from the rank behind him. Turning, he saw a grey-haired soldier called Dick Tomlinson struggling to break free from his comrades. O'Connor leaned towards Patsy Macmahon who was also in the rank behind him. 'What's up with Dick?'

Macmahon shrugged his powder-blackened shoulders. All around the square men were now turning to look as Tomlinson's tormented voice rang out. 'Let me go! Leave me alone, can't ye?'

Fighting wildly, the man suddenly tore himself free and ran out in front of the square. Among others, O'Connor tried to grab him. 'Dick! Get back.'

General Lambert was spurring his horse across the square. Realizing he was about to order his men to fire on the deserter, Wellington caught his arm. 'What's his name?'

'Tomlinson, Your Grace.'

Wellington moved sternly forward. 'Private Tomlinson. Return to your duty! At once.'

Tomlinson took no notice. He was standing in the no-man's-land between the British square and the astonished French cuirassiers who were making no move to attack him. Muttering to himself and making gestures of despair, he was divesting himself of his equipment. As he threw away his cartridge belt, his tortured face lifted and his accusing voice reached friend and foe alike.

'You've never met before . . . any of ye! Then why d' ye do such harm to one another?'

Lambert could contain himself no longer. 'Come back, Tomlinson, or you'll be shot.'

Muttering to himself, the grey-haired soldier stumbled towards the cuirassiers who drew aside their horses to let him pass. 'I can't do it, sir. I can't kill any more.'

As Lambert turned to shout an order, Wellington put a hand on his arm and shook his head. Tomlinson, the one remarkable conscientious objector at Waterloo, disappeared among the French horsemen.

Macmahon was staring at O'Connor. 'I never thought Dick was a looney.'

A cynical voice made both men turn. 'Mebbe he's the only sane one here.'

'Amen to that,' a second gruff voice reflected. As other men muttered their agreement and O'Connor squirted tobacco juice thoughtfully into the trampled grass, there was an angry shout from behind them.

'What's the matter with you men? Sergeant-Major! Get them into action again!'

There was a roll of musket fire, a thunder of hooves, and once again life was normal as men tore savagely at each other's throats.

CHAPTER EIGHTEEN

The battle had now raged for nearly seven hours. As the sun set, storm clouds began massing and men remembered a powerful wind sweeping columns of ash and filth down the ridge. Some said there was one immense thunderclap as if the heavens had split; others said it was an ammunition dump exploding at the back of the ridge. Wounded men lying unattended on the battlefield prayed for rain but none fell.

On the mound at Rossomme Napoleon had his hand raised to protect his eyes from the wind. An officer on a horse lathered with sweat rode up alongside him. 'Marshal Ney requests more cavalry, Sire.'

The sick man's voice was acid with bitterness. 'More cavalry? The fool has used my entire reserve without success. Tell him to use the six thousand infantrymen he has kept waiting for the last two hours.'

In an attempt to gain an overall picture of the battle Wellington, de Lancey, and three staff officers had ridden up a small hillock six hundred yards behind the ridge. Although fierce fighting was still taking place behind the pall of smoke ahead, one of Wellington's younger officers who had just returned from the ridge was jubilant.

'His cavalry are defeated, sir. They are moving back all along the valley.'

The report was true. In the dogged red squares the French cavalry had met their match and had at last been ordered to abandon their attack. There was no disgrace in their withdrawal. Unsupported by infantry or adequate field batteries, they had fought with superb courage. In a way Napoleon was a victim of that courage for, by refusing to concede defeat until their dead lay all over the ridge, they had both destroyed themselves as a fighting force and given Blücher precious hours to reach the valley.

Not that Wellington's army had fared any better. In total its losses were even higher than the French. But although desperately few redcoats remained to man the ridge, those that did had gained such morale from their victory that only death could defeat them now.

An infantry officer riding a captured French horse rode up the hillock to Wellington's side. His left hand rose in salute: his right arm was dangling helplessly. 'General Lambert requests reinforcements, sir. The French are now sending infantry at the ridge.'

The Duke's horse shied as a flurry of wind swept down the ridge. Wellington soothed it, then glanced at the wounded man. 'Tell General Lambert I can only send him my compliments. Then go and have that wound attended.'

As the man rode away the Duke rose in his stirrups to survey the smoke-covered ridge. His telescope paused on a field to his right where the smoke was densest. He frowned at one of the staff officers. 'Why is that square of infantry lying down? Get them to their feet.'

A fresh gust of wind, more powerful than the first, made the five horsemen brace themselves and blew the distant pall of smoke away. Wellington raised his telescope again and then motioned to the officer who was about to ride away. The man said afterwards it was the first time he had seen the Iron Duke show emotion.

'Do not bother, sir,' he said curtly. 'I see it cannot be done.'

Far down the valley Blücher had suffered a setback. As weary unit after unit continued to arrive, he had managed to drive a French brigade out of Plancenoit. This had brought Prussian artillery within range of the French Headquarters, and when cannonballs began to fall among his Imperial Guard, which Napoleon had carefully held in reserve for the *coup de grâce* on Wellington, the Corsican realized further steps had to be taken to ease the German pressure.

The unit he sent out to attack the Prussians was his Young Guard. It was made up of men in their early twenties, some of them sons of the grim Old Bearskins waiting behind Rossomme. Others were the descendants of soldiers who had died fighting for the Emperor during his long reign. Fresh, full of youth and idealism, they drove hard against Blücher's tired infantry and threw them back.

The news came as a massive tonic to the Corsican. With the Prussians checked he could give Wellington his full attention again. If La Haye Sainte could be taken quickly, artillery could be rushed up to the farmhouse and would swiftly annihilate the maimed British regiments clinging to the ridge above it. His infantry and cavalry could then pour through the gap and roll up the entire British line. God help Blücher then – he would drive the old devil and his minions all the way back to Königsberg . . . A message was sent to Ney. Take La Haye Sainte! Regardless of cost. Take it!

There had been no respite for the British infantry. The main cavalry charges had no sooner ceased than the tireless Ney had attacked the ridge with the 6,000 fresh infantrymen he should have used earlier. Leaving their squares to form a line along the ridge, the redcoats had thrown them back with over 1,500 casualties. But they had also suffered losses – losses they could not afford – and Wellington's tone was unusually sombre as he paused on the hillcrest with his diminishing staff.

'I'm very nearly at the end of my tether, de Lancey. We're too thin on the ground to hold them much longer. And now he seems to have his mind on the farmhouse. If he takes it my centre is broken.'

At that moment a cannonball bounded up from the ground and struck de Lancey in the back. The thud and crack of bone could be heard yards away. The young American was thrown several yards from his horse, staggered to his feet, and then collapsed. Everyone present ran to his side. He stared at them and then at Wellington, who lowered his head to listen to his whisper.

'Pray ask them to leave and allow me to die in peace.'

Soldiers were called over and told to carry him in a

blanket to the farm at Mont St Jean where a surgeon was operating on the wounded. As the broken, ashen-faced man was borne away Wellington, who had known him since he was a boy, climbed bleakly on his horse and rode back to the ridge crest. No one knew to whom his murmur was directed. 'Magdelene will have to be told ... Picton, Ponsonby, and now de Lancey! This is the saddest affair I have known.'

Below, new columns of French infantry could be seen marching up the shell-blasted road towards La Haye Sainte. On receiving Napoleon's order, Ney had for once obeyed him to the letter and collected several battalions of infantry and units of field engineers who had been told to bring with them every entrenching tool they could find. Cheated from victory all day, Ney did not intend to fail this time even if he had to take the farmhouse apart brick by brick, and there was a grimness about the marching columns that boded ill for its gallant defenders, Major Baring's King's German Legion.

Major Baring had been under attack at La Haye Sainte since noon. Ammunition was now running so low that at his last check he discovered he had only four rounds per man. He had sent a messenger scrambling back up the ridge with an urgent request for more but none ever came. Some say it was a staff oversight: others that the Germans paid the price because they were issued with rifles instead of muskets and the only wagon carrying rifle ammunition had overturned on the Brussels road. Whatever the reason, the courageous defenders were doomed before the vengeful Ney could reach them.

They still fought with passionate fury, expending all their ammunition and then engaging the French with sword and bayonet. But as French soldiers smashed in doors and windows with huge axes and poured into the burning buildings, Baring realized the futility of further resistance and gave the order to withdraw. Altogether only Baring and forty-two men of the nine companies who had originally garrisoned the farmhouse got back to the British lines. With the French infantrymen bitter at the losses the strongpoint had inflicted on their comrades, many of those captured were slaughtered before the French officers could intervene.

Back at Rossomme Napoleon was a new man. The key to Wellington's defence was his at last and, if he moved swiftly, so was the battle. His legendary energy was back and blazed like a blowtorch as he sent dispatch riders racing all over the field with his orders. The two companies of the 95th British Rifles who had occupied the sandpit at the side of the Brussels road were swept away. Horse artillery came racing across the valley, some taking cover behind the broken farmhouse walls, others deploying on the slopes of the ridge itself. Cavalry, hastily reorganized, galloped after the cannon to give support. Long columns of infantry followed. The Corsican's plan was to bring pressure to every point of the British line while he exploited his success in the centre. To bleed Wellington further, he threw in even heavier attacks against Hougoumont, compelling the Duke to reinforce the garrison.

The close-range artillery led the massive assault. Forced to remain exposed to repel any sudden attempt at a breakthrough, the Allies suffered terrible losses. Gun after gun went silent, its ammunition exhausted or its gunners killed. Some were unable to fire because the barrels became overheated: on average British guns fired over 800 rounds apiece that day. The gaps between the line of infantrymen widened as the shot raged among them. Divisions shrank into brigades, brigades into mere companies. When cavalry attacks came, junior officers found themselves in command of regimental squares.

The wound that was bleeding the British to death was the road junction above La Haye Sainte. Knowing it was the target for Napoleon's killer thrust, Wellington had no option but to keep it reinforced, even though the artillery hidden behind the walls of the farmhouse cut men down like a scythe mowing grass. The 27th Inniskillings were sent to the key spot, the junction of the two roads. Some troops near by faltered under the murderous fire but although the Inniskillings lost half their number they stood firm.

Visibility was down to eighty yards: the enemy seen only by the flash of cannon and musket.

A desperate effort was made to regain the farmhouse. The Prince of Orange, Commander of the 1st Corps, galloped up to Ompteda and told him to lead a battalion of his German Legion in a counter-attack. Moreover, they were to march *in line of battle*. Ompteda, a kindly Hanoverian who, like the Free French 150 years later, was fighting to free his homeland and who had two teenage nephews in his legion, had noticed a strong force of cuirassiers waiting in the smoke for such a move and protested they would slaughter his infantrymen. When the Prince, young, arrogant, and inexperienced, repeated his order, Ompteda begged permission to march his men forward in a square to give them some protection against the cavalry. The Prince refused and Ompteda had no option but to lead his men forward to suicide. The cuirassiers, thirsting for revenge against Wellington's infantry, galloped along the line of helpless men and slashed them to pieces. A few British light dragoons tried to save the Germans but the odds were too heavy. Ompteda was later found in the garden of the farmhouse, a musket ball through his throat. Ordered to lead his men to their death, he had made certain of finding it with them.

The loss of the entire battalion left another gap in Wellington's centre. He was also suffering from wholesale desertion. Kruse's brigade had evaporated under the fierce artillery fire. The Cumberland Hussars, headed by their colonel, turned and rode off to Brussels where they caused even greater panic in the city by declaring Wellington was defeated. An artilleryman, sent to bring forward a battery of Dutch guns, was amazed to discover that thousands of Allied soldiers were not only taking shelter in the woods but cooking themselves a meal there. The only cavalry left in the centre of the line were two squadrons that survived from the brigades commanded by Somerset and Ponsonby, and they spread themselves out to make their numbers seem larger.

By this time Wellington could see Blücher's units engaging the French at Plancenoit. The sight was like water to a desperately wounded man. His urgent need was for reinforcements to shore up his left line so that he could stiffen the centre. To explain the desperate situation he sent Freemantle, one of his aides, to the Prussians.

The message, received by Marshal Zieten, had the reverse effect to the one intended – interpreting it to mean Wellington's lines were collapsing, the Prussian pointed out to Freemantle it would be foolish to pour good money after bad. Other Prussian officers disagreed and an argument broke out among them as to where help should be sent – to Bülow who was heavily engaged with the French at Plancenoit or to Wellington who might be a lost cause on the ridge of Mont St Jean.

In the meanwhile Wellington had no choice but to sweat it out. Uncertain whether he would receive direct help on his left flank and gambling that Napoleon's main thrust would come somewhere between Hougoumont and La Haye Sainte, he decided to cut his losses and concentrate his remaining strength nearer the centre. In a bean field near the crest of the ridge he called Uxbridge and Somerset towards him.

'While I've an ensign and ten men left I intend to stand,' he told them. 'Call up the last of the reserves, Chassé's Dutch-Belgian division back of the line. Send Vivian and Vandeleur's cavalry over here. I'm abandoning my position on the left.'

As the two officers showed their surprise, Wellington went on: 'If we make ourselves as tight as stone, and if Blücher comes, we might still do something.' He pointed at the ground beneath his horse. 'I want what remains of us here.'

Uxbridge was looking grave. 'You know he still has his Old Guard in reserve? Fourteen battalions, according to a French deserter.'

He received a cool stare. 'I have heard. They have a good reputation, have they not?'

Someone laughed. Around them bandaged, grimy-faced men were seen staring at them and whispering. The Duke showed impatience. 'What's the matter with those men?'

Somerset called over a junior officer. As he was questioning him, Lord Gordon rode up. Seeing the beans he dismounted and plucked a pod. He broke it open and showed it to the Duke.

'They're good beans, Wellington!'

The Duke turned towards him. 'If there is one thing in the world I know nothing about, Gordon, it is agriculture.'

Gordon shrugged at Uxbridge and put the beans in his mouth. Somerset turned from the junior officer. 'It seems they do not want to wait for the next attack, Your Grace. They would rather try to finish it quickly by attacking with the bayonet.'

The men received Wellington's dry grin. 'Tell them I admire their enthusiasm. But the rascals will remain where they are or get a flogging.' His eyes moved to Uxbridge. 'Have every gun brought here. At full gallop.'

As Uxbridge rode away, Wellington accompanied him for a few yards. His voice was low. 'It appears I have lost the battle, Uxbridge. Only night or Blücher can save me. But at least I'll die in the place I have chosen for myself.'

Ney was jubilant. Entrusted by Napoleon to lead the Army in spite of what had happened between them in the past, he had led each cavalry charge with fanatical fervour. Some critics would say if he had exchanged that fervour for coolness he might have made more gain, but none could fault his resolution and courage. He had risked death a hundred times, only to face the humiliation of leaving the ridge still in the possession of the cursed red squares. Fresh from his failure at Quatre Bras, desiring above all things to rehabilitate himself in the eyes of the man he loved, Ney had begun to believe there was a curse on his efforts.

Now, however, his reward was there for the taking. The smoking, ash-covered ridge was littered with shattered cannon, abandoned equipment, and corpses. Wounded in their hundreds were dragging themselves towards the woods. The last obstacles to victory were the decimated British regiments and their thin line of cavalry, and a quick sweep of the telescope was sufficient to reveal their pitiful condition. Attrition had done its work at last, and all that was needed now was the *coup de grâce*.

But Ney's men were also battle-shocked and exhausted. His skirmishers were the remnants of d'Erlon's defeated divisions, his cuirassiers survivors of the regiments who had hurled themselves all afternoon at the ridge. To execute the kill Ney needed the Old Guard and he sent a colonel racing back with the message.

The Emperor, after retiring to Le Caillou to have his piles treated, had now established himself where normally he would have been all day – on the mound at La Belle Alliance that overlooked the entire valley. Unfortunately for Napoleon the crossroads and the centre of the ridge were now entirely hidden by gunsmoke. Thus he could not see the frailty of the British position but he could see down the valley where the reinforced Prussians had counter-attacked and were overwhelming his Young Guard.

The colonel begged him to send his Old Grumblers across the valley to Ney at once. The old Napoleon would have had no hesitation. Only ninety minutes remained before darkness fell. Unless he could defeat Wellington in that time he must have known he would lose the battle and with it his throne. There was no point in holding back reserves for future contingencies. The correct move was to gamble all, in one bold throw for victory.

Yet he hesitated. Perhaps it was his newly-found admiration for the tough British infantry that deterred him. Perhaps – although his own military sense should have told him it still remained the correct move – he underrated Ney's request because it was carried by a mere colonel. Perhaps, in pain, and with the wear and tear of so many campaigns behind him, he was suffering from the loss of nerve that affects all fighting men sooner or later. Whatever the reason, he made the fatal mistake of procrastination.

'More troops,' he snapped at the colonel. 'Where do you expect me to get them from? Do you expect me to make them?' Instead he ordered two battalions of the Old Guard to Plancenoit, where they quickly proved the worth of seasoned troops by driving the Prussians out. Only when he was satisfied his right flank was safe again did the Corsican turn his mind back to Ney's request.

By that time thirty minutes had passed and much had happened. Zieten, who had finally agreed to lead his troops to the British left flank, had been misled by the hundreds of wounded men and fugitives he had seen streaming back from the ridge. Convinced the British front had collapsed, as he had predicted earlier, he had started marching his troops back to join up with Bülow who was engaged with the Young Guard. The horrified Müffling had noticed the move and ridden desperately after him. In the argument that followed, the fate of Europe once again balanced on a knife edge. Finally Müffling convinced the reluctant Zieten and the Prussian led his troops back towards Wellington's left flank.

Wellington still appeared near defeat. The French had by-passed Hougoumont, were engaged near the top of the ridge with his exhausted infantry, and on the far left had swept well beyond Papelotte. On the other hand the short delay had given time for Chassé's reserve division to reach the ridge. The white-faced men, seeing the thousands of wounded, the heaps of debris, and the piles of corpses, could hardly believe Wellington was still holding the ridge.

Meanwhile, another messenger had reached Napoleon from Ney. His uniform drenched in blood, he was a cavalry officer who had been hit by shrapnel during his dash across the valley. As he rode unsteadily towards Napoleon, the dying sun broke free of the clouds that had hidden it most of the day, and sent its red rays slanting across the mound. Dismounting, the cuirassier had to clutch his saddle to prevent himself falling. Soult took the dispatch and handed it to Napoleon. The Corsican read its contents aloud. 'I urge haste, Sire. They are so bled their heads are down. If you will bring the Guard you can walk straight through them to Brussels.'

The Emperor's hand came down with a smack on his knee. Rising he turned eagerly to La Bédoyère. 'With Plancenoit safe, we are ready. Send news all along the front that Grouchy approaches.'

Along with the rest of the staff officers, La Bédoyère gave a start. No contact whatever had been made with Grouchy; in fact he was still miles away deeply engaged with Thielemann's corps, the rearguard Blücher had thrown out. By this time he had realized the urgent need to link up with Napoleon but Thielemann had found an excellent defensive position behind a wide stream, and Grouchy could find no way of disengaging his army without putting it in danger. All he had been able to do was send Napoleon some reserves and they had little chance of reaching the battlefield before nightfall.

Seeing La Bédoyère's hesitation, Napoleon became impatient. 'Do as I say. I need the troops in good heart when I lead the Guard forward.'

As La Bédoyère and his fellow officers rode off to spread the falsehood, the young cavalryman broke into a paroxysm of coughing. As bright blood ran down and stained his culotte, Napoleon moved towards him in concern. 'You are badly wounded, sir?'

Fighting his cough, the young officer turned to him with a smile. 'No, Sire. I am killed. No matter – I have died for you.'

His knees buckled and he fell at the Corsican's feet. As Napoleon stared down at him, the dying rays of the sun gave his eyes an unnatural brilliance. He motioned Larray over and as the surgeon bent over the dying man, he turned to Flahaut, his aide-de-camp.

'You can write now to Paris, Flahaut. Give them the time and say I have broken through Lord Wellington's centre. The battle – no, say the war – is mine.'

CHAPTER NINETEEN

The stage was set for the final act. The sun was almost down behind the woods at Hougoumont and its rays were tinting the sea of smoke that filled the valley. Here and there the effects were beautiful: the smoke turning mauve or shimmering pink. Birds returning to their nests were black arrowheads against the fading sky. Night was less than ninety minutes away.

To those who had fought all day it was a bitter moment. To survive when all one's friends have died around one, to know darkness will ensure one's salvation, and yet to have to fight again in those twilit minutes is something that can break the strongest man. One has allowed oneself to dream again of a warm hearth, of loving arms, of the laughter of one's children. And instead there comes the rhythmical tramp of boots and the menacing shouts of those who might yet snatch away tomorrow.

The Emperor's Guard were on the march at last. His *élite* corps, the veterans who had fought for him on the icy steppes of Russia and in the torrid heat of Italy. The men with their great moustaches and bearskins who had never been known to bend or break. The Immortals, as they were called. In recent years seldom used by the Emperor until he was ready to execute the death blow.

He led them through the smoke on his white horse. Men yelled 'C'est la Garde', and as the news raced along the valley weary French soldiers felt their limbs lighten. The Old Grumblers were on the move at last. It was the prelude to victory.

They came up the Brussels road as if they were marching on parade. Five battalions of them in close, eight-men ranks. Sauret could be seen among them, his grizzled face impassive. The line regiments had made hard work of it but now the Emperor would have his victory before nightfall.

Rata, the drum-major, led them, hurling his baton high in the air and crying 'The Emperor'. Six thousand gruff voices behind him echoed the cry. The line of young drummers tapped out the march. The Guard's band followed, twenty-four musicians playing *La Grenadière*. Men felt shivers run down their spines at the martial sound. Dying men rose on their elbows and tried to touch the legs of the Emperor's horse as he rode past.

The British artillery, Mercer's battery among them, had

now got the range of the oncoming columns. Shells burst among them but the Guard stepped over their dead and marched on. It was an advance that contained professionalism and *élan*, confidence without haste. The Guard knew they were the *élite* of French soldiery and it showed in every move they made. Not for them colourful uniforms; they wore their faded battledress. The place for fancy uniforms was in their packs, to be worn on their victory parade through Brussels.

Napoleon was riding with Ney, La Bédoyère, and the curly-haired Cambronne, a tough and loyal Guards' officer who commanded the 1st Chasseurs. The Emperor's staff followed closely behind. Ney, hatless, his uniform torn and covered in mud, was unrecognizable as a marshal of France. Yet for the first time that day he looked happy. The battle had been brutally hard and frustrating but at last the fruits were ready to be picked. Above all else was the mood of his Emperor, who was behaving as if his part in the abdication was forgotten. It was like the old days again and Ney asked for no greater happiness.

On their right side was a column of the Guard, on their left one of the supporting eight-pounders. Nudging Ney, Napoleon pointed at the Guardsmen. Huge in their bearskins, with their faces half-covered by great moustaches and side-whiskers, they looked creatures made for war, magnificent but slightly inhuman. As he leaned towards Ney, the Corsican seemed to be speaking almost in soliloquy.

'It would take me another twenty years and all my sixty battles to create their like again. Their love is my strength. Yet every battle, every year, I march them off the earth.'

A cannonball struck the ground not fifteen yards away, bounded forward and smashed a gap in the column. As the impassive Guardsmen closed their ranks, the alarmed Ney and La Bédoyère walked their horses sideways in an effort to protect the Emperor. As Napoleon spurred impatiently forward, Cambronne swung his horse directly in front of him. The tough Guards' officer was grinning.

'Sire, if you expose yourself to this gunfire any longer I shall order your own Guard to nail you up in a box.'

Ney added his own plea. 'Please, Sire. Your loss would cost us the battle and it is almost won.'

Napoleon hesitated, then surrendered with a good-humoured laugh. 'There is spirit in them still!' As he allowed his horse's head to be turned he leaned towards Ney. 'Lead them over the hill to Wellington's standard. Your courage today deserves that honour.'

As his staff followed him to the quarry by the roadside an agitated cavalry officer rode up. 'Sire. The Prussians are on the east ridge.'

The Corsican's reply was savagely sarcastic. 'You bring me news, sir.'

There was a sudden roll of gunfire to the east. La Bédoyère gave a start. 'Could that be Grouchy?'

Napoleon shook his head as he stared bitterly up at the eastern ridge. 'I made one mistake in my life – I should have burned Berlin.'

Another column of the Guard was marching past. Their great cheer on seeing him gave the Corsican new heart and his fever-bright eyes turned on his staff. 'I have only been beaten once on the field of battle – at Marengo. I lost it at five o'clock, then I won it at seven. Blücher has come too late. The battle is with Wellington and it is won.'

The news that the Old Guard was moving up to attack had spread to every unit on Wellington's ridge. The British troops received it with mixed feelings. After their dogged defiance all day, and with Blücher near at last, the realization that defeat and death might still cheat them was crushing. On the other hand – and perhaps only soldiers and ex-soldiers will understand this – they were fascinated as they watched the grim, disciplined legions moving towards them through the haze of gunsmoke. Very few of the British infantry had met the Old Guard in action. They had fought the French in Portugal and Spain and the Old Guard had always been kept near the Emperor. But they had all heard its claim – to be the greatest soldiers on earth – and to a professional fighting man that was a challenge. Old sweats like O'Connor could be heard growling: 'Let the bloody bastards come.' With half their comrades dead or wounded, revenge was one factor. Another was relief: a direct confrontation would end the bloody affair once and for all. But the third factor belonged to professionalism. The British infantry had its own tough pride and here was the greatest challenge in its history.

With Uxbridge, Wellington had returned to the elm tree although the French artillery was again sweeping the ridge. The gunfire was filling the valley with smoke but occasionally it would drift aside and reveal the relentless, oncoming columns. Wellington's expression was composed as he turned to Uxbridge.

'If he had sent them at me half an hour ago I could not have stopped them. Now at least we have a chance.'

Short although the respite had been, it had given time for Zieten's advance troops to take over part of the left ridge. Wellington had used the relieved troops to reinforce his centre and also deal with the many French skirmishers who had been harassing his artillery. Once they were cleared, his cannon had been able to move forward and silence the French batteries at La Haye Sainte that had done such damage to the centre of his line. Thus the only artillery protection now available to the advancing Old Guard were the field batteries moving up on its flanks.

The columns were now no more than five hundred yards away, coming straight up the road towards La Haye Sainte. As they passed the quarry, Ney, leading them on horseback, inclined left and took the way up through the open fields over which his cavalry had charged that afternoon with such little success.

No plausible explanation for this move has ever been given. Possibly, knowing the Prussians were moving in towards his right flank, Ney thought the opposition from the British would be weaker towards Hougoumont.

It was a mistake. It denied the Guard the shelter of the road cuttings and took them over open fields that had been churned into liquid mud by the French cavalry. The slopes were also littered with the corpses of their compatriots. But it was not the Old Bearskins' way to question their leaders.

Stepping over the dead, they began widening their ranks as they approached the hillcrest. Veterans of many battles, they knew the value of firepower and soon they were in columns of sixty men abreast. With intervals between the companies they soon formed a line four to five hundred yards long.

On the ridge Wellington had ordered every man who could be spared to take cover from the furious French bombardment. Evidence suggests he had guessed Ney might strike at this sector of his line for he had already stationed an arc of thirty cannon there and deployed his troops four deep so they could provide maximum firepower and yet have a chance against cavalry should the French throw any remnants against him. When he saw it was two battalions of Maitland's red-coated Foot Guards who were going to receive the brunt of the attack, Wellington stationed himself in the field behind them. There, ignoring the gunfire, he was in a position to see over the ridge crest.

The French artillery ceased as if a switch had been thrown. In the momentary silence the Foot Guards felt their hearts beating faster as French drummer boys began beating out the dreaded *pas de charge*. Grimy and calloused hands on whose courage and loyalty the fate of Europe rested shifted ammunition pouches and gripped muskets tighter. The moment of truth was very near.

Every gun Wellington could muster, including a Dutch-Belgian brigade, was pouring fire down on the advancing battalions. For a while they disappeared into the smoke and behind undulations in the valley. When they emerged on the final slope they were formed into two great columns, one directly opposite the Foot Guards, the other, slightly smaller column, nearer the centre of Wellington's line. Eight-pound field pieces were firing from their flanks and some units of cavalry following in the rear. Rejuvenated French line soldiers were also coming up in support.

The two columns, muskets at the port, advanced until they were only fifty paces from the crest of the ridge. Sweating gunners fired double charges of grapeshot at them over open sights. The effect was like wind swaying a field of corn. Ney, leading the larger column, had his fifth horse of the day shot from beneath him. Jumping up, he ran forward, shouting: 'Forward! Forward! These last few yards will give us Europe.' Ignoring a last salvo from the British gunners, the sea of bearskins flooded over the hillcrest.

The sequence of events that followed can never be established with any certainty. Regiments, even companies, were hidden from one another by gunsmoke, and fear distorted men's own experiences in their memories. What seems certain, however, is that the smaller column of the Old Guard had considerable initial success. Two British regiments recoiled before it, collided in their retreat with two other regiments, and the whole disorganized mob was driven back across the fields. With the Old Guard in possession of their cannon, it seemed quite possible for a few minutes that the French would be able to spread westward and roll up the entire British line.

The situation was saved by Major Dawson Kelly. Sent by Wellington, he arrived in time to see the infantry commander, Halkett, receive a musket ball through the mouth. One of the demoralized units was the 73rd, Kelly's old regiment, and he took charge of it himself. A popular officer, he brought new heart to the men and the other regiments rallied behind him. The crisis was over and the right flank of the Old Guard held just in time.

The larger column, led by Ney, went over the ridge crest directly opposite the Foot Guards, who were hiding behind the bank of the low cutting. The artillery defences were quickly overrun, some gunners standing their ground until they were bayoneted, others obeying orders and running back. Directly ahead of Ney the ridge appeared empty except for the fleeing artillerymen, a few horsemen, and the debris of battle. All along the line, resistance appeared to have ceased or to be on the point of doing so, and Cambronne yelled his triumph to Ney.

'It was a rearguard only. They have run!'

None of the veteran soldiers behind him was surprised. Had they not brought their beloved Emperor victory on fifty battlefields? Some officers in the front rank began to link arms and sing 'La Victoire est à Nous'. The song spread to the men behind them. Because of the dense smoke rolling across the valley few noticed the long column of British soldiers marching down the slope to their left.

It was the 52nd Regiment led by Colborne. A soldier with a reputation for daring ideas, he had been watching the French advance against Wellington's Foot Guards and decided that if he could line his regiment along the great column's flank, its fire, combined with the frontal fire of the Foot Guards, should be enough to break even the Old Guard.

It was a daring move because unless it were carried out quickly and faultlessly it would leave huge gaps on the ridge which the French could exploit. Nevertheless, Colborne had received permission from his brigade commander, Adams, and with his 52nd Regiment augmented by parts of the 95th and 71st Regiments he was marching into position.

If few men noticed the distant line of British infantry through the rolling smoke, still fewer took notice of the lean horseman at the rear of the ridge who, as the French column began pouring over the crest, spurred his horse up to the sunken lane and leaned down.

'Maitland! This is your time. Get ready!'

The front rank of the Old Guard was now less than forty paces away. Drifting smoke and ash turned them into huge, almost mythical figures. A moment more and then Wellington's order rang out sharp and clear.

'Now, Maitland! Now!'

As one man the Foot Guards rose up from behind the low cutting. The shock to the French was profound: the red-coated English soldiers seemed to spring out of the very ground itself. Muskets at the ready, in a precision as perfect as if they were on parade, they stood staring eye to eye at the astonished Old Guard. Then a trumpet blast sounded and a shout from Maitland.

'Aim!'

In perfect precision the Foot Guards lifted their muskets and sighted them.

'Fire!'

A disciplined, synchronized volley crashed out. The French column stopped as if it had struck an invisible wall. Men who a second earlier had been full of strength and triumph were transformed into human wreckage. Ney, miraculously unharmed, ran screaming along the line.

'Get at them! Forward!'

A second volley from the Foot Guards answered him. Hands clapped to shattered faces, knees buckled, men fell in hundreds. Sauret, surrounded by dying comrades, spat his defiance at the erect redcoats. French officers, some desperately wounded, tried to make their orders heard over the din and the confusion.

Meanwhile the French had now noticed the advancing four-deep line of British soldiers extended along their left flank. Realizing the danger, desperate officers yelled at the outer ranks to wheel and open fire. They had barely got their muskets to their shoulders before Colborne's men fired a volley that brought a hundred of them down. Before the column could recover, the second rank stepped forward and delivered an equally shattering volley.

The Foot Guards on the ridge had also fired again. Ney was yelling like a madman as he urged his men to advance but wiser heads among them were trying to deploy right and left in the hope of finding a less defended sector. Other survivors were bravely trying to return the fire but the pressure from behind made accurate aim impossible. Psychologically it was the exact moment to attack and Wellington did not miss it. He leaned over the bank again.

'Now, Guards! Up and at 'em!'

With a great cheer the Foot Guards, later to be immortalized as 'Grenadier' Guards for their repulse of the French grenadiers, leapt out of the lane and charged with fixed bayonets. Hemmed in by dying men, some held upright by the dense pressure, French soldiers were unable to defend themselves as the bayonets stabbed home.

No soldiers on earth, not even the lion-hearted Old Bearskins, could have withstood such a shock and then such an onslaught. Down the slope, conscious his attack must be pressed to the limit if it were to succeed, Colborne was leading a savage bayonet attack on the shattered left flank of the column. Assailed from the front and with a murderous buzzsaw biting into its side, the column began to fold back on itself. As congestion grew in the centre, panic began to grow and spread. Like a gallant oak tree stricken by lightning, the Old Guard was at last facing defeat.

CHAPTER TWENTY

La Garde recule! From Hougoumont to Papelotte the news spread as if telegraphed. Soldiers of line regiments who had rallied when Napoleon had led the Guard towards the ridge felt their blood run cold. If the Old Bearskins were retreating, their fate was sealed.

Other shouts were heard. 'We've been betrayed' was one as French soldiers realized they had been told a lie about the nearness of Grouchy's troops. With faith in their officers destroyed, morale collapsed and with it the will to fight.

The cry *La Garde recule* reached the quarry where Napoleon and his staff were sheltering. Conscious it was the cry of doom, the officers were afraid to look at the ashen-faced Corsican. When he did not move or speak, and as the defeated veterans poured past the quarry, Soult approached him gently. 'Sire. We must move back. The Guard is broken.'

The Corsican's intake of breath was a sound of pure agony. Swinging away, he clapped his hands over his ears. 'You lie, Soult, you lie! The Guard cannot be broken. C'est un roc de granite!'

To the west Papelotte had fallen to the Prussians and in Plancenoit they were destroying the remnants of the two Old Guard battalions that had been sent to stop them. The Prussians, who had suffered similar atrocities when the

Guard had driven them back, were taking their revenge and slaughtering all prisoners. On the outskirts of a shadowy wood Blücher, his injured leg heavily strapped, paused to stare into the smoke-filled valley. Gneisenau was alongside him and behind, almost invisible with the dark wood as a backdrop, was a battalion of black-uniformed Prussian infantry. Lowering his telescope, Blücher leaned towards Gneisenau.

'Wellington has them on two sides – we and Zieten will strike on the third.' He turned to the troops behind him, his voice rising. 'Raise the flags high, my children. And remember, I want no pity – no prisoners. I'll shoot any man I see with pity in him.'

There was a great cheer. As black flags rose like hideous birds over the massed Prussian ranks, the soldiers burst into the rousing Lutherian hymn *Ein Fester Burgist Unser Gott*. Blücher waved his sword forward and the Prussians plunged deep into the valley.

Ney, who had been swept down the slope with the rest of his men, was desperately trying to halt the retreat. His voice was hysterical as he grabbed at running men. 'Stand! Only another hour. Do you hear me, damn you – stand!'

He finally succeeded in halting a corporal and half a dozen of his men. They stared in amazement at the wild, red-headed figure in the tattered uniform of a marshal who tried to turn them back to the ridge. 'Stay with me! I am Marshal Ney. Stay and see how a marshal of France can die.'

He started back up the bullet-swept slope. The six soldiers glanced at one another, then ran on after their comrades. The corporal hesitated, then followed Ney and caught his arm. 'Sir. There is no one to go with you.'

Ney tore himself free, stumbled, then ran on. The corporal caught him again and this time held his trembling arm firmly. 'Sir, it's no use. The Guard – they're finished. They're in full retreat everywhere.'

Through its mud and filth, Ney's white face glared at him. 'Salaud! You lie!'

The corporal turned him gently round. 'See for yourself, sir.'

As the truth struck him Ney seemed to turn into stone. Then he made a retching sound and swung away. The corporal led him like a blinded man towards the quarry alongside the road.

It was eight-thirty. Wellington had galloped from his position behind the Foot Guards to the elm tree and had his telescope trained on the scene below. Although among the shadows and the smoke a few brave French units could be seen trying to fight a rearguard action, the vast majority were in full flight, men throwing away their packs and muskets as they ran. Snapping his telescope closed, Wellington nodded at Uxbridge who was on horseback alongside him and took off his hat. Standing in his stirrups so that he was silhouetted against the evening sky, he waved it forward three times in the manner of a huntsman laying on a pack of hounds.

It was an order that could not possibly be mistaken by all who saw it and its effect was electric. The Allied cavalry let out a tremendous cheer, put spurs to their horses, and went hell-for-leather down the slope. Artillerymen forgot their exhaustion and started their batteries thundering forward. Dazed infantrymen found a new life as the news swept along the ridge and ran down the hillside as fast as their weary legs would allow. Even some of the wounded, cheering thinly, stumbled after them. As they left the smoke of the ridge behind to discover it was a fine summer evening, men saw the impossible had happened and the entire French army was in retreat.

After the fluctuations of the day and the nearness of defeat a mere half-hour ago, it was a moment of delirious triumph. Even Wellington showed emotion as he watched the wave of Allied soldiers flood down on the shattered French. His hand, clapping down on his horse's neck, made the animal start. 'Damn me, Uxbridge, if I ever saw thirty thousand men run a race before.'

Uxbridge smiled back. 'Shall we join the race?'

'By God, we will, Uxbridge. We will indeed.'

The battle was almost over but death did not cease its reaping. Instead, as though conscious time was running short, it redoubled its efforts. Mercer's gallant battery that had fought so well all day was struck by murderous gunfire just when it was about to follow the advance. The attack came from a Prussian battery that believed they were French. Before the error was rectified the broken-hearted Mercer had lost half his men and 140 of his magnificent horses: the virtual destruction of the troop of which he had been so proud.

Down in the valley the carnage was heavy. Some of the more experienced French soldiers fell on their knees when cavalry overtook them and bowed their heads in surrender. Most of these were spared if the cavalrymen were British but the Prussian hatred was too strong and helpless men were sabred and lanced by the hundreds. Nor was the slaughter one-sided. The superb French artillery on the southern slope was not yet overrun and was giving maximum covering fire to its retreating troops. With the Allied forces now fully exposed in the valley the losses were as heavy as any during that day.

Wellington, Uxbridge, and Somerset, with three aides in attendance, were discovering the accuracy of the French fire as they followed the advance across the trampled fields. As grenades exploded and the black specks of cannonballs hissed past, Gordon noticed the group of horsemen and came galloping over.

'They're like wasps, aren't they, Wellington?' he shouted merrily. 'They can even sting out of their arses.'

At that moment a cannonball passed over Copenhagen's neck, causing even the impassive Wellington to jerk back. Angry with himself, he turned sharply to Uxbridge. 'Put the cavalry against those guns, Uxbridge. They're doing too much damage.'

For a moment Uxbridge did not speak. Then his low but calm voice made the others stare at him. 'I've lost my leg, by God.'

All eyes were now on Uxbridge's knee which the cannonball had shattered. Wellington's response had the un-emotional banality he tended to assume when shocked or upset. 'By God, so you have.' Urging his horse alongside the wounded man, he helped Somerset to support him until the aides galloped up. Soldiers were called and Ux-bridge was carried off the battlefield for amputation.

Not all of the French army was still in retreat. Although Napoleon had been unable to check the wholesale flight, he and Cambronne had managed to rally some of the Old Guard and under their protection the Corsican had retreated towards La Belle Alliance where his last reserve, his Imperial Guard, was awaiting orders. There Cam-bronne, a bloody bandage around his head, made frantic efforts to protect him.

'Stand and form a square,' he shouted. 'Form a square to defend your Emperor!'

Augmented by the remnants of the Old Guard, the Imperial Guard backed into position. Surrounded by their fellow countrymen in full flight, they were like an island in the path of a collapsed dam. A thousand strong, each man knew his life span could now be measured by the time it took the enemy cavalry to cut down or disperse the mob that lay between them. Yet not a man protested as they formed the square. Both Sauret and Chactas were present. The huge grizzled Sauret, with his head bowed and his arms resting on his musket, was in the elegiac pose of a gladiator waiting to die.

Inside the square the object of all this devotional sacri-fice was riding back and forth like a man possessed. 'I lost Marengo at five o'clock and won it at seven. I tell you Grouchy will come and he will have their backs.'

Soult gave La Bédoyère a significant look before answer-ing. 'Sire, Grouchy cannot save us now. You must either surrender or escape.'

Napoleon halted his horse. 'Surrender! I am not re-hearsed in surrender.'

'Then you must escape while there is still time, Sire. There is no other alternative.'

The bandaged Cambronne rode up. There was con-
demnation in the way the distraught Corsican turned on
him. 'Everything was won, then everything was lost.
Twenty years have gone in one afternoon.'

Cambronne winced, then laid a hand on the Emperor's
rein. 'Sire, you must go. You were not born to be cannon
fodder.'

'To be born isn't everything. A man must die as well.'

'I know that, Sire. But your enemies must not have your
body.'

The laugh was bitter. 'Why not? Because they would
stuff it and put it up on show for a penny a look?'

Ahead, an evening breeze had rolled aside the smoke
and allowed a glimpse of British cavalry and advancing
field cannon. As the smoke closed back Drouot rode
frantically across the square. 'Sire, you must come away.
While there is still time.'

He received a look of dislike. 'Am I the only man here
condemned to live?'

Without further argument, Soult snatched at the bridle
of his horse and led it through the south wall of the square.
The Emperor's staff followed and in the open fields outside
closed around the Corsican like a bodyguard before
galloping away into the murk.

The French guns were silenced and the Allied cavalry
began attacking the square. In their shakos the grizzled
Guardsmen were like great bears hurling off the attack of
wolves. Veteran after veteran fell to sabre or lance, but
their comrades stepped over their bodies and filled the gaps.
Calloused hands rammed down powder and ball, powerful
shoulders drove bayonets into the bellies of horses. In the
smoke and gathering dust the veterans became spectral
figures, superhuman in their strength and courage. But
infantrymen were now appearing among the Allied cavalry
and even men who were oak trees could not survive the
volleys that were poured into them.

The square grew smaller. Sauret's face was grey with
exhaustion but still his ferocious bayonet kept the cavalrymen at bay. Chactas was bleeding from three wounds but

although on his knees he somehow kept his musket firing. Dying men called the name of the man whose love of power had brought them there to die.

Suddenly a trumpet rang out. Horsemen and redcoats drew back as an officer rode forward with a white flag held high on a lance. As the firing on both sides ceased, the British drew farther aside to reveal two field cannon lined up forty yards from the square. Loaded with grapeshot, they looked overwhelmingly lethal through the haze of smoke.

Wellington and Colborne had ridden up behind the guns. Colborne frowned as he turned towards the Duke. 'We're doing murder, sir.'

Wellington showed no resentment as he inclined his head. 'We are doing our duty, Colborne, which in war is usually murder. But I agree. Give them a chance to lower their colours.'

Colborne spurred his horse towards the lancer who was now only thirty paces from the motionless square. Checking him, he rode a few yards nearer. His address was in French.

'Brave Frenchmen, no men could have done their country more honour than you today. As further resistance is futile, the Duke of Wellington asks you to save your lives and surrender.'

Sauret spat his defiance to the ground. Cambronne, right up in the front of the square, noticed the gesture and gauged the mood of his men from it. Putting his hands, one red with blood, to his mouth to make a megaphone, he shouted his defiance.

'Merde!'

A hoarse laugh and cheer broke out from the veterans. Colborne, his cheeks very pale, gazed at the defiant square for a moment before lifting his hand in salute. Then, turning abruptly, he rode back to Wellington. 'I do not want to see this, Your Grace.'

The Duke's face was equally pale. 'Nor I.'

The two men turned and rode westward. A few seconds later there came the deafening crash of the cannon and a dense cloud of smoke rolled forward and hid the square from sight.

CHAPTER TWENTY-ONE

Colborne's men lay exhausted on their packs near La Belle
Alliance. A near-full moon was rising and those still able to
keep their eyes open could see the black mass of Prussian
infantry marching past on the Genappe road. Those too
tired to watch could hear the tramp-tramp of their booted
feet. All were too weary to attempt any communication with
them. To exist, to lie in the mud and to *be* was more than
enough for the British infantry at that moment.

Then cheering was heard down the hillside. It grew and
soldiers heard shouts of 'Blücher, Blücher'. A colour sergeant heard the outcry and staggered to his feet. At his
hoarse order men began to rise around him.

Horsemen came clattering up the *pavé* road. As their
silhouettes appeared against the rising moon, cheering
British soldiers were seen taking off their hats and waving
them.

Colborne's colour sergeant moved into the centre of the
road. The group of Prussian horsemen paused alongside him.
Their leader, an old hussar with a bandaged leg, reached
out for the colours and kissed them on both sides like a
man kissing a friend. The cheer the gesture brought from
Colborne's men was now loud and uninhibited.

A group of mounted British officers rode out from the
shadows of the inn. Their leader, tall and lean, doffed his
hat as he approached the old man. The Prussian made a
stiff bow. Then formality broke down and the two men em-
braced one another. As he hugged Wellington, Blücher shook
his head.

'What a business, my Lord Duke! Twenty years it took.
What a business!'

Wellington nodded. 'It was hard bargaining, Prince. And
without you it could never have been done.'

'We drew blood, Wellington, but you cut the throat.' The

185

fierce old man gave a chuckle. 'You had the full bucket of it. You made history for your England today.'

He received Wellington's dry smile. 'I can't say how history will regard it – whether it was a battle we won or he lost.'

Speculation of this nature was never Blücher's way: his impatience to get after the fleeing French showed in his glance down the road. 'We'll give them a run in the moonlight, Wellington. A run they'll remember.' Turning towards his infantry he let out a shout. 'Stamp on them until your boots split, my children. Test the pulse of every corpse with your bayonet!'

Wellington was clearly disturbed by the Prussian's jaunty ruthlessness. 'Sir, the French have fought me most honourably all day. I beg you to allow those who are left to go home.'

There was almost suspicion in the look Blücher gave him. 'Of course, my Lord Duke, of course.' He swung round his horse. 'But while we are talking we waste the moon. This will be a fast night, Wellington.'

There was a commotion up the road. A party of Prussian lancers, a grim sight in their black uniforms and Death's-head helmets, were galloping back to the inn. Their leader was carrying a plush-lined bicorned hat on his lance head. Blücher snatched at the hat.

'What's this?'

'We found it in the ditch, sir. A wounded officer says it belonged to him.'

Blücher's voice turned eager. 'Then he might be on foot! Find him and hang him on the nearest tree.'

The party of lancers raced off. Others came clattering up the road, pushing aside the marching infantry. Saluting Wellington and giving a chuckle, the old man spurred out to meet them. His exultant shout rang along the hillcrest. 'They run before you in their thousands! Remember Ligny and take no prisoners. Forward!'

The clump of trees was stained red by the fire the Guardsmen had lit. Raindrops from a passing shower hissed as they dripped into it from overhanging branches. A young French officer, followed by a comrade, walked nervously towards the small, hatless figure who, hands clasped behind his back, was staring into the flames.

The officer coughed. 'Your Majesty!'

When Napoleon did not answer, the young man found a desperate courage. 'Your Majesty, you must not stay here. There are too few of us to protect you. We have a carriage waiting on the road.'

Still the Corsican did not move. The officer took one look at his face, then drew back embarrassed. Moving like a sleep-walker, Napoleon picked up a stick and prodded the fire. As a cloud of sparks rose, his muttered question made the young men exchange compassionate glances.

'Where is Grouchy? We must find Grouchy.'

A party of horsemen galloped across the field. With Ney and Flahaut at their head, they filed through the trees to the fire. Ney, a wild and almost unrecognizable figure, sounded frantic as he leapt down beside Napoleon.

'Sire, there are units of Prussian cavalry approaching. They are li' e devils from hell – slaughtering all prisoners, even burning alive the wounded sheltering in cottages. You must leave before they get their hands on you. Your travelling coach is waiting at Charleroi.'

'Charleroi?'

There was neither life nor intelligence in the Corsican's question. Recognizing shock when he saw it, Ney caught his arm and led him across the field towards the road. Flahaut, leading the horses, followed them. As Napoleon stumbled in the long grass, his distraught face turned to Ney. 'Grouchy must fall back on Rouen. Massena will march to the Loire. Marshal Rapp – where is he? He must stay on the Rhine. France must have borders. Has no one a map?'

As Napoleon halted and turned to Flahaut, Ney tugged urgently on his arm. 'Sire, please hurry. The Prussians cannot be far away.'

A carriage stood on the road. A small guard of cuirassiers with drawn swords waited in attendance. As the three men approached, they ran forward to open the carriage door.

With a sigh Napoleon slumped into the seat and closed his eyes.

'I feel I am suffocating.'

Ney, leaning into the coach, nodded sympathetically. 'You are a little pale, Sire.'

It was a remark that seemed to fuse together all the elements in the Corsican's despair. His eyes opened and blazed their torment at Ney.

'I am pale, am I? You surprise me, for the wound is not deep. I have only lost an empire and seventy thousand men!'

Seeing Ney was to become the target for Napoleon's bitterness and wishing to save the weary soldier more pain, Flahaut drew him away. As the two men moved towards their horses, the Corsican's mood changed and he leaned from the coach. 'Do you think they will hang me? Or will they be satisfied with a bullet?'

Ney's voice was as gentle as a woman's as he turned back. 'They will do neither, Sire. France will never allow your death.'

The small figure sank wearily back. Seeing the tears in Ney's eyes, Flahaut, the scholar, nodded quietly at the carriage. 'You are right. They will chain him like Prometheus to a rock, where the memory of his greatness will gnaw him forever.'

There was gratitude in the glance Ney gave him. Half a minute later the carriage and its accompanying horsemen vanished into the night.

The rain had ceased and the moon was high when Wellington rode back across the battlefield. Somerset and Percy, one of his few aides who had not been killed or wounded, rode with him. For the first time that day Wellington was showing signs of distress, and Percy motioned Somerset to rein back and allow the Duke to precede them.

In the cold light of the moon the scene was one of pure horror. Bodies lay in mounds or like abandoned sacks in the rye. Here and there a man would rise to his feet, stagger a few yards with outstretched hands as if blind, then collapse again. Others were dragging themselves about on shattered limbs in the hope of finding a pistol or bayonet to end their agony. Crippled horses sat on their tails, whimpering, or lay kicking in pain. Sodden paper from torn state documents and dispatches lay everywhere. The faint breeze brought the sickening smell of sweat, vomit, gunpowder, and blood.

Although musket fire rattled to the south the battle had long since left the valley, and the sound that cannon and musket fire had hidden for so many hours was now heard in its own right. With over 40,000 casualties lying within two square miles the agony of the wounded rose on the night air like some dreadful organ note.

Wellington paused by Cambronne's square where many of the French veterans still lay in their defiant formation. Officers in their white trousers lay near their dead horses. The gay drum-major, Rata, lay bloody beside his shattered drum. Urging his horse reverently around the inside of the square, Wellington moved on as if paying the dead the tribute of a review. Sauret came into sight, a stricken oak of a man with his calloused hands still gripping his musket. Chactas, yet to be found by Maria, lay slumped over another grenadier, his white hair moving gently in the breeze. As Wellington gazed about him, Percy saw his lips were moving silently.

Down the valley, vague dark shapes were flitting among the dead and wounded and more were arriving by the minute. Some were women searching for husbands or sweethearts. Others had different reasons for their presence, for although the fighting had ceased, the killing had not. Corpses already lay naked in the moonlight, stripped even of their false teeth. As the ghouls crept forward, knives in hand, helpless Frenchmen called piteously for British soldiers to come and give them an honourable death.

Stippled clouds crossed the moon. Near Cambronne's square a French soldier's scream bubbled away as a scavenger's knife slit his throat. With a cry of horror Percy turned his horse and gave chase. His pistol shot, perhaps the last shot fired in anger at Waterloo, reverberated across the valley. Dark figures, many of them women, melted alongside their victims until the three horsemen rode away.

Their own dead lay thick on the ground as they reached the slope of the ridge. Towards the crest some had already been laid out in rows. Duncan's body was among them, the fine limbs the girls had admired at the Brussels ball now still and waxen. To the three battle-shocked officers the rows of dead seemed to stretch beyond the light of the moon itself. Wellington's distressed voice made Percy start as he rode half a horse's length behind him.

'Pray God let me have fought my last battle. I have lost many of my dearest friends today.'

As he paused on the hillcrest Percy saw that tears were glistening on his cheeks. Clouds crossed the moon again and as their shadows swept down the silent ranks, the dead seemed to stir in protest at their misuse. Shuddering, Wellington turned his horse sharply and rode away.

There was no sound of revelry as they entered the British encampment behind the ridge. Men were huddled within the circles of their camp fires as if afraid of their own shadows. Somerset questioned a colonel who, conscious of Wellington's presence, sounded apologetic. 'I don't know why, sir. It seems a strange way to behave after a great victory.'

All three men stiffened at the cold voice behind them. 'You think so, sir? Then know that I share their strangeness. Today they witnessed the disease of Man, and such a sight leaves only a fool undisturbed. Respect their fear and pray that one day you might understand it.'

With a nod to Percy, Wellington turned his horse and rode back alone to the inn at Waterloo. As the three men watched him go, the organ note of the dying came swelling upwards on the night wind.

WATERLOO

Frederick E. Smith

A superb novel based on Dino De Laurentiis' most spectacular motion picture starring **Rod Steiger as Napoleon and Christopher Plummer as Wellington.** Frederick E. Smith fills his magnificent canvas of The Hundred Days with the fury and sound of battles and the drama of human emotions.
Pan Original (25p) 5/-

the field of WATERLOO

A magnificently produced souvenir by Paul Davies contains diagrams, illustrations and maps, many in full colour, which brings vividly to life The Hundred Days–Napoleon's last campaign. Photographs of uniforms and weapons of the opposing armies together with a complete list of the Allied and French military commanders and a battle-plan make this a fascinating and graphic companion to Dino De Laurentiis' magnificent film—Waterloo.
Pan Original (25p) 5/-

A SELECTION OF
POPULAR READING IN PAN